Stevie Davies, who is the Royal Literary Fund Writing Fellow at Swansea University, is a novelist, historian and literary critic. She is a Fellow of the Royal Society of Literature and a Member of the Academi Gymreig.

Her first novel, *Boy Blue* (1987) won the Fawcett Book Prize in 1989; *Primavera* (1990) confirmed her literary reputation; and her shattering breakthrough book, *Arms and the Girl* (1992) received universal praise. *Closing the Book* (1994) was on the longlist for the Booker Prize, and the shortlist for the Fawcett Book Prize. Her fifth novel, *Four Dreamers and Emily*, described as 'poignant, funny and luminous...immensely enjoyable, lit by comedy and wisdom' (Helen Dunmore, *The Times*) was published in 1996; and of *The Web of Belonging* (1997), shortlisted for the Arts Council of Wales Book of the Year Prize and the Portico Prize, the *Independent* commented, 'There are good writers, there are very good writers. And then there is Stevie Davies in a class of her own'. Her previous novel, *Impassioned Clay* (1999), was shortlisted for the Arts Council of Wales Book of the Year Prize. She is also the author of *Emily Brontë: Heretic* (1994) and *Unbridled Spirits: Women of the English Revolution 1640–1660* (1998). The Women's Press publishes all these books.

Also by Stevie Davies from The Women's Press:

FICTION

Boy Blue (1987)
Primavera (1990)
Arms and the Girl (1992)
Closing the Book (1994)
Four Dreamers and Emily (1996)
The Web of Belonging (1997)
Impassioned Clay (1999)

NON-FICTION

Emily Brontë: Heretic (1994)
Unbridled Spirits: Women of the English Revolution 1640–1660 (1998)

STEVIE DAVIES

THE ELEMENT OF WATER

First published by The Women's Press Ltd, 2001
A member of the Namara Group
34 Great Sutton Street, London EC1V 0LQ
www.the-womens-press.com

This paperback edition published 2002

British Library Cataloguing-in-Publication Data
A catalogue record for this book is available from the British Library.

ISBN 0 7043 4730 X

Typeset in Sabon by FiSH Books, London WC1
Printed and bound in Great Britain by Cox & Wyman, Reading, Berkshire

Foreword & Acknowledgements

I am grateful to the Society of Authors for the generous Writers' Foundation travel and research grant, which supported the writing of this novel.

I should also like to record my gratitude to Heinrich Stricker, Director of the Goethe-Institut, Manchester, for valuable and unstinting help, to the librarians of the Goethe-Institut and to Ursula James for checking countless queries on my behalf. I owe a great debt of gratitude to Malcolm Sargent, then of the Department of Continuing Education at Manchester University, for his gentleness, tact and humour in helping me take my first faltering steps to reclaim my German; then to the teachers at the Goethe-Institut for developing it so that I could read and speak with reasonable fluency. I thank Professor Ian Kershaw, authority on the Third *Reich* and author of the definitive biography of Hitler, for his generous advice. I am grateful to the staff of the Public Library, Plön, Schleswig-Holstein, for their help, and to the Training School for Naval Officers, Ruhleben, Plön, for permission to view the establishment and for supplying a delightful young cadet to guide me round. I thank the staff of the *Marienkirche*, Lübeck, for the information they kindly provided. Any inadvertent mistakes of fact or deliberate blurrings in the cause of fiction, are, needless to say, my sole responsibility.

Although it is true that Grand Admiral Dönitz and the Rump of the government of the Third *Reich* did retire briefly to Plön, where he was named *Führer* at Hitler's death, and that the Ruhleben naval camp, having been taken over by the British in May, 1945, did become a British forces boarding school, which I attended as a child, the plot and characters of *The Element of Water* (apart from well-known political figures) are pure fiction.

to Margaret Drabble

'Our future lies on the water.'

Kaiser Wilhelm II

'Far away, our *Führer* Adolf Hitler has a beautiful villa. It is located high up in the mountains and is surrounded by an iron fence. Often people who would like to see and greet our *Führer* stand in front of it.

One day the *Führer* came out again and greeted everyone in a very friendly way. They were full of joy and reached out their hands to him.

In the front row stood a little blonde girl with flowers in her hands, and she said, in her clear child's voice, "Today is my birthday."

Thereupon the *Führer* took the little blonde girl by the hand and walked slowly with her into the villa. Here the little girl was treated to cake and strawberries with thick, sweet cream.

And the little blonde girl ate and ate until she could eat no more. Then she said very politely: "Thank you very much!" and "Goodbye!" Then she made herself as tall as she could, put her little arms round the *Führer*'s neck, and gave the *Führer* a long, long kiss.'

Baldur von Schirach, *Primary School Textbook*, 1935

'We must give fanatical adherence to Hitler and the National Socialist State. Any deviation from this is a laxness and a crime. I would rather eat dirt than allow my grandson to be brought up and to be poisoned in the filth of Jewish culture . . .'

Grand Admiral Dönitz

'But the whole thing's quite appalling.'

Admiral Canaris, 1938

'I'm not sure I want my son to put the State first [but] no children look stronger and more beautiful than those little blond angels one sees in the country. It's a terrible confession to make but I honestly think that if Michael hadn't shed that dark hair he was born with, I wouldn't feel so proud of him. He might be mistaken for a little Jew!'

'Sept 3: England has declared war on Germany . . . My head is splitting and I feel ill with nerves.

Sept 4: I feel better today. The German navy torpedoed and sank a British liner. That will show them.'

Elisabeth von Stahlenberg, *Diaries*, 1933, 1939

'. . . hands off the British Empire is our maxim and it must not be weakened or smirched to please sob-stuff merchants at home or foreigners of any hue.'

Antony Eden, 1944

1

Lake Plön, April–May 1945

Michael Quantz transiently haunted the lakeside, pausing, screwing up his eyes against the sheen of grey light. Waves spilt at his feet, drizzle fell with calm steadiness, and he found himself at a standstill.

One rarely indulged the luxury of thought nowadays. All did without sleep, catnapping in odd half-hours or getting caught short, jerking to consciousness with a mouthful of sourness, a staleness of cigarette smoke, lungs coated in a raw residue of tar, sweat caking the body within its uniform. Jolted awake, there was surprise at having been taken by the permanently denied sleep, which stalked like a predatory lover to whom no upright man should surrender.

All looked pasty, cadaverous, defective, under the unforgiving light. The businesslike efficiency of men working at top speed took on a blue blur through the cigarette smokescreen; naval uniforms seemed dusted with powder, like bloom on fruit, and everyone looked off-colour. Admiral Dönitz's unnervingly competent secretaries kept up a martial tempo of typing, brisk, fresh-looking. Their fingers marched on the keys, processing messages, each one more urgent, more abysmally meaningless than the last, intermittently glancing up at the clock above the admiral's door.

What time is it? What time? How much time do we have?

Time pressed and something must be done: some last-ditch push to ward off total defeat, although it was numbly known that defeat was already total.

Quantz moved between the twin naval camps: 'The Trout', with its arc of half-completed buildings, and the fancy training school for lower officers at Ruhleben on Lake Plön. 'The Trout' was the hub of Germany, now that Berlin was a tomb, Dresden ash, Frankfurt flattened. There on the border of Lake Suhr, in the middle of nowhere, Admiral Dönitz, with two hundred officers and four hundred men, kept motley court, his eyebrows permanently raised as if anxiety had set hard, feigning a mask of determination. Multiple phone calls drilled the ear drums, radios emitted despair, telegraphs whirred in messages of domino-collapse as the east moved west and the west moved east; and Dönitz, rigid and narrow at his desk, blindly searched the faces of his officers.

Quantz, trained in the Canaris school of Intelligence but long returned to the Navy, couldn't quite slough his habit of cynical observation. His role was outsiderly, that of a high-powered mercury. He bore handwritten notes from base to Ruhleben on a pushbike, and was mildly entertained as he emerged to see the rump of the Cabinet borne into 'The Trout' in a clapped-out Volkswagen. The cadet on guard duty had raised the barrier and shot up his arm with an immaculate *Heil*.

Ministers were billeted in the swisher houses of Plön and Eutin. Krosigk in his capacity as Finance Minister; Dorpmüller representing traffic; Thierack, arbiter of Justice, where money had no value, traffic was at a standstill and justice had been dead for decades. Ribbentrop took no part, though like the rest he was familiar to the gaping townswomen in Plön, who stood in the cobbled marketplace and watched semi-mythical heroes come and go as if the town had been converted into a set for a film. Ribbentrop swept in and out of Haus Junghans and Himmler came and went daily from his headquarters in Lübeck: panicked, cornered, lethal. Parties of SS-men in their black glory roamed. Marines without ships. Pilots without planes. Speer kept tucked in next to Dönitz, having swapped his ramshackle trailer above Lake Eutin for 'The Trout'.

As The Rump sped in, Michael pedalled out. The road between the camps was, as usual, a site of heaving chaos, choked with refugees and lorries laden with wounded troops. This was Dönitz's doing, this feat of evacuation, as German civilians and soldiers were salvaged from the Baltic and shipped to the western zone in hundreds of thousands. Human misery flooded north-west, away from the Russians, into a dwindling territory of hope, where Dönitz was still striving to be delivered of his good idea.

Michael negotiated his bike through wagons and prams, as they laboured through the beauty of the spring woodlands. A bespectacled old man with a cloud of white hair, resembling a professor who has absent-mindedly mislaid his shoes, padded past. Then a girl unloosed lank hair, which tumbled down her back from its roll, and, singing, suddenly pulled her blouse up over her head in one lithe movement. *Stop it, just stop that rude nonsense*, the mother grumbled feebly, a token resistance, because decency takes a while to die and you have to say something. But the girl's bared breasts caught the light and Michael's eye; he braked, mesmerised to watch her brief rapturous dance, arms gracefully extended, whirling on the spot. And singing. Mind gone, he presumed, raped or whatever, along the way. *Come on, Effi, put your things back on*, the mother pleaded. *Be a good girl for Mummy*. And she stopped, staggered disorientated and, catching Quantz's eye, flashed him a smile that would have been tearingly beautiful; would have been, except that her teeth were entirely gone.

No teeth. No teeth and called Effi. Mind gone. Quantz pedalled off distraught, because she was called Effi, and her mind was gone and her teeth too. He found his eye combing the oncoming crowd, for signs of his Effi and his Wolfi, who somehow seemed more mortal.

***

It was the fake normality of the Navy that impressed. While Germany was escaping from Germany, rolling the carpet up behind itself, the chap at the barrier of Ruhleben insisted on seeing Michael's papers.

'I just came out of here half an hour ago. You saw me go.'

'Sorry, sir. Identification, please.'

No teeth. Not one in her head apparently. Her smile so wide it revealed the cavernous emptiness of her jaw. And called Effi. Breasts beautiful, ripe; no teeth. Mrs Effi Quantz had no breasts to speak of, but her teeth were good, hardly a filling. Whereas his own mouth was full of horror. Crumbling decay, of which he had noticed he was conscious, because he tended to cover his mouth with his hand and avoided smiling.

But Effi must be safe, surely, even in Kiel, with an impregnable cellar like that. She and Wolfi. Although he had shown her little love... With a pang of shame, he dismounted and delivered his message at the main block, where all was quiet and businesslike. Commander Pauckstadt's adjutant thanked Captain Quantz, assured him he would pass the note across at the first opportunity, the Commander was rather tied up at the moment. All orderly and disciplined, the U-boat people being quietly spoken, with 'no side', as Michael put it to himself. They just got on with the job in hand: the scuppering of the submarine prototypes, one-man exploding suicide boats, in the lake. They were sabotaging their own suicide boats. Michael would not think further of Effi.

Ruhleben still seemed spanking new, its white barracks proudly erected on the eve of the war, centred by the flagstaff, a nautical whimsy, fitted out with rigging and a crow's nest, the great crossbar hung with flags and an intricate complication of ropes, so that the camp emulated a great ship on a wholly becalmed ocean. How the Plön townspeople had loved it when the Navy moved in; loved becoming a garrison town again after a gap of seventy years. Plön had been put back on the map. The intense optimism of the times had brought folk out in militaristic raptures: the Nikolaikirche bells had pealed carillons, flags had rippled and shanties been sung; sailors had been lavishly kissed by the Band of German Maidens.

The town had been full of uniforms: SS, SA, SD, the Marine-SS, Hitler Youth, Marine Hitler Youth. But there had also been visits by poets, artists and foreign delegations, wined and dined in the elegant Ruhleben mess, there on Lake Plön, a sheet of water the shape of Africa. Ruhleben Barracks still glittered in the sun, but broken-down lorries now clogged its quadrangles, tackled by engineers whose ingenuity reached levels of improvisation which must count as genius, Michael thought, in such circumstances. No spare parts, no oil, no petrol and, when you had mastered these difficulties, nowhere to go.

Sailing boats were moored at the jetties, jostling for space. Michael stood looking out over the breadth of water. The girl with the breasts had stirred his senses, and he was conscious of smelling the strange fishiness of the lake. A pleasant, lively stink that brought to mind the smell of a girl's sex. Girls, his weakness. Any girl. Young preferably, slim or voluptuous it didn't matter. The salinity of the moist terrain between their legs. And when he had tried licking and nuzzling Effi there, where they loved it, she had stiffened and closed her legs against the explorations of his obliging tongue. Closed her legs like a pair of blunt scissors. Turned her back and plunged her head in the pillow, mortified.

But you'll like it. That's what women like.

How do you know, Michael? she hadn't said. She had kept dumb, played dead from the waist down; from the neck up, come to that.

If I were you, he hadn't said, *I'd get the benefit of my experience and be grateful for it.*

You don't love me, she'd snuffled.

Oh Christ. Change your tune, the record's stuck. Had he said that, or just thought it? She would remember, if he had. He had called her *Rigor Mortis* in his mind. Michael flinched on her behalf, looking out over the lake, cruised by black-headed gulls, with their blood-red bills; velvet coots skimmed the surface. At breeding-time the skies were clamorous; bird colonies came in dark clouds and the air thronged with wings like an eclipse. The birds mated, nested and brooded on the fish-rich islands; so Heini the young lieutenant had said, his whispery voice rising in an ornithological passion which had amused his pals. *Love birds*, he'd said, *just love them*. That was what he'd joined the Navy for. *Gull Island, that is*, he'd said, and pointed. *The storm gulls breed out there, where there's no vegetation. And you can see the sea swallow, on the gravelly banks of the islands, all the way from tropical Africa. And wild geese. Look, there they are, wild geese.*

It had gone quiet; the knot of men had looked out over the waste of waters, into the non-human world.

And when autumn comes, the earnest young nature-lover had said in his hoarse voice, *one day you'll see the geese leave, all at once they go. They all migrate. In V-formation.*

So that's where all our planes have buggered off to, said another. *Frigging well migrated*. Knowing Quantz would turn a deaf ear.

Think I'll have a go at migrating, Heini's pal Günther had murmured. Pregnant looks had been exchanged.

Dönitz's vicious naval police were kept busy catching and hanging deserters. One day the hanged lad on a beech tree just outside the barracks turned out to be Günther. Heini came sobbing to Quantz: *But that's Günther. They've hanged my Günther, Michael*, violating all the codes of rank by grabbing him with his Christian name.

They had buried the boy. Michael had shaken Heini by the shoulders. *Bloody well pull yourself together, lad. Get a grip*. But Wolfi came to mind, his boy babied and over-mothered in Kiel, gentle as the young ornithological lieutenant, dithery, flat-footed and cannoning into things. Such sweetness of spirit as Heini possessed, combined with a noddleful of useless knowledge, seldom made for long survival.

So Michael was roughly tender with the weeping youngster, and snarled to him to keep his head down till the Brits came.

***

The water's lappings acted as a soporific. Michael slept and dreamed awake. The rhythm implied a banal existence, a peaceful monotony, which repeated itself like a dull lie. The lie slid into the spirit with a dissolving effect, like a pill on the tongue. He watched the water pucker with drops of sweet rain that clung in a mesh of fine droplets over his jacket: out there it was so pearly with mist that he could not see to the other side.

Before the war he and Paul Dahl used to cycle out from Lübeck with their rods and bait, for the choice fishing. Perch and tench, bream and salmon. Michael remembered the women smoking eels, and how he and Paul had gorged on the acrid flesh until Paul was sick – he was often ailing in those days, his mother worrying constantly about his delicate stomach. Michael had patted his spewing friend's back with one hand and pinched his own nose with the other. Paul then sat down all quivering and white, on a fallen willow stump overgrown with weeds and moss. But mostly they'd fished, watching the creatures spasm in their silver death-throes on the floor of the rowing boat. Old Franz Mützenbrecker had owned the estate, which he had sold to the Navy, as a patriotic duty. They had cleared the woodlands and built roads and supply-works.

The thought of Paul made Michael wince. From a seraphic Lutheran chorister, a good chum, though none too bright, Paul had ripened to the purest filth...

Michael would bolt. They were all doing it, if they had any sense.

He could get quit of rank and uniform, boots and badges, grow his hair over his collar and take to the life of a peaceful...peaceful what? Village schoolmaster? Did they still have village schoolmasters? He would decamp, pick up Effi and Wolfi, and bring them back here. Start again, the three of them. He picked up a downy breast-feather from the sand and closed his palm around the delicately curling softness. Rural life would suit him well; suit them well. The scent of resin from the forest told him so, its soundness, its balm. The canopy of chestnuts and ash, beech, birch and willow made you feel safe.

Yet the woods crawled with refugees, coughing, hacking timber to build fires. You saw the smoke rise, and at night the naval police went round ordering the refugees to put out their fires, to blackout. The village had all but doubled in size; sleepers lay on floors, in sties, sheds, in the school, the hospital, the pharmacy, on straw. It would get worse.

Michael hunkered on the dun sand, among a litter of sailors' fag ends and the patternings of birds' footprints; a complex code of comings and goings. Water rippled in at his feet, then doubled back into the lake that now looked gelid, clotted. Oil from the scuppered subs cast its rainbow coat on the shore like a slough. It was curious to think of what this lake contained: Michael had seen chaps tossing badges, weapons and helmets into the lake, before scarpering. He had not acted to stem these gestures of common sense in a world where dedication to absurdity was both norm and rule.

The admiral . . . which admiral? From Canaris he had passed to Dönitz. From the double-talker to the single-minded yes man. And how Canaris had almost survived, almost, but hadn't, overcame Michael again, with a sensation that dull adaptation to perpetual crisis could not numb. Anguish; near to love. He shrank into himself; crouched like a beetle whose instinct to burrow under a stone is balked not by fear or obligation but by sheer disorientation. His memory misgave him. He possessed too many eyes and tongues.

This polyglot fluency was what had recommended him to the Little Admiral. Portuguese, Spanish, Italian, English, French and Russian were languages in which Michael could express himself with varying degrees of ease. It was the gift of mimicry that did it. How Canaris's eyes used to light up when Michael came out with some phrase that brought to mind the warmth of the Mediterranean, a fluid ambivalence with which no true German could feel comfortable. It had made for a bond. Teutons could only feel safe strictly bound in the rigours of their own tongue's laws. Gradually all other tongues would be swallowed in the global stride of German, which not only obeyed its own strong rules but maintained a duty to parade these grammatical laws on its sleeve, facing outward like badges. His countrymen's insularity was odious to the supple-tongued, bilingual Canaris, who, hidden beneath his sombrero, had ingenuously imagined himself unrecognised as he'd toured Spain. How charming he could be, the Little Admiral, the ironist, and they had hanged him like a puppet (for so lightweight was he, that he could not easily die, so had said Michael's informant, but twitched on the line for a quarter of an hour).

The other admiral was now the dogs' master. Michael saw the logic of Dönitz's position (but it was an ill logic, solipsistic): hold on, hold out, keep fighting in 'Fortress Schleswig-Holstein', evacuate the Baltic, and wait for the British and the Amis to turn against the Soviets, as turn they would. *Turn they must, turn they will*, stated Dönitz, and kept on saying the same, in conjunction with the words *duty*, *honour* and *loyalty*, as though infinite repetition at the edge of an abyss would incite everyone to jump in. Dönitz's conviction was that the British would turn to us. *They will need us. We have an army, here in Schleswig-Holstein. They and we are on the same side, we think alike, they will need us to fight the Bolshevik Menace.*

We have an army! thought Michael. That's a good one. We have the ghosts of shadows. The halt and the maimed. We have regiments of casualties. Oh yes, and don't forget the remnant of our heroic Belly Regiment, the conscripted contents of a hospital for stomach complaints. He relished ironies and was given to minting them, but in the present case invention was beggared. Irony was the land in which they all resided, stony-faced before the virtuosity of the Fatherland's mirthless witticisms.

The British were pounding on the door of Hamburg. Bombers darkened the sky. He would fetch out his English and polish it, ready for the arrival of the Britons.

Nowadays it was Michael's own tongue that he felt impotent to master. It felt hidebound as a dead language, pith dried on a sapless tree. His tongue stumbled as he recalled faltering when first called upon to translate the warlike deeds of Carthage and Rome, nations he had as a youth considered fictions invented by sadistic Latin masters. Nowadays he caught himself thinking phantom thoughts in wisps of French or Spanish. His native language fell away; its joints snapped, for it had hobbled too long on crutches of circumlocution and euphemism. Having pledged itself faithfully to show its subjunctives on its sleeve and to parade its genders and cases in categories of a bureaucratic exactitude and pointlessness, it was now reduced to the incessant barking of a tethered hound, *Ich kapituliere nie. Nie kapituliere ich.*

Paul Dahl's sole tune: *Never, we shall never give in.*

It had given Michael's stomach a turn when his boyhood friend fetched up here at Plön, with a squad of deathsheads, who had somehow managed to buff their boots and buttons despite the journey north on roads choked with refugees. The Golden Pheasants, bigwigs in their Mercs and Horches jampacked among the little people, thumbs on hooters, driving them off the roads, and still they came, and kept coming, skeleton-children, bundles of rag containing old people, a bust of Julius Caesar bouncing on the open boot of a Daimler, and bursting through this throng, Paul Dahl and comrades in a Volkswagen running on potato fuel.

The blood had rushed to Dahl's head upon seeing Michael Quantz: he was one of these milky complexioned men who blush so easily, his wheat-pale hair nearly white, like a girl's. With his fellow lickspittle, Karl Müller, there stood the inseparable friend of Michael's childhood. On the white sand at Travemünde, building sandcastles, their mothers gossiping in wicker sunchairs, they had crouched close as brothers. Michael had not thought it strange that Paul's father kept a room as a shrine to his ancestors, but accepted this as children do accept vagaries and obsessions, in a world where all is novel. Not that he had envied Paul his father, for while Mrs Dahl had doted, Mr Schoolmaster Dahl had been dissatisfied with his thin-skinned younger son. He bullied and threatened; humiliated and scored cheap points off the boy. *Come here, blancmange; come along, milk pudding*. Michael had regularly done Paul's homework for him. The two children, dressed from earliest days in sailor suits, had been destined for the Navy. But Paul had spat in his father's eye, and got out of range, opting for a profession of butchery instead.

It had been Dahl and Müller who passed on the news of the Little Admiral, with gloating they took no trouble to hide. Michael had watched rather than listened to Dahl spouting. He was still a well-nigh perfect animal. He had risen in Himmler's brotherhood by virtue of blond, obsequious good looks, and perfect blood which showed through the translucent skin with exemplary purity. Not a lot of beard to shave off. The hair off-white. Albino perfection. As Dahl told him of the hanging of Canaris, he raked his hand through his hair and Michael remembered how Paul had caught his first wife dyeing their child's hair blonde: denounced the one as an adulteress and the other as a Slav bastard and got shot of the two of them.

Michael's guts squeezed; he remembered his last meeting with Dahl, performing bestial duties in Russia. He'd be reduced to dyeing his flaxen mop brown before long and passing himself off as a Ukrainian slave-worker. Murderous barber.

Dahl had a cold sore at the edge of his mouth, which had crusted and cracked. His fingers wandered up to pick at this blemish to his beauty, which he would be angrily aware of: worse than any woman for vanity.

'I regret,' said Admiral Dönitz's aide to Dahl and his comrades, 'we have neither present use nor messages for you. I suggest you link up with your leader in Lübeck. You will find him at police barracks.' He did not look up from his desk.

***

'What poor little sausages we are,' Dönitz had said, in Michael's astounded hearing, 'compared with the *Führer*.'

Then the poor little sausage became the new *Führer*.

***

They were whispering in the vestibule when Michael arrived back at the nerve centre of 'The Trout'. The neglected chins of clean-shaven men wore bristly five-o'clock shadows; their eyes were bagged with grey pouches. Nerves had been impossibly strung for so long that if ever they were to slacken, the men's sinews would perish like rubber bands. Michael reached for his cigarettes.

God will pass judgment on us, Canaris had said six years back, on viewing the massacre in Warsaw. *Our children's children will have to bear the blame for this.* He had kept Quantz and others watching, noting, reporting, his conscience crawling, yet made no stand. He petted his dachshunds. Fondled his Arab mare, as she nuzzled her nose in at the French windows for sugar lumps, her silken mane white as his hair. Only this month Canaris had swung. Such a tiny man, only five foot three, the puppet-master died like a marionette, naked, and the 'traitors' were cremated, nothing left. So said Dahl and Karl Müller in chorus.

Michael lit up and turned to the window, looking out into the darkening parade ground, wedged with lorries and staff-cars. But the admiral still swung from a meathook in his mind.

Dönitz could be seen framed in the doorway, white to the gills. His *aide de camp* bent over his shoulder as they read and reread a message from the Bunker. Speer, sitting bolt upright in his chair, passed his hand over his mouth in a curious movement as if to wipe off a fatuous and compulsive smile.

'The *Führer* has named me,' announced the admiral to the assembled company.

Nothing was said. It was as if the *Führer* had named as his successor a wooden doll.

'Is he dead? What do you make of it?' Dönitz faltered to Lüdde-Neurath. He turned to him almost with pleading. 'It doesn't say so. What do you make of it?' he repeated.

Lüdde-Neurath scrutinised the message, shook his head, handed it back. 'You are named his successor, that's certain, sir.'

'I am named,' repeated Dönitz, stunned. 'I am named.' Ashen, he received this anointing. 'So I shall have to continue with our beloved Leader's ... in the event that ... '

The admiral juddered to a full stop, as if he had run out of fuel before journey's end. Speer, Minister for non-existent Armaments, recovered aplomb, and assumed a shade more deference. Without being fulsome, he emphasised the high admiral's unique competence for this difficult office. The office, thought Michael, that is only a nameplate in finest Gothic gilt lettering, on the door of a bombed-out room.

'I am authorised, as you see, to take all measures necessary to secure Northern Command against the enemy. Written authority on the way. Quantz, what is the precise time?'

'Six forty-two, sir.'

'We must recall Himmler,' Dönitz twitched. 'He must be told. He won't like this, my God, he won't like this one bit. Call him in, would you, Lüdde-Neurath. Better station some troops ... just in case.'

His hands visibly trembled. 'So much work,' he sighed, but the word *work* seemed to revive him. He repeated it, assigning to himself, correct Karl, the sacred duty to obey himself, Supreme Commander Elect.

***

Michael reluctantly joined armed U-boat men stationed in the surrounding wood. Standing sideways behind a stout chestnut near the guardhouse, he caught the wink of a star: the North Star, was it? He recalled the trick he learned at school whereby only if you hold the star at the edge of your eye and look at another will you focus it clearly. He forgot why that should be. Behind him in the barracks there was total eclipse, windows blacked out. A sliver of moon.

Like a snapshot, Michael kept seeing his Little Admiral hanging naked. The abject humiliation of that; its hint of atonement. The man was risen, quit of debts, beyond harm. But Michael intended to survive. He had not slid and slithered all this way, shedding greasy skins as he went, to meet his end in some senseless shoot-out between rival gangsters. A tract of bracken behind him would serve as cover. He heard the purring of engines long before the unlit cavalcade was visible. They all heard, ears on the strain. Michael held in his belly.

A motorcade of open Volkswagens roared in from Lübeck, three dozen of Himmler's seasoned butchers aboard. Engines off. Macher – he saw Macher – leap out into the silence, a lynx on the pounce. But instead of bloodshed, there was merciful anti-climax. Lüdde-Neurath stepped out smartly to welcome the SS guests, his Knight's Cross gleaming faintly in the moonlight, the most disarmingly conspicuous of targets.

'Good you could get here so promptly. Your chief with you?'

Down stepped the five-foot-seven-inch conquistador, flabby hips, pouched cheeks like a marsupial, the skin of his chinless face like putty.

Macher and five butchers were escorted to Dönitz's presence.

'Please,' requested the admiral, 'read it for yourself.'

Himmler, heir-in-waiting, read the wire pronouncing Dönitz head of the Thousand Year Reich, paled, sat down, rose, bowed, then called into play his old-world formality and aloof geniality.

'Allow me, then, my Leader, to be the Second Man in your administration.'

Through the night, as Dönitz and Himmler confabulated, Michael drank Hennessy in the mess with their aides, Lüdde-Neurath and Kremer, in company with Dahl and his fellow filths. All night the Little Admiral hung from a beam directly above Michael's increasingly squiffy head on a thread, a *deus ex machina* peering down with detached amusement on the insomniac crew and their games of double bluff and murderous camaraderie.

Michael heard enquiries after Paul Dahl's family. He watched Paul weep.

'I shall never believe it. I shall never believe our beloved Leader can die. I shall be loyal to the grave.'

Michael turned upon the blotched face the hag-ridden sleeplessness of his insight. He got a clear view of the void at the centre of a man who is loyal to the grave.

'But your family, your immediate family. Are they in a safe place?'

Paul shed tears. 'The *Führer* is my family. And if he should fall, I am an orphan. We are all orphans. Where could we go? Where would be our home?'

Michael's teeth began to twinge. Horror thrilled round the nerves of his jaw, a mouthful of corruption. As he looked up, wincing, he got a swift view of Dahl's bared teeth, flawlessly perfect. And the stuff at Minsk all came up: the bloodying, blooding, of his memory. Michael had seen *that*, that which was not named, which was simply 'that'. He had reported his view of 'that' to Canaris, and the Little Admiral had not blenched, because 'that' he already knew, but (his shabby uniform crumpled, with what looked like egg on his lapel) had sighed and called out 'Sweethearts, come, come,' to the ubiquitous dachshunds, plump from titbits, and had put up a merely token resistance when Quantz had begged to return to sea duty.

'What is it, Quantz?' asked Lüdde-Neurath.

'Nothing. Just bloody toothache. It will go off in a minute.'

'I have some tincture somewhere. Does the trick for me.'

'It's going off,' insisted Michael faintly. Brandy unstrung him but the power to rationalise was returning. After all, he, Michael, had done nothing but report, investigate, communicate, liaise...

He would get the necessary internal repairs done, when all this was over. And it was nearly over. Everyone had false papers up his sleeve, ready to dive into the Navy or duck into civilian life, or to spirit himself abroad along webs he'd been building for months. Michael's tongue licked queryingly round the dodgiest of his teeth. A mouthful of corruption had not progressed too far beyond the dentist's renovation, a filling here, a gold crown there. Surely not.

Watery, lachrymose eyes stared from Paul's face, yet Michael recognised a sly flicker of smugness in his childhood friend's sideways glance, which assured him that Dahl had indeed taken care of his own. 'We as individuals do not count,' parroted Dahl. 'Only Germany matters. The Amis will turn on the Soviets, you'll see. The *Reichsführer* has been putting out feelers. He has many friends in the civilised nations, all sorts of strings to pull, our network runs from the Vatican to... you'd be amazed. He will get us out of this temporary hiccup.'

'But Dönitz has been appointed...'

'Come, come,' cut in Dahl, his voice a shrill rebuke. 'We all know where the real power lies.'

They all breakfasted together. The politeness was enough to make anybody's fillings twang. Himmler ate like one half-starved; Michael was staggered at the way he shovelled it in. Then he sat and talked, talked, talked, drumming hectic fingers on the table and, in those moments when he made way for another speaker, raised his upper lip to tap his front teeth with his fingernails. Dönitz, hardly able to touch his rolls and coffee, remained quiet. Polite. Heedful. Chary of the forces his rival still commanded. *And besides*, thought Michael, *they agree. For the most part, they agree.*

Thank fuck, the Chinless One was going. Himmler pulled on his white leather gloves, flexed the fingers. Dahl did likewise. Himmler straightened his tunic around plump thighs, body craned forwards as if suffering stomach gripes. Dahl held open the door for his master and followed him out into the dusky sunrise.

'I doubt whether Mr Himmler,' explained the admiral, tacitly stripping him of his title, 'will be a member of our government but we shall need to keep in close contact.'

***

1 May. Bormann's telegraph, eleven hundred hours, Hitler dead.

Confirmation that afternoon. *Let it come*, thought Michael. He could not quite focus the feeling but imagined that they'd all been queuing in the cold outside the bread shop and found (what they dreaded learning but in point of fact had known all along) that there's not a crumb of bread there, never had been, never would have been, all a hoax. At least the queuing was over.

Michael was aware of the soft thud of a peaked cap on the desk as at some stressful moment Karl Dönitz unconsciously put it on his head, then removed it, to scrape his fingernails through his hair as though something under there itched. He was about to broadcast to the nation: *German men and women, soldiers of the German armed forces!* he muttered to himself, preparing. His voice was tinny. *Our* Führer, *Adolf Hitler, has fallen... His mission in the battle against the Bolshevist flood-storm is valid for Europe and the entire civilised world.* Michael, mechanically sorting papers for incineration, viewed Dönitz sidelong. He saw a naval officer, stuffy, upright, falling back on a Prussian code of honour in a world soiled beyond redemption; a lackey who'd never sought high political office shooting into what had been a firmament but was now only a void. He saw a grey soul utterly at sea, floating by virtue of his own hollowness, lost on a waste of waters.

The admiral replaced the doeskin hat, with its large and floppy peak, positioning it over his forehead in regulation manner. The Head of State picked up his maroon fountain pen to amend a word. *Army! The* Führer *has appointed me as his successor... The oath of loyalty which you yielded to the* Führer *is now due from each one of you to me...*

In viewing the baring of that head, Quantz experienced a shuffle of alarm. Sleeplessness made some strut of his inner framework give and homesickness washed through his breast: not for Effi, but for Mama (for whom he had felt a regulation scorn) so long in her grave. The life-guaranteeing, the necessary one. But Mama was dead.

And Dahl saying, *We are orphans*. Infantile.

But the fatty breakfasts, how he missed those, the eggs, sausage, ham, black bread, butter and cream; and the way Mother used to sit him on her lap, a comfy, plump woman; and the rolls warm from the oven, all fluffy and breathing steam when you broke them open. Effi would be all right, down there in the cellar: these old merchants' houses were built like fortresses, and he knew she'd stocked up; her legs were like a wishbone and she clung to the child, as if the child could save her. Michael's chest seethed.

Ceasing to sift the papers, he calmed himself by looking directly over at his chief, who glanced up, forehead furrowed, beneath the outsize brim. Why did he keep donning and doffing his cap? Quantz was aware of the smallness of the man, the dwarfing largeness of the dark halo.

***

Back at Ruhleben, Quantz presided over final scupperings, the bird-obsessed Lieutenant accompanying him. Two of their men had waded in after the broadcast, in full battle kit, wearing the Knight's Cross, rifles above their heads. Their pockets must have been full of stones, to militate against any last-minute inclinations to swim. It must have taken them an age to get far enough out. Nobody bothered to retrieve the bodies. They killed themselves tidily, beside the jetty of the swimming area, drunk down into the glossy shadow of its struts.

He asked Heini about his family. Heini murmured that he had had no news about his mum and dad since leaving Berlin. A qualm of agitated memory beset Michael. Effi, meagre and homely in a wrap-around green dress, with her rather hooded, guarded eyes, querying, *So you no longer care at all?* Effi in Lübeck with the toddling lad, always hanging on to Mama for dear life, a handful of skirt in his chubby grip, his thumb threaded through her buttonhole. *You'll make a milksop of him*, Michael had warned, but not in an unkind tone. He had chucked Wolfi under the chin, and the boy had squirmed away.

He's all I've got, Effi had snarled back, bonded to the boy with fierce tenacity. *You've got your women.*

Michael had cared, but failed to care enough. Now he

shook, at the lakeside, with grief over Wolfi and a need to cherish Effi, for whom he had made so little effort and to whom he had always told, with unforgivable casualness, the truth.

2

Lake Plön, September 1958

How deep? Isolde Dahl wondered. The volatile water slapped at the foundations of the jetty; she crouched to watch its surface slide her image into elongating lozenges, focusing on nothing stable. The struts plunged to sandy depths; though one could not see the bottom, only a geometry of timbers, whose perspective held out until a nebulous greenness foiled the eye. It must be really deep. And because one's view failed at a certain depth, it appeared that the rectangular jetty marking off three sides of the swimming area was like a raft riding the waves.

Isolde stood up and, with both hands resting on the wooden rail, smooth from a history of many hands, looked out into the haze of silver lake. The bordering forests were misted by the same pallor as the immense sheet of water. Over there, straight ahead, lay the Danish border, beyond lake, pines and hills more soft and slight than the beacons of Brecon. A hidden world of invisible plains and polders. She screwed up her eyes. A rowing boat made a tiny point of motion on the still trance of the lake, and she could just see miniature oars dip and rise, dip and rise, with the suggestion of a wake forking out behind the boat.

She was new and off balance. Had not bargained for the militariness of the school, the way its bright buildings stood to attention around the central quadrangle, over which a flagpole towered, in the shape of a mast. *Quaint*, she had thought, and then *daft*, for a squad of schoolboys was being marched out in full naval gear by a po-faced man to whom she would later be introduced as the head, Mr Patterson. A man in civvies, moving with stiff, straight legs beside his callow squad. She lugged her cases out of the main building. When she turned round, the cadets had been halted by a larger lad, appointed to bawl orders. And one was shimmying up the rigging. Up he went and down. Then another. And another.

Like monkeys, Isolde thought. She had foreseen hockey but not military drill when coming out as a teacher to the British Army Over the Rhine. Perhaps that was naive.

'Miss Dahl! Miss Dahl! You can't carry those on your own! Just hang on a mo. We'll get our good Heini to help you out.'

Now the lads were shuffling sideways, now forming up, now raising the Union Jack and slamming to attention with a salute.

The man called Heini, with his owl-spectacles, emerged to scoop up her cases.

'Sorry, miss,' he said. 'You shouldn't be struggling with those.'

He was youngish, sweet-looking: walked with something of a limp and spoke English with a strong German accent, like Isolde's mother's, but without Renate's distaste for the tongue. His air was apologetic.

'Thanks so much,' she said. 'I'm all in.'

'Unfortunately, your block is the furthest out, miss, nearest the lake.' He spoke with hesitant deference, as though personally responsible for the long walk.

'I'm sorry,' she said in German. 'I don't know your name. We haven't been properly introduced.'

'Good gracious,' he said. 'Good gracious.' And stopped, overwhelmed.

'Funny name.'

'No, miss, of course that's not my name,' he replied solemnly. 'Heini Fuchs. School groundsman. It was just, well, just nobody speaks German here.'

He seemed so flustered that she returned to English. 'How long have you been here?' she asked.

'Years. Many years. This is your block, miss, over here. I am by vocation an ornithologist,' he amazed her by saying. 'Not much call for that nowadays, so I stayed put when...when I came here. The school was kind enough to take me despite my minor war-wound. It is enough,' he explained with earnest sincerity, 'to be near my birds. We are just by the North Sea, you see, and the perfect environment for many species of . . . '

And they were off into an ardent realm of coots and ducks, seven, at least seven, different species of gull, wonderful creatures, he said, but to Isolde, native of Swansea, gulls were of limited interest. Her nerves fluttered as she encountered the monumental facade of her block, eye-like dormers peering from the fortifications of a high-sloping roof.

'Was this always a school?' she asked.

'It was built as a Marine Academy. For young German naval cadets to learn the ropes. After the war, the English took over. This was the HQ of your occupation troops.'

'Not mine,' came in Isolde.

He coloured up; deposited the cases at the door. 'Oh no, I didn't mean yours personally, of course, miss. I meant,' he fished around for the appropriate phrase, 'Eight Corps, to be precise. And after that Ruhleben became Connaught Barracks. And then this excellent boarding school.'

'Pity,' said Isolde. Heini looked astounded. He was evidently accustomed to the politely arrogant patriotism of the British communities stationed in his country. His flummoxed face, its roundness emphasised by the round specs, reddened. 'What I meant was, it's a pity the name Ruhleben had to be lost,' she explained quickly. 'Meaning, "Peaceful Life".'

'Indeed! Yes, indeed!' His face lit up. She found herself liking him, with a sudden gentle stirring, which she had not felt since Denis.

'And . . . have you a family?' she asked.

He had a wife and three young ones. Just like Denis. She watched him walk away, that slight limp only accentuating the tall, flexible body, with a certain chagrin. She had had to bite back the word 'pity' again, when he owned up to the nest just outside Plön, with the three tenderly loved fledglings. He had such a sincere, pleasant manner that she had been immediately drawn to him. How mam would fume. Rant. Blow her top. The very first German Issie comes across, she is stirred by. The characteristic recklessness Renate so deplored and feared and recognised was lightly breathed upon.

However, Heini's passion was reserved for birds and family, Isolde realised, and she was not planning to destroy anyone's nest. Nests did get destroyed though.

***

She had, as instructed by the hard-faced matron, 'made herself at home' by dumping her bags in her narrow room beneath a portrait of the Queen, and headed for the lake. The silver wedge of water visible from her window called irresistibly.

On the jetty, Issie turned again to look down into the enclosed water, her mind murmuring the same theme over and over: *You'll never work in an independent school in England again, Miss Dahl, be sure of that.* Tears filmed her eyes like an archaic habit, for the wound was now more chronic than acute: it didn't smart in the same way, yet it still dismayed her. For it was not her fault, as they had implied. It was his fault too, wasn't it? But it did not count against Denis in the same way, for a strange cluster of reasons: because he wore a tweed jacket, a collar and tie, a small moustache and a diffident, gentlemanly expression. Mary Wright's could not have done without its maths teacher, a family man of previously impeccable credentials, the tedium of whose classes seemed somehow to guarantee sterling worth, so kindly a man as to hesitate in reprimanding the first years for running on the stairs. And for such a clement, prim chap to be found with his hands inside the blouse of a young woman of voluptuous physique and European antecedents had left the headmistress and her deputy in little doubt as to the apportionment of blame.

Although Issie had received notice to quit and the stinging prediction, *You'll never work in an independent school in England again*, it was Denis she'd smarted for. She had felt along her very nerves his gentleness beside her, and the fragility of his frame, and had blurted, *It wasn't his fault.*

We are aware of that, Miss Dahl.

The way her surname had been stressed and mispronounced as *Doll* rebuked its foreign stamp. Its inheritor, for all her Welsh accent, did not belong. Could jolly well go back where she came from, the scandalised told-you-so in their eyes implied, tacitly pointing out that she had been given a sporting chance to prove herself and been caught out cheating, as, sadly, persons of foreign extraction will.

Issie had jutted her chin and shown some spirit, despite all. The pain of being parted from Denis had stabbed at her heart; she did believe she loved him and hoped he loved her, nor was she convinced that in 1958 illicit love should count as a hanging offence. So she had stuck out her chin, waywardly truculent, chip off the old block, and had told them it was love. If it was love, she'd said, it couldn't be a crime. She shouldn't be condemned for love.

Don't be childish, rapped the disgusted riposte. *Mr Taylor is a married man.*

Yes, and a mathematician, an Englishman, a father of three, equipped with jacket, moustache, pipe and set-square: what argument had Isolde against all this moral equipment? She had stood there blushing, while the head and deputy had stared, fascinated, at the mother-of-pearl buttons on Isolde's bosom, which they had watched her fingers scramble to do up. Denis crept back to Doreen, in remorseful gratitude.

But she had felt that he would write.

The lake creamed into shore, its green tide bearing beads of foam, a bobbing pine cone, a feather, like occult messages all sent streaming in one direction. Isolde crouched, with the sun on her back, as the feather fled under the boards, viewing in her mind's eye a phantom letter with Denis's costive handwriting; seeing herself snatch it from the pigeonhole and plunge it secretly into the pocket of her skirt.

The crossing from Harwich to the Hoek had been by night-ferry. Issie had stayed up on deck much of the time, headscarf flapping round her face in the bluster, giving her lips little stinging hits with its tail. Her thickly petticoated skirts were beaten into foam beneath her belted mackintosh, as she stared through a welter of night, watching the phosphorescent furrows of the boat's wake as they ploughed away from England and Denis.

He wouldn't write. She didn't honestly think he would...

Issie began to walk away from this thought, along the outermost jetty, where swimmers' footprints laid a cryptic, evaporating trail along the warm planks. She passed a notice marked 'DANGER!' and an orange lifebelt. Out at the rim of the enclosure on a high diving board, the figures of two young men stood against the sky: senior boys, the cream of whom were really full-grown men, broad-chested and narrow-waisted, hands on hips as they assessed the green abyss. Agile in their beauty, they poised and looked down from the arrogance of altitude at a cluster of girls perched on the edge of the pool. Sun threw tendrils of light off the water on to the tanned skin of their legs.

One young man abruptly leapt into the air, arms raised as if in semaphore, somersaulted in a tight ball, then flashed down into the water, with a concise spray of foam. His slick head burst up, seal-like, above the surface; he shook it and blew water out of his nose. Issie watched his lazy freestyle cover the pool's breadth. It must be freezing cold, for the lake shelved deeply. She shivered with longing to be in there too. Water was home: it was Pllwch Du and Rhossili on Sunday morning before the trippers arrived, virgin sands washed clear of castles and the vestiges of yesterday's encampments; herself running barefoot down the beach, corrugated like the ripples of the sea. She would show those English bastards how to dive.

The moment of contumely buoyed her up and she forgot to feel lost. It affected her like the premonition of a time when this whole Denis business would appear a farce in which she had played an embarrassing but forgettable part.

He wouldn't write...probably. But then he might, now that he knew she was gone for good and he was safe. He might perhaps write to say sorry; that it had mattered to him, despite the shame of losing face before the head, his own forfeiture of dignity, letting the side down.

Was it just the postwar scarcity of males that had drawn her to the unglamorous Denis? No: because he had shown interest in her, as a person, not just the lusciousness of her body, the powerful darkness of her face, with its high cheekbones and almond-slant eyes. In whispered conversations, he had asked about her history, listening carefully, in his calm fashion.

From Germany, originally, she had told him. *But I don't feel German. I feel Welsh. I am Welsh. My mother and I came to Swansea as refugees before the war. I don't remember it all that clearly, I was very small.*

And your father?

Stepfather. Owen. He's a lovely man. The original one I don't know.

How do you mean, dear?... You don't know?

Mother doesn't talk about him and somehow there's an unspoken prohibition on asking. I found some torn-up photos once. I was poking round, as one does. I thought that might be him. Dashing and tall-looking and fair.

Some of the pictures were in colour. She had conveyed the jigsaw scraps to her room, locked the door, and spent illicit hours recreating the putative father. He was a stunning blond; really, his hair was sensational, you'd have thought it was dyed, she reflected, matching the bits of him so that his reconstituted self stood now beside a glowing red-brick church, now on a bridge, beneath Neptune and his trident, now in a black leather belted coat, legs astride, arms folded, head bare, beside a heavy monument with twin spires. Her mother had known, with that hound-like instinct of hers, that Issie was up to something.

What are you doing in there, sweetheart? came the honeyed voice.

Homework.

Pause. Uncertainty. *Well, don't overdo it.*

The man's ash blond hair had somehow disconcerted Issie. It beggared her mother's brighter blonde. Not natural. But not dyed either. Something wrong with it, as if all the colour had been leeched away, near-white like old age crowning a young man's threatening, virile beauty. And she had never liked that kind of face, it seethed in her, the sense of something coming up from this patchwork picture, coming up in herself, and she had nicked the photos from Renate, and Renate would nose this crime out, she always did, and Isolde's hands shook, with . . . why was she feeling hot shame? Probably he was not even her father: what could her dark hair and eyes have in common with *that*? Yet her gaze had drunk him up too; even in the moments of revulsion, she could not have enough of the conundrum of the handsome ruffian in the boots, even while seeing that she had muddled the pictures and that the faces didn't quite add up.

Tada's home, Renate's voice came up the stairs, along with the scent of brisket cooking in its fragrant juices, and it had been odd how the blinds closed in Isolde's mind; she had lost interest and, shaking the bits into an envelope, had returned them secretly to Renate's drawer.

***

Don't imagine you'll ever get work in England again.

No, nor in Wales either, or Scotland.

Certainly not in Scotland.

Ireland had evidently been considered beneath mention.

Isolde plumped down on the edge of the jetty and, shedding her shoes, tested the water with her toes. The longing to strip off and plunge in rose like a thirst she didn't dare slake. To be drunk down into that cold element, and strike out with strong, muscular strokes, showing off her unfeminine crawl . . .

God, what a ruction there had been when Renate was made aware of Issie's decision to take the job in Schleswig-Holstein.

'Whatever will you tell your mam, *bach*?' Owen had asked in the Oystercatcher, taking a nervous mouthful of beer and replacing the glass carefully on the beer mat.

They were forever tiptoeing round Renate's susceptibilities but Issie could never remember why. Renate exuded martyrdom. Yet Issie could not see her mother as a victim: this lush, commanding woman who towered above the Welsh aunties with the sole exception of Lennie, and equalled most uncles. Only with Owen did Renate drop her guard; the domineering manner seldom asserted itself and she submitted to his reign of stoic gentleness with every appearance of contentment.

But even here lay an element of prohibition. Renate's high forehead spoke of burdensome secret intelligence, won far too late and at high cost, knowledge tainted with dark apprehension. She fussed over Owen's health, as if he were sure to be wrenched from her by whatever malign spirits controlled the world. And she would fight them every step of the way, prevent ambush by coddling and feeding him: for God's sake, the poor chap was weighed every week on the bathroom scales like a baby and begged to plump himself up a bit. Owen was naturally gaunt and wiry but he must be fattened.

In lulls of cold detachment, Mama would sit at the dressing table, pale hair down her back, head propped on one hand, staring not at herself but into retrospective space. Issie could not construe the abyss in those eyes; that limitless withdrawal both scared and repelled her, as Renate's arrogance did the rest of Owen's family.

And then the peculiar because passionate ambivalence of her mother towards herself, alternating ironic tolerance of the little creature and its foibles, with rigid discipline and phases of desperate possessiveness, holding up Issie's wide face to the light with too hard a grip, interrogating it with more hunger than the child could possibly fulfil.

Liebling... and a host of other endearments in German, which had, Issie felt in adult life, an operatic quality. Other people's mothers just took them grumblingly for what they were – whereas a sense of an elusive *someone else*, *somewhere else* had haunted her. Why couldn't Mam spit it out? It couldn't be that bad.

The trouble was, it could. She had read about the death camps and so on. So it could be that bad. But Issie was Welsh, not German. Issie was the new generation, free of *all that*. Her own speech bore no vestige of an accent, though her mother's could still be thick, marking her out as a foreigner in an area where even the English were foreigners, and whereas tribal intimacy could encompass family feuds of fabulous longevity as an aspect of bonding, it winced away from strangers. Especially a busty Kraut who knew her own mind, flaunted sunburnt skin in skimpy floral sundresses and made no secret of regarding her husband's family as the bottom of the barrel.

'If you could just be a little more . . . tender of my sisters' feelings,' Owen would suggest.

'Bear with their prejudice and provincialism – that's what you mean, *ne*? Yes, all right, for you, Owen, I'll try to *shrink*.'

Shrink she couldn't. Issie watched her explosively keeping her trap shut while the *antis* wittered. Issie adored the *antis* and could see nothing demeaning in their unlettered, cosy conversation. On a pouffe at *Anti* Margiad's coal fire, she let herself be blessed by the continuum of ordinariness, summed up in choirs of knitting needles and the accompanying gossip which seemed at one with the coal smoke in the shabby room tinged with damp. Renate acted hoity-toity in this air that suffocated her; that was the only way her self-respect could articulate itself in such an alien world.

The *antis* tattled ten-to-the-dozen in bubbling Welsh as they pottered in the kitchen. Issie, conscious of the lost look in Renate's eyes, was nevertheless enchanted by the lashings of lovely gossip, and would join in, but softly, whispering so as not to upset Mama.

'Displaced persons,' Renate had once confided. 'That's what we are.'

'I'm not.' Meaning: you be if you want to be but leave me out of it.

'You don't see.' The Mumbles train had chuntered round the arc of the bay. Issie, looking out at the glistening crescent of mudflats and an incoming tide, had felt totally at home.

'I'm Welsh,' she'd affirmed, loudly, so that the other passengers travelling to the pier and lighthouse could hear. As if offering them all a sight of her passport.

'Are you? Well, that's good.' Mama had reached for her hand and squeezed it; now Mama would have to be displaced on her own. 'My little Welsh *cariad*.' Renate tacitly agreed to the division between them and Isolde felt her vitality ebb.

The train had stopped at Oystermouth, folk getting on and off.

'I'm the same as what you are,' Issie had stated with bleak loyalty.

'Shall we have fish and chips at the pier? Ice cream?' Renate had suggested with new gaiety. It had been as though Issie had released her own energies for Renate to rise upon. 'What shall we have? We can have whatever we like.' She still childishly marvelled at the lifting of rationing; a penance of stint completed.

'I'm not bothered.'

'What's up, little love?'

'Nothing.' The train had pooped and started off again on its leisurely chuff round the bay. Isolde, pouting, had looked down at her knobbly knees. The scent of her mother's cheap cosmetics was rather overpowering. There had been a pause and then the brainwave hit her. Before she could think to put on the brakes, she blurted, 'Are we Jewish?'

'*Jewish?*' Renate swivelled, in astonishment that moved rapidly to affront. 'No, of course not. What's got into your head now?'

'I thought we might be Jews, that's all. How do I know?'

'Do I look like a Jew?'

'*I* don't know. I don't know what one looks like.'

'No, well, never mind.'

Now it was Renate's turn to withdraw. She breathed heavily and falteringly as Issie devoured a cornet in the seafront restaurant at Mumbles Pier, squinting out at the tide powering its way in, until they seemed to be floating on an ark above the waters. The sea pounded the rocks satisfyingly, throwing jets of spume into the air. As Renate's spirits had fallen, Isolde's had convulsed, and she became belligerent and raucous. She clamoured to have a go on the roundabout; whined for a swim. She had ignored two tears that bled from Mama's eyes, to be thumbed away in a gesture of self-contempt.

***

How could one tell the difference between unspeakable guilt and mute violation? Perpetrator and victim dived for the same cover: numb, exilic silence. Sitting in the warm haze of the bar Issie badgered Owen.

'I can't tell you, see, if she won't.' He'd shifted from haunch to haunch on his stool. 'It would be a breaking of her confidence. Let's talk about something else now.'

Issie had bent her head and said nothing. Her silence was a condemnation, a reply in its own terms to the barrage of silence with which her questions had been met by both parties.

'I've brought you up as my own, Issie, my one ewe lamb. As far as I'm concerned, you are my own. Never had the gift of the gab. Not my style, see. But can't that be enough for you? It is for me.'

'You've meant everything to us, Tada,' she muttered.

It had not been clear that Owen had caught her reply, swivelling round to squint at the clock. But his pale blue eyes, so striking in the unremarkable, rather weaselly face, had snagged in hers, and she had seen, with a squeeze of the heart, that he was moved. For a moment nothing had mattered save that he had been her rock. Surely in his own person, she had all the history she needed? Her restless inquisition had stopped there, at his habits and fads, his liking for lamb and mint sauce, his propped socked feet on the fender as he dozed of an evening. She had been replete with the generosity of her portion in life, even while suffering a qualm at knowing him mortal. Each had looked away in a different direction.

The foggy hubbub of the pub, with its beery gales of

laughter and babble of anecdote, embraced them in its tepid fug. Owen had downed his half.

'Walk it off on the beach? Get some good sea air in our lungs. Eat a mint, shall we, *bach*, for our breath?'

They had stumbled across the pebbly wilderness down beneath the parapet, bending to glean winkle or razor-shell, gutted of moist life. Salty gusts tossed gulls back to breast the current. Issie stood in the flow of wind, looking out, and was suddenly overcome by the smell of the mudflats, rank with evisceration and decay. The exquisite mother-of-pearl shell on her palm was the husk of a life only, a life digested into other lives, themselves devoured. The marine odour combined with the moody mobility of the cloudscape, light dissolving into a looming grey bank. The smell told now of rot, now of vitality, indeterminate between womb and gut.

'Try to break it to your mam gently like,' Owen had counselled as they'd toiled up the steep hill into Mumbles.

***

Renate could not see why any rational person should choose to quit Wales for Germany. And Schleswig-Holstein: had she heard rightly? Her own daughter wanted to go to Schleswig-Holstein? That place? Did she know what kind of people lived there? Very low people, cold and reserved, speaking gibberish of *Plattdeutsch*. She felt faint, she must sit down, it would kill her, she knew it would.

'It's an opportunity,' Isolde explained.

'For what? Opportunity for what?'

'Well, for seeing something of the world. Anyhow, it's not a German school, it's an English forces school.'

'I particularly do not wish that you go there. I wish you do not.'

'But I particularly do want to go.'

'Yes, and don't we all know why? To spite me, your mother. That's why. Because I went to all that trouble to get you out, *you* insist on going back. Despite having such wonderful qualifications – we scrimped for you, did you notice? We went short ourselves to put you through Froebel. You go to . . . that place . . . just to get back at me.'

'Of course not. That's nonsense.'

'Oh, so I talk nonsense, do I?'

'Yes.'

'You are punishing me . . . for something that was not . . . my . . . fault!'

'I am *not* . . . punishing . . . you! What would you need to be punished for?'

Renate had gone white, resorting to a crude, ragged voice that sent tremors down Isolde's spine. And look at your *hair*!' she screamed preposterously. 'It's like a . . . bird's nest!'

'What the hell has my hair got to do with it?'

'It's greasy, that's what.' She choked. 'Look at you.'

Emotion had dishevelled her English accent and grammar, revealing what she most wished to abandon, her linguistic roots. When Renate raged like this, Issie generally knuckled under.

'If you don't like how I look,' Issie retorted, 'that's up to you.'

'You are a cold, ungrateful girl!'

'*Me* cold!'

'Yes. You. After all what I done for you.'

'What? What have you done?'

'Owen, she asks what I've done for her! Where are you going? Oh, that's right, run away – go on, skedaddle when the going gets tough. Didn't even fight in the war like a man, him, no, he was in a Reserved Occupation. Real men don't turn tail, they stand by their women, real men fight!' She pursued him into the corridor where he was lifting his jacket from the peg. 'Where are you going?' and she actually made as if to collar him, her aggressive lunge accompanied by a look of pleading fright.

'Out for a drink,' he mumbled. 'Out for a bit of peace.'

'But you've just come in from a drink!'

Yet off he had trotted out of the front door, which he gently latched.

'Oh, leave the poor bloke alone.' Issie hated it when Mama, roused, seemed to revert to some primitive code that held it offensive for a man to be so inoffensive. You could see any day what 'real men', tanked up on booze and brotherly bondings, did to their hangdog wives. 'He's a lovely man.'

'Yes,' Renate paused. 'He is. A lovely man. What for do you want to leave him then, *Liebling*?'

The storm had abruptly abated, the wind going out of Renate's sails with a banal deflation. Isolde plumped down in an armchair.

'I don't want to. There's been ... a bit of trouble at school. Man trouble.'

She bet her mother wouldn't press her to any shameful disclosures. Renate stared, eyes bulging slightly. They sat, spent, at either end of the dinner table, Isolde doodling a pattern with a knife on the tablecloth with its field of pallid cream flowers and the ghosts of long-ago stains.

'I suppose,' Mama said, tucking wisps of pale hair behind her ear, her voice small in defeat, 'you are looking for roots.'

The terribly blond man in the photos flashed into Issie's mind: she had picked up a discharge of pure fear from her mother, as clear as a radio signal.

She replied gently, 'Honestly, no. I've got roots. Too many roots. I'm all root. I'm leguminous. All the *antis*. *Mam-gu*. *Tad-cu*. You and Owen.'

'You do not go with my blessing,' Renate stated, recovering.

'Okay. I understand that.'

'Okay is American slang, not correct Queen's English.'

***

'Freezes your ballocks!' called the boy in the water to the boy vacillating on the board. 'Come in and try!'

Yes, it would freeze your balls, thought Issie, if you had any to freeze. Her toes curled as she inched her instep into the icy greenness. The girls tittered, passing round their frisson at the diver's virile brag, just as he had intended. Down sped the second diver with no preliminaries, straight in, splitting the surface. There was a long pause, during which he failed to re-emerge and all that Issie could hear was the clucking of water around the spars beneath her. She churned her feet as she scanned for him.

'Miss Dahl, I take it?' The voice had a nasal, reedy timbre: Mr Patterson, headmaster, out patrolling his colony, wearing his academic gown. In this warmth and amid all this beauty, he seemed in his subfuse gloom an anomaly. 'No, don't get up. Please. Don't you find it a jolly place?'

It was, Isolde agreed anxiously, very jolly.

'And how are you settling in?'

'Fine, thank you.'

Wasn't he hot and sweaty, in that gown? The sun had relaxed the back of her neck and bathed her arms in milky warmth. It spangled on the water through which the boys now swam decorously to and fro under Patterson's tutelary gaze, executing pleasureless lengths in a brisk crawl as if clocking up merit points.

'So what do you think of our little outfit?'

'It's a lovely setting.'

'We like it. Of course, Jerry built it. Started as a Nazzy naval base; we took it over. So think of that, Miss Dahl! Where you are sleeping now, Jerry once slept. Jerry messed in our Refec and *Heil Hitlered* where my cadets now salute the Union Jack. There's justice in it, don't you think? Things do come round. We fished up a quantity of their gear from our lake, you know – Nazzy helmets, grenades, uniform buttons, all sorts of memorabilia.'

'The water's very clear,' Issie observed.

'Oh yes, clear and clean. Are you a keen swimmer, Miss Dahl?'

'Very keen. It's my only vice.' She flashed up a grin, to guage how human he was. It appeared he wasn't.

'Good, good. We are in favour of physical fitness. Hiking, swimming, riding – we encourage it all. You will find us a spartan crowd, perhaps, compared with the types you're used to, and the youngsters frankly rough. Officers send their children home to the public schools, naturally enough, leaving us with other ranks – chiefly other ranks, though there's a leaven of the better sort. We sprinkle them about a bit, to, so to speak, diffuse their civilising influence.'

'I see.' Issie's feet were numb and now she withdrew them, scrambling up so that she was standing next to Patterson, a barefoot figure in the lee of his angular tallness, shrouded in the black vanity of the gown that maintained caste and status. His left eyebrow, she saw, had a pronounced twitch. Had England spat him out too? Had he been advised to pack his bags and vamoose, to hector the riff-raff of the British Army's children, because he wasn't considered up to scratch?

'Can't you just imagine it, at The End?' he asked, and the gauntly middle-aged face assumed a boyish zest, as if about to unpack a chest of toy soldiers. 'Do you know, I often stand here, Miss Dahl,' and he rocked to and fro rather near the edge. 'And I think of Doughnuts. I imagine Jerry on the run, and our boys marching in. Coldstreams, Royal Dragoons, Scots Guards, can't you just imagine it? And this was Northern Command HQ, no less. Something for us to be proud of, I tell my cadets. An honourable tradition to keep up.'

Issie feigned pride and she wondered about the doughnuts.

'Modestly proud, of course.'

'Of course.'

'And out of Connaught Barracks, Edward the Confessor's School was born. We have a tradition to live up to, Miss Dahl. You may have noticed my sea cadets?'

'I did. They were climbing the rigging.'

'If you interest yourself in Things Military, perhaps you would like to see my collection?' he asked ardently. 'I call it the Doughnuts.'

'Is that because of the Americans? GIs?' She swallowed a giggle.

'There were no Americans here. This was the *British* Zone, Miss Dahl.' He looked politely puzzled. 'Because of the admiral.' He searched her face for signs of enlightenment. 'The German high admiral.'

'Oh, of course.' She hadn't the foggiest what he was talking about.

'Of course, we're on the same side now. A common foe. Over there. Look east, Miss Dahl.' He pointed with his finger, and she felt bound to follow its direction. All she could see was the green spire of the Nikolaikirche and the prince's palace, white on its wooded hill; a trinity of swans gliding over the water, their reflections liquefying beneath them. Peacefulness incarnate. All Mr Patterson could see, apparently, was the Iron Curtain and an incipient mushroom cloud. 'Of course we're nearer Them in Germany than at home,' he said, and then, as if unwilling to terrify so raw a recruit, hurried on, 'But you'll be weary from your journey. Enjoy the Indian summer. We don't usually swim at this time of year. Jolly good butterfly, Baxter,' he congratulated a youth crashing up and down the pool with a bucking back.

Spectral in that black gown, he haunted the rip-roaring young like a *memento mori*; flapped back to shore. Issie heard him calling, 'Mr Quantz! Both Mr Quantzes! A word, please,' to two men standing there, a young and an older one.

Her feet soon dried in the sun and breeze which carried a minty scent in buffeting drifts across the water, under the sky's blue ache. The scent aroused her senses without proposing any fulfilment. She began to tell someone in her head about this beauty and to describe the menthol air, the lake and the grey–blond sand that bounded it. She told the someone in her head (crossing the shore, stippled with the heelprints of swimmers) that she was going back now to her quarters to unpack; going to nest; to make an Isolde-shaped space for herself, placing her belongings on shelves where once young Jerry had stowed his kit, in one of these great white monumental blocks, screened by pines, somewhere in the hills toward Denmark.

The young Mr Quantz, a dark, slight but tall figure in perhaps his late twenties, looked up shyly and smiled as she passed. 'Good day,' he said.

'*Guten Tag*,' she replied, and both the Quantzes turned their heads to stare.

3

Lake Plön, September 1958, April 1945

Quantz stopped in his tracks, in the midst of remarking to Wolfi and Mr Patterson that there was a child new this term who could play the harp, but a regrettable lack of harps. He was arrested by the tall, well-made woman who said, '*Guten Tag*.' She walked with a certain heavy grace, a carriage rare among the fashionably hip-wiggling young Englishwomen, her hair a mass of soft, bouncing curls. And she spoke in German, with a shy, confederate little smile.

His son was also staring. Wolfi's eyes followed the stranger appreciatively as she walked in thin shoes over the roots eroded out of the pathway under the trees.

'Miss Dahl,' observed Mr Patterson. 'Our new languages teacher. Keen sportswoman, she tells me.'

They chatted briefly about the harpless harpist; timetables for piano and flute lessons. Wolfi volunteered nothing but murmured assent to whatever the headmaster said to him; this was his normal mode of expression but luckily, thought Michael, the English had a tolerant acceptance of shyness and found silence in a foreigner an acceptable form of tribute, which they mistook for deference. It was a pity, however, that Wolfi left his father to speak for him, since his command of English was flawless. He could make an impression if he chose. A complex of worries about Wolfi's lack of social grace, his sexual preferences if any, and that unacknowledged burden shouldered from childhood, hung just beneath the surface of Michael's mind, a slick of algae in a pond. But the way Wolfi's eyes strayed during Patterson's tedious monologue after the young woman's disappearing figure was surely a good sign. He noted it mentally in his shortlist of hopeful thoughts about Wolfi, under the heading 'Normal'.

The headmaster, hands behind his black fusty back, took leave; followed the same path back through his domain.

'Luscious girl,' Michael observed to his son, man to man.

It was the kind of complicity he would have given his eye teeth to have shared with his own rigidly starched father, but Wolfi, typically, flushed in mute offence, turned away his head and walked on staring sideways into the green gloom beneath the canopy of trees. Bizarre that this sensitivity on Wolfi's part should mirror the expression of prudish outrage that literally curled Michael's father's lip at the very suspicion of concupiscence. For the difference was nearly total: the one a code of rectitude which had scarred the father and coarsened his skin to hide; the other a thinness of skin, a fastidiousness born of too close a bond with his mother, a sundered bond. But common to both, Michael thought, was fear. Fear of the mess, the delinquency, the loss of control of sex. Exactly what Michael relished. He watched Wolfi's lithe figure stalk ahead, getting out of range. His silence sealed his thoughts into a privacy which resented all invasion but could not bring itself to separate from its source in his father.

Not yet. Presumably one day Wolfi would break the knot; bound free. Michael did not like to admit to himself how much he depended upon Wolfi's quiet presence. Rather his silence and reproach than the hollowness of a forsaken house.

Michael allowed his son to move ahead. The suppressed anxiety on Wolfi's account dogged him, dragged at him; the endless imminence of the unsaid. And the haunting proximity of Effi drowned in the face of their son; floating up from shallow burial. Wolfi's eyes, not in themselves much like hers, in their rather remarkable pale brown with yellowish flecks, somehow managed to maintain a simulacrum of her expression. Somewhere between hurt and bafflement: the product of which was accusation, alienation. *Luscious girls* had been Michael's weakness, yes, but that was normal to the point of unavoidable in a male – venal, meaningless. Effi had dumbly insisted upon taking it all to heart.

Morbid of her. But beyond the grimed sheet of glass he had interposed in his mind between himself and Effi, he knew her affront and gross pain intimately, as if they had been transferred to himself from her rotted body in the ruins of Kiel. Fingers of her anguish fumbled at him, stopped the throat of his blithe carnality. He had been so gripped by it for a over a decade that his own urges had largely shrivelled. Effi had won, posthumously, yet never knew her victory. Practically gelded him by dying.

Wolfi turned for a second, granted the amnesty of a half wave, and dodged off down a side path through the timber, to open out space for himself.

But what outrageous garb the young man affected in his off-duty hours. The affable English headmaster had looked him over from head to foot with sartorial disbelief. Tight blue jeans revealing narrow hips and a bulging crotch. A shirt that looked to Michael's eye more like a blouse. Off Wolfi had roared to Hamburg in his friend Hansi's souped-up, clapped-out VW, bought from a departing GI. Returned not only with this decadent rig-out but with The Haircut. A quiff, was that what they called it? To which Wolfi appeared to have dedicated his soul. Quantz observed him slicking it back earnestly with water or oil, head to one side, eyes narcissistically intent on his image. *Are you a nancy boy then?* he had silently enquired as their eyes tangled in the mirror. *Or just an over-age Elvis fan?*

Michael had the gumption to keep his thoughts to himself. He idled on, past the point of Wolfi's disappearance, rounding the path to the glade where he had met Maria.

The name took him by surprise. The clarity of the fugitive face. He came upon the lost name by some unaccountable step that led from his vulnerable son. The last girl who had offered herself to him had been Maria.

***

He would dump his kit in the lake and slide away, submerge.

The British stormed eastwards and northwards. Minute by minute they made ground. The Dönitz typing pool typed faster. Messages radioed, wired and telephoned fatuous imperatives across a landscape of desolation. Dönitz got ready to bolt. He let Hamburg fall; Lübeck gave itself up to the west in concussed relief.

Michael's mind whirled. Cynical, dextrous, polyglot and thirty-four, he had every intention of surviving. And that his family should survive. Had never been taken in by claptrap but had ridden with it, an eel among sharks. He prepared for his manouevre. He would fall back on his languages. Who wasn't thinking in parallel with this? You could read it in their hooded eyes.

Maria was nobody in particular.

In lulls between sky-darkening squadrons of British planes flying north-east, the lakeside became a tenuous refuge, granting the illusion of perspective. Michael's false papers were ready. He dumped his uniform in the lake. Sleeplessness lent the experience a certain cinematic vividness: beneath the waters buttons winked like coins no longer current, belt and badges plopped into water that already held weaponry, Iron Crosses, helmets, scuppered baby subs and a violin, which Michael spotted bobbing on the waves. Who would ditch a violin? Yet, so far gone was he, that the lapped violin seemed in strange harmony with the scene, only fractionally more peculiar than the other jettisonings.

One part of his mind assessed the instrument and told itself: *It's just an old fiddle, not a violin. Junk*. Still, there was a wild picturesqueness in the bronze-brown curves of its body that tickled his mind to vague romantic reverie. Someone's gesture of despair. Total recidivism, art restored to nature: wood, glue and gut. Would its fragile hull fill and go down or be washed up as driftwood, swollen and deformed?

He shambled yawning into a green womb of elms and yews, stunned by the extravagance of the morning chorus; lay prone on a quilt of ivy. A herb that grew profusely in the woods bathed the place in minty scent. The last thing he heard before falling asleep was the foghorn-booming of a bittern, love-sick in some remote reed bed, like a ship stranded in a sound...

Struggling into consciousness, he felt the hairs on the back of his neck prickle: he was being watched. Let down your guard, let it down even for a moment, and you are done for. He rolled over, towards the thicket, but then relaxed, for it was only a girl by a tree, with a basket. No spare flesh on her. Shadowed, saucer eyes, very blue, in a tanned face. He beckoned and she came, soft-foot. He put out his hand to her as one might to a shy animal.

'*Guten Morgen*,' he said politely.

'*Guten Morgen*,' she echoed.

'And who might you be?'

No answer. A dither of her free hand on the body of the basket, as if moving to shelter precious contents.

'I've got chocolate,' he said, and smiled at the melted look on her face. '*Pralin*, the real thing, do you like marzipan?'

He could fetch her foodstuffs from the mess, if... he foraged in his pockets.

She was ready. Willing, and knew the score. She lay straight down, and hoisted her skirts to splay her legs, opening the vulnerable territory that was anyone's to colonise, for bread in the mouth. She shut her eyes and waited.

He looked down upon a faceless face. A doll's disquieting absence of expression as the girl lay passive under dappling shifts of light. She had good skin, he noted, no cold sores or rashes, for she was not malnourished. He roved with the pad of a forefinger over her cheek and traced the strong, square eyebrow. That was all he did. Her eyelids gave a convulsive flicker and a spasm of anxiety passed across her face. Her stoicism in the face of a stranger's probing finger commented on Michael's carnality and opportunism. Her automatic capitulation to the terms of his bargain, with its graceless absence of preliminaries, gave his heart an unexpected squeeze. It must be wearing civvies that did it, calling up prewar proprieties long abandoned.

She could not be more than sixteen, if that, he thought, saying, 'Sit up. Eat something first. What's your name? How old are you?'

'You mean my German name or my Polish name?'

She gazed at the chocolate in Michael's hand with that ecstasy of craving he recognised that turns your legs to jelly and brings you to your knees so that you will say anything, do anything, to get what you want.

The kind of ravening hunger Michael had only ever felt for want of a fuck, but then he had never gone short of food.

'So you come from Poland?'

She clapped her hands over her mouth: the sudden sight of sweets had loosened her tongue. An escaped slave then, one of tens of thousands carted east to Lübeck in goods-wagons, to build U-boats and torpedos, munitions and ships.

'So where's your badge, little No-name?' he asked.

'What badge?' Eyes very wide and blue denied all knowledge of the letter 'P' that must have been sewn above her right breast.

'Did you run away? It's all right, I won't tell.'

Her sudden outburst into baffled lamentation took Michael by surprise: 'My mum, she told me she wasn't my mum any more, *Go back to Poland, scram.*'

At first Michael didn't cotton on. Then he realised: one of the poor blonde spawn Himmler's Lebensborn squads had grabbed from the gene-pool in the east and imported to Germanise. Increase the stock. Not that it hadn't come as an uncomfortable surprise to Himmler to discover amongst the 'degenerates' tens of thousands of Poles with every Teutonic characteristic in his book. Blond, blue-eyed babies handily placed for distribution to barren German mothers.

He passed across the *Pralin*, warm and crushed from his pocket. She gnawed it like a dog a bone; hadn't seen sweets for years, and acted as if this were not the least but the gravest of her woes. Like a child.

The thought of Wolfi sparked in his mind. And how the sky-darkening squadrons all seemed to be flying toward Kiel. And Wolfi so puny for his age, his lungs creaking with asthma and always wailing with earache in the nights as a toddler, so that the doctors had twice to pierce the eardrum to let out the muck, and the child had lain so still in his hospital bed, with the pain gone, holding his teddy; he saw his son's hands and wrists sticking out of the pyjama sleeves, and that was Wolfi, whom he had managed to sequester from the compulsory youth organisations, in Kiel now, where the planes headed.

'I am eighteen years of age,' stated the girl, as if to a committee of inquiry.

'Like hell you are,' he said, eyeing the unripe outline of her breasts beneath the coat a size too small, which didn't meet at the front. Her wrists stuck out too, her vulnerable wrists. 'More like fifteen. If you guzzle more of that on an empty stomach, you'll throw up.' She set the rest aside, out of the sun by a tree trunk, where she could angle glances at it. Her skin was tawny, wisps of hair escaping the ginger-coloured kerchief over her head. She appeared on close inspection sturdy and her hands were brown and broad, nails ingrained with dirt, as if with much manual toil. The powerful hands were out of proportion to her size; could have spanned, he thought, well over an octave on the piano. Her clothes were little more than sack. 'So how old are you actually?'

She thought she might be fourteen. She wasn't sure. Nobody had told her. Only last week Michael would have had her anyway, but today he wavered. It might be his last chance. This had been his maxim for years. You have to do it or eat it or lick it or fuck it while you can. She was hardened; barely reacted to his reconnoitring palm beneath the calf of her bare leg.

'Can you get me sausage, mister? Can you get me bread? I'll pay you, I'll wait here under this tree, and pay you – anything you want. Can you show me the way to my country?'

She spoke as if Europe were a province of huddled

villages, in which a wanderer might encounter signposts at a crossroads: *To Poland*, *To Czechoslovakia*, and hope to hike from country to country by suppertime. But borders had been annihilated. There was nothing for supper and Europe poured across territories like a flood inundating plains.

Michael removed his hand from Maria's leg. He lacked appetite, after all. It was over now. In this anticlimax lay a curious relief. Now he must recall his taboo languages. Teutons disdained effete French, dog-Russian, pig-Yiddish, whorish Polish, which he now rushed to embrace. This was what she had to barter: not her body but her tongue. Language would save his skin and Wolfi's and Effi's.

'I'll tell you what you can do for me,' he said.

'Yes please, anything.'

'Oblige me by talking in Polish. I used to be quite a linguist.'

'Oh,' said the girl, shocked. 'Polish is not allowed. We are told to forget Polish, which is what the scum talk.'

'It's your mother tongue, though. You can't forget your mother tongue.'

'Mister, I will forget anything I am told to forget.'

'All that's over now,' said Quantz. 'You can forget all that forgetting business. Plenty of Americans are Polish Americans. Start by telling me your name – your Polish name.'

There were so many layers of forgetting required. She was all at sea.

Syllables began to slide off her tongue; her native language expressed itself in baby talk and nursery rhymes. Maria was her name but that word floated in memory; it did not attach. On the farm they called her Helga. She had learned to answer to Helga and it would smart when she peeled off that label, like a sticking plaster. Helga-Maria sat in her sack-dress, light through wavering treetops washing over the brown arms clasping her knees. Her eyes, suspicious of yet another sadistic trick in a world of unfathomable perversities, were blue but void of brightness, like drowned lights. Michael listened to the outpouring of words with a pleasure insubstantial as the sipping of long untasted wine. Her cadences seemed to melt in his ear, to soften and liquefy the heavy burden of her story. Maria had worked on a farm, and been treated as family, and drunk milk straight from the cow. Now the woman she called Mother had turned her away, saying, *Walk home to Poland*.

Which way was Poland, please? she wanted to know.

In halting Polish, Michael told her to wait for the English, then get herself on a transport; she was headed in the wrong direction in any case. If she carried on north, she'd get to Denmark. If she headed east, she'd land straight in the arms of the oncoming Russians. Her face fell; she looked round in terror. All bearings fell away.

'Don't forget your chocolate,' he reminded her.

'Can I speak German now?'

'Yes, go on. And eat up.'

Instead, Maria took the chocolate reverently, as if fingering some holy wafer, and wrapped it back in its covers. The sun glinted off the wrappings as she tucked it into her basket.

Michael returned to barracks with the intention of fetching her supplies but there at the barrier was a British jeep, at the head of a small convoy of tanks and lorries. The guards had cleared off. As if on cue, Michael walked forward, enquiring, 'May I assist? I speak some English.' He did not need to emphasise his omni-competence, indeed, that would have counted as suspicious bad form: his accent declared it. The khaki officer's face brightened at the sound of a cultivated English voice. Michael set about making himself indispensable, with courteous, manly diffidence that never erred into the abject. It was his chance and he seized it. He thought keenly of Wolfi, Effi. Planned his foray to Kiel. The little Pole he recalled in passing, a blurred face among displaced hordes. There were thousands of Marias, wandering the map, stray leaves from a blighted tree.

4

Lake Plön, 1958

In the night Issie could hear the young ones sob, huddled in beds whose mattresses were treacherous collaborations of three military biscuits, under grey blankets and starched sheets. The night throbbed with stifled grief and the assaults of the older on the new and younger, mobbing them as if homesick tears called for swift reprisal. Small quarries were chased down corridors and stripped, doused in cold water. *Back to bed!* a wearily angry voice ranted. *Get back to your beds, and, you, put your clothes on, who has done this, what do you mean by it?*

How could any of them know what was meant by it? They expressed their devotion to British civilisation by turning on the most vulnerable, harrying those who could least stand up for themselves. Isolde heard heels thud as they fled to their dormitories. She felt now, listening to the scuffles and rebukes, as if she were still travelling. So her belly had churned as the ferry hit the swells; as the train had crawled across the plateau of the Lüneberg Heath, and she had consumed a dry Welsh cake out of greaseproof paper, its floury dryness coating her palate. Disembarking from the train at Plön Station, she had stumbled, seeing the vast lake at her feet, a few metres from the platform, as if the sea had followed her. A momentum of displacement continued.

All seemed provisional, in this world of transients. Her narrow room suggested an antechamber to somewhere else, supervised by the young Queen wearing star and garter over turquoise satin. Her upper arms were bare and one pale-gloved hand rested on the other.

Where we are now, Jerry was once. Mr Patterson's gloating.

But I am Jerry, Isolde thought.

In the open wardrobe, full skirts hung limp, like items on a rail in a second-hand shop, waiting for someone hard-up enough to claim them.

I can always go home.

But she couldn't. The thought of Renate waving her off on the train, eyes blurred with tears, her rictus smile, was enough to put her off that. Goodbyes had been said, and goodbyes were costly rituals. You worked up to them, putting your affairs in order, like a little death. You went round all the *antis*, *mam-gu*, *tad-cu* and the neighbours, making speeches and avowals, and completed a last walk along the front, seeing it all for the last time, committing its detailed beauty to heart. You held out against Mama's fatiguing admonitions and tearful silences, before collapsing in a corner seat of a train carriage. Issie had pulled away from Swansea station, Owen walking, then trotting alongside as the engine built up steam, until her hand slid out of his. *Let go, Tada*, she was saying anxiously at that very moment, fearful he would get dragged along and hurt; and there he remained, just ahead of her mother, a diminishing figure as she craned out of the window; he called out, *Put your head in, my beauty*. It wasn't until near Neath, looking out at the scarred hills, that Issie realised she had finally cut free.

Her thoughts raced back across heath and sea to Denis, on whose account she had been cast adrift. What was he doing now? Now was nine o'clock in the time-zone she had quit. He'd have had his supper by now, presumably: the aproned woman to whom he had made eternal vows would have laid the table for one husband and three small sons. Now the mother clapped her hands to call the family to the table, setting down plates of roast chicken, and Denis sat obediently in his allotted place, smiled at the boys, whom he served with greens, though perhaps they didn't like vegetables and the little one, Sam, squirmed on his chair... Issie's imagination grew a room within the room into which she peered as if through plate glass; an England within a Germany, each as foreign as the other.

Probably the child would have eaten his cabbage without demur. Most likely, Denis and Doreen would have the kind of children who actually liked greens, belonged to the Wolf Cubs and fussed with tweezers and magnifying glasses over stamp collections. And it was to this charming family that Isolde had proposed to take an axe, cleaving their table from end to end.

***

The refectory was a roaring sea of children. She seated herself beside the other teacher of languages.

'Foul row, isn't it?' said Susan Brierley. 'Sleep well?'

'Not much. Most of the kids seemed to be crying at the tops of their voices. I felt like joining in.'

'Poor little tykes. Well, they soon get used to it. *Ja, bitte . . . und Kaffee für mich.*'

Issie was amazed at the food: it was spectacularly good, and plentiful. German cooks dished up the breakfast at high table, a mixture of egg, bacon and potato baked in a tray, and as much of it as you could pack in. Thick-lipped jugs of cocoa and coffee steamed on the table.

Susan broke open a warm roll and spread it with thick butter.

'One thing you can say for this place, and perhaps there is just the one thing, is the food's decent. We've got the same cooks that cooked for Admiral Dönitz. You don't know about that? I'm surprised Our Leader hasn't filled you in on the gen. His absolute favourite topic.' She raised her voice malevolently. 'I was just telling Miss Dahl, Mr Patterson, about Admiral Dönitz.' She pronounced it 'Doughnuts', solving a riddle.

'Doesn't Miss Dahl know about Admiral Dönitz?' He craned eagerly forward. 'Gracious, Miss Dahl. In that case I must enlighten you. Admiral Dönitz was eating his breakfast hereabouts just thirteen years ago, perhaps the very same farmers' breakfast we are enjoying now – think of that.'

The eaters round the table chewed on, suppressing groans, offering perfunctory signs of brooding upon the breakfasting admiral.

Issie hadn't a clue who Admiral Dönitz was, and it showed.

'You *are* familiar with the history of the final stages of the war?'

'Oh – in a rather vague way. Hitler in the bunker and so forth.'

'Ah, but that was not the end of the Third Reich, Miss Dahl,' said Patterson with zeal. 'Not by several weeks. Let me fill you in.'

Susan sat back to allow Patterson's monologue to flow across her bosom to its victim.

'High Admiral Dönitz was named by Hitler as his successor. Naval chap, U-boat strategist of distinction; came north when the Commies closed on Berlin, and established HQ just over the way from here. Couldn't believe the game was up. None of them could. So up comes Dönitz, and Keitel and Jodl (not heard of Jodl, I can see it in your face, I'll fill you in on Jodl . . .'

Susan smirked at the thought that Isolde would have to be Jodled as well as Dönitzed.

'. . . another time). Anyhow, up they come with a ragbag bunch of henchmen, to be followed by Hitler's Last Will and Testament naming Dönitz President of the Reich, Minister of War and Supplies, and Commander of the Armed Forces. Only question is: what Reich? What war? What supplies? What armed forces? Down to boys they were, Miss Dahl, lads with pitchforks. And up comes Speer, he's in Spandau now, ha! Lucky to be alive; only Allied justice saved him. Anyway, he was here, and a group of Gestapo nasties, briefly: and do you know what they called it, Miss Dahl? Northern Command. Commanding what? What was there to command?'

'Nothing?'

'Worse than nothing,' he corrected her. 'Starvation. Bombsites. Scorched earth. A living grave.' Then, without a pause or change of tone, he went on, 'I see you've managed to drag yourself out of the arms of Morpheus, Miss Williams.'

The fair-haired newcomer unfurled a napkin and was snapping her fingers at a cook, who came at the call of her elegant insolence without a flicker of his features, but his whole body (Issie felt) protested.

'I say, have you got any farmers' breakfast left, waiter? Just enough for little me?'

Issie heard him complaining as his white-aproned figure retreated into the kitchen: *Bin doch gar kein Kellner... bin Koch!*

'Frightfully sorry, headmaster, I was fagged after my journey. Any coffee left in that jug?'

'Only it puts the staff out, you see,' stated Patterson in a level tone.

'Yes, of course,' she said, smiling in his eyes.

'Miss Dahl, our new languages teacher – Miss Lynne Williams represents music and dance.' Patterson named this effeminate subject with a wince, in much the tone with which he might have pronounced the word, *brassière*. 'She liaises with Miss Brown and Mr and Mr Quantz, father and son, our two German teachers of piano.'

'I think I met them yesterday.'

'So you did. Sound, quiet chaps: "Decent Germans", so to speak, like our good Heini and Herr Poppendick. You see, we do Miss Dahl, view ourselves as ambassadors here, in our small way. Hence the school anthem.'

'Ah?'

'"Ambassadors". You will hear it sung at assembly.'

What hair, Issie was thinking, *what hair*. She could not help gazing at that ash-blondeness, with a pang that twisted envy with unaccountable shock. Under the window, it soaked in light and radiated it, silken-fine as a child's. Her page-boy style swung with each turn of her head. For all Lynne's skittish rudeness, she hypnotised even Patterson. The returning cook seemed to pause momentarily over the mass of pale hair as he set the plate down before her. Yet Isolde thought he must have spat in it first. She would have spat in it.

'Too kind,' said Lynne, not really thanking him, tucking in with a fork. 'What about some fresh coffee? I can't drink this stewed muck.'

Issie felt mesmerised distaste. So apparently did the

flock of German matrons at the bottom of the table, speaking fast and covertly in a thick dialectal brogue Issie could not easily penetrate, and which she had the idea was used as a code against the English.

'So,' said Lynne, between mouthfuls. 'Here we all are again. Jolly old Fräuleins jabbering mumbo-jumbo... up with the lark... army brats bawling... your petticoats starched so that they stand up on their own... Admiral Dönitz still going strong... jolly uplifting if you think about it.'

Patterson blanked her off. He rose and prowled the tables, hands behind his gowned back, lulling the children's hectic babble wherever he set foot.

'So where might you be from?' asked Lynne. 'Somewhere in Wales, issit, Taf?'

'I was teaching at a school in Kent.'

'She's been Dönitzed, Keiteled and Jodled,' said Susan. 'Already. And it isn't even half past eight.'

'God, feels like frigging six. Any chance of a booze-up with the Krauts at the weekend?'

Patterson was back, leaning tenderly over Issie's chair, so that she got an intimate glimpse of his nose hairs. 'Since you're interested in the history of the base, Miss Dahl, you may care to see our collection of Nazzy memorabilia?'

'Thank you. That would be lovely.'

'If you've finished, Miss Williams (and perhaps you could bestir yourself at the proper hour tomorrow), the remaining three hundred and twenty-four of us can disperse to our several duties.'

***

Issie took her first day's classes. Few of her pupils entertained the notion that German was a language useful for speaking to people: it was just another gratuitous torment requiring analgesia. Most scarcely deigned to recognise that they were living in a foreign country. They lived in an enclave of military Englishness.

'Let us imagine,' suggested Issie brightly to the second year, 'that we want to go out to a restaurant and order a cup of coffee? How would we ask for that? Come on, I'll be the waiter. What would you ask me? Yes, you, what was your name, Peter, what would you say, how would you ask for a cup of coffee?'

'I wouldn't, miss, I'd go to the Naafi. I wouldn't drink the German coffee.'

'Why ever not?' Issie was rash enough to ask.

'Germs.'

'Very silly, Peter. The Germans are a most hygienic people,' Issie replied, through snorting laughter. 'What about you . . . the boy next to Peter. Ask me for a coffee.'

'Why, have you got one, miss?'

More braying from the back and cranings round from the front. Issie thought she'd try the girls.

'Please, miss, we don't drink the German coffee,' an earnest voice piped up. 'The milk's unpasteurised, miss, so we could catch TB, my dad says, so we aren't to have their cream, that's what my dad says.'

'Well, I don't think that's actually the case, Jean, but let's obviate the problem of tuberculin testing by asking for a cup of coffee *without* milk or cream. Say after me: *Eine Tasse Kaffee ohne Sahne, bitte.*'

The class dolorously bleated this phrase after her. Perhaps it would prove easier on her nerves, after all, simply to stick to the curriculum, without attempting to father on the children of a perished empire a belief that other races might engage their curiosity and regard. These children, who were 'posted' to 'camps' around the world, never ventured outside the tent of hackneyed Englishness. They transported their England with them and pitched it wherever they bivouacked, a haven of ignorance, a haunt of belligerent fear.

Shadows lay under eyes red and swollen with the night's tears of homesickness. After all, their defiance was little more than bravado.

Giving in, Issie stuck to the textbook, resting her voice while they did an exercise, scratchy nibs dipped in inkwells sunk in the desks, heads propped on grubby hands. Some looked unkempt and greasy, as if they needed taking care of. Wasn't that what the Fräuleins were supposed to be doing?

'*Gebt mir eure Hefte*,' she instructed them as the bell went. '*Ja, die Hefte! Gut*, Maureen. See, Maureen knows what a *Heft* is – an exercise book.'

'Her mum's a Jerry,' said her neighbour, with a sneer. 'That's how she knows. She wouldn't know it otherwise.'

Not knowing evidently counted as an innocence from which the wretched Maureen must be forever barred, a half-alien clutching on to the English portion of her mongrel inheritance. Issie felt common cause with the freckled girl but had the sense not to show it. She collected in the books without bestowing any token of favouritism. The children returned to the refectory, where they were served great jugs of cocoa for elevenses, with a hunk of cake.

Lynne Williams lit up a cigarette from the stub of her colleague's.

'Our Leader doesn't usually bother us at break,' she said. 'We put our feet up. Fag?'

Issie shook her head.

'Don't smoke, Taf?'

'I never took to it.'

'The sporty type?'

'Hardly.'

'What caused you to come out to this squalid little dump?' asked the fair-haired one. The butt of her cigarette was blotched with crimson lipstick.

'Is it?'

'What?'

'A squalid dump.'

'Fags out, he's coming. Your time to be Dönitzed, Taffy.'

***

'You're not acquainted with the history of the place?' asked Patterson, conducting her with long strides, as if he had her in custody.

Issie could see he hoped she would admit to being a dry well of ignorance, into which he might funnel information. His haggard features betrayed an excitement at once abnormal and routine, as he prepared to display to a novice his trove.

'That's the High Admiral, Miss Dahl, on the wall. What do you think of him?'

They were standing in what seemed to Issie a Nazi shrine. Helmets, guns, swords and medals were displayed on walls and tables, the whole being dominated by Dönitz's portrait, imperious in braided uniform, wearing an outsize hat.

'He looks . . . foxy.'

This was Issie's first and indeed only impression.

The face before her had the withheld, impassive look common to public figures posing for the camera. His thin, prim lips, big ears, sharp chin and close, small eyes told nothing about the man within, except that the man within (if such a being existed) had no intention of showing himself. He looked, to Issie's eye, like any man in uniform; personality buried deep beneath the surface. Not a person at all; an icon. He looked like no one.

'Foxy? Ah . . . you mean shrewd? Well, there's no doubt he was an inspired naval commander and strategist – not a genius, no, no, I wouldn't go that far,' Patterson mused judiciously, as though personally acquainted with genius and competent to detect it. 'No, but he possessed an Iron Will – totally reliable, professional – U-boat mastermind – but he had a flaw. And his flaw was – do you know?'

'No.'

'Fanatical, suicidal obedience. Believed in the heroic master-race – adored the *Führer* like a woman – bad error of judgment.'

'I thought obedience was meant to be a virtue in a military man?'

'Aha. Very true. But there is obedience and obedience.'

He did not offer to elaborate, nor did Issie push the question. Englishmen just understood these distinctions, by virtue of being Englishmen; and if Englishwomen didn't, that was because, though English, they were somehow or other perpetually off-side. Fagged at the prospect of being shown each trophy individually, she wished he would just get on with it.

'Did all this come out of the lake?' she asked.

German lakes were full of secrets, Patterson said. He had personally trawled up . . . oh, for instance, this helmet.

'*Wehrmacht* helmet, found in the swimming pool area,' he said. Then, like a milliner he urged, 'Try it on if you like. Go on, Miss Dahl, try it on.'

An iron-headed Isolde looked back at herself from a mirror. Wavy hair sprouted from the base of the casque; a ludicrous sight. Was this an essential part of the ritual of being Dönitzed? It must be. Here captives stood at Patterson's mirror playing soldiers, having the chinstrap securely fastened by practised fingers.

Some young German had worn this helmet for real not fifteen years ago.

The iron felt cold round her head; she fumbled to break free of the leather strap. Some phrase about dead men's shoes stirred in the sediment of her memory.

'Remarkable what they chucked in their panic,' said Patterson. 'Valuable items, some of them. Rare pieces. And each has a meaning. One can read them like a secret language. Take a look round and anything that *particularly* interests you, I will explain, in so far as my limited knowledge allows.'

At random, Issie picked out a medal in the shape of a cross, complete with a ribbon with hooks and eyes.

'This?'

'Interesting choice, Miss Dahl. You have an eye for the subtleties. A Knight's Cross, to be distinguished from the Iron Cross First Class and the supreme accolade of the Grand Cross. Note, however, the peculiarities of this little beauty. Should have a silver frame: this is silver-plated zinc. Central swastika should be iron: this is brass. Any ideas why? No! Well, this tells the *cognoscenti* that it belonged to a navy man – these being non-rusting metals, you see. And here, a pet of mine, a U-boat clasp in bronze, which tells me that its owner was a torpedo mechanic . . . collar patches, shoulder cords, cuff titles – am I boring you, Miss Dahl? – cap badges . . . Can't you imagine them tearing the stuff off their uniforms as our boys came pounding up into Schleswig-Holstein, hey?'

He chortled at the piquant thought; replayed the routing of Jerry like a favourite inner film. Patterson's life would be empty, a dull round of bossing and bureaucracy, without the war.

'Fascinating,' Issie offered a wilting homage.

'"Lest we forget" and all that. We mustn't forget, must we? Good for us to remember,' he said, almost pleadingly.

'Yes. Yes, I suppose so. That's the received wisdom anyhow.'

'It is wise. It is right. We don't want what happened repeating itself, do we?'

Isolde wondered whether, in that case, it mightn't have been better to chuck the whole lot. She watched Patterson's fingertips lift and stroke his valuables. Presumably he eyed the trophies in a spirit not wholly alien to that of their owners; he flaunted captured decorations and gave new currency to old lies. For this was homage, wasn't it, this shrine? This compulsive fondness? Thus a musician might stroke piano keys; a lover his mistress' breast. She supposed upper-class Englishmen who'd fought in the war might have such hobbies, for reasons opaque to her generation.

'What did you do in the war, sir?' she enquired, as this inkling of light dawned. A false dawn, as she instantly discovered.

'Ah, well, I was in a Reserved Occupation, you know. Not able to take part in the fighting, though naturally I... was bitterly disappointed.'

His voice trailed off. He replaced the medals in sequence. A tic plucked at the skin beneath his hooded eye, and she felt she had involuntarily touched a sensitive spot, nervous inner tissue inside the carapace. Why did such men wear their skeletons on the outside? What were they afraid of?

His bent torso expressed a flat abeyance of gusto, a species of defeat.

'Well, there you are,' he said, straightening up, reaffirming his stature. 'Spoils of war.'

'Did Admiral Dönitz have an Iron Cross?' enquired Issie, to cheer him up. Glancing out of the window, she saw Heini, the groundsman, mowing the lawn around the great bronze bell in its house. He was a sweet man, she thought. As she looked, the younger Mr Quantz strolled across to him in his shirtsleeves, hands in his pockets, past the flower border, where a notice said 'Keep Off The Grass'. His casual air, as if he was not going anywhere, just existing, aroused pleasure. She liked the way he drew one hand through his thick brown hair. His pianist's hands looked, she thought, sensitive. He mitigated, in his sauntering, the dullness of admirals.

'Good question! Glad you asked. The admiral was highly decorated. Let me show you.' He drew her, his hand beneath Issie's elbow, away from the window and back to the picture. She could just see the younger Mr Quantz interrupt Heini with some quip. The fragrant grass cuttings stopped whirling and the two men both swayed back from the hips, laughing, like a flower opening, she thought. A flower opening. 'There – you see – crossed swords, worn between the oakleaves and the cross.'

Mr Patterson was perky again, as if he had dipped into the murk of the lake to retrieve another treasure from its slime. 'And we have documents. Would you care to see our documents?'

That word: *Dokumente*. The scary word that validated you as *bona fide*, not alien; the word she and Renate carried between them in the dark pouch of a shared but cryptic memory. At the post office in Mumbles or at the fishmonger's, in a tiz, Mama would scrabble in her handbag for her purse: 'Oh, Issie, I've lost my . . . oh, here it is. Thank *God*.' A fraught exhalation that was also a communication to her daughter of that just-in-the-nick-of-time feeling; a splayed hand on her heart, absurdly overreacting. Renate was the most careful person in the world about possessions. The purse could not be lost. But if it *were* . . .

This was the sensation Patterson's word 'documents' brought to Issie: the tumble of heart-in-your-stomach when Owen drove the Morris too fast over a hump-backed bridge, a momentary unnerving.

But the younger Mr Quantz was still there, lodged in the corner of the window, quietly chatting. She liked the way he stood, easy and flexible; liked his supple tallness, and presumably he hadn't the disability of a wife and three small sons tucked away in the village. Too young. Mr Patterson followed her gaze and made for the window. As if they had eyes in the back of their heads, the two men parted; Heini pressed on with his mowing.

***

'So you've been done?' observed Lynne eating *Strudel* daintily with a fork.

'How do you mean?'

'Dönitzed. You've been Dönitzed. Rhymes with blitzed. You have that gaga look about you – anyway, I saw Our Leader marching you off and in his case, it could only be for one purpose.'

'So go on,' said Susan. 'What did you get – the sword in its scabbard or the tin hat?'

'Tin hat. And medals. And lecture.'

Boys at a table beneath an open window were trapping wasps in a glass, with honey for bait. Their knives caught the light with a dim sheen as they sawed the creatures in half. Their eyes were bright with sadism. One of the cooks, a burly man with thick eyebrows and a ready smile, stood over the boys, shaking his head. Issie heard him murmur in remonstration: '*Wer Tiere quält ist ein Unmensch*.'

The wasp-torturers paid no attention, regarding the cook as a non-person. Their hands grabbed for hunks of succulent chocolate cake. Issie blushed hotly, and then wondered why. She was ashamed of the cruelty of English boys, and felt impugned, for Englishness was supposed to mean decency, fair-mindedness, a certain steady level of kindness. She strode over to the table.

'Don't you know the creatures suffer?' she asked the lads. The table was a graveyard of dismembered insects.

'Why, miss, do you like wasps?' one asked, his mouth

full. ‘Do you want stinging?’

‘No, of course not, and don’t be rude, but I don’t want them to suffer. Do you know what the cook just said to you?’

‘Nope.’

‘He said it’s inhuman to torment animals.’

Actually, he had not quite said that. She returned to high table, having scraped the remains of the wasps into the glass with a knife. He had said *Unmensch*. How did you translate that? Subhuman?

‘What have you got there?’

‘Medicine for Patterson,’ said Issie. ‘If he ever Dönitzes me again.’

‘No, you won’t get another dose. That’s your initiation. The kids in my block are busy initiating each other every night – the big ones scrag the little ones. And there’s a quick turn-over, what with their being constantly posted, a steady supply of new victims. I like to think that the real bastards go off and get beaten up at some other dump. It satisfies my sense of justice. Well,’ Lynne dabbed the corners of her mouth with a napkin, ‘there’s Darwin for you.’

‘They’re so horrible to one another,’ said Issie wonderingly. ‘I mean, well, children are cruel and all that, but these . . . ’

‘Think the toffs are any gentler at Eton or Harrow?’

‘Well, no, but . . . ’

‘It’s their parents,’ stated Lynne, as a sociological fact which did not admit dispute. ‘They don’t know any better.’

‘But they haven’t got parents around. If they had parents . . . ’

‘They’d be just as vile, but the parents would join in the bashing.’

‘But it’s some kind of mass bereftness. They’re like part-time orphans all driven in on one another. I found a lass this morning in the lav – Rachel – her eyes were almost closed with crying and when I coaxed her out she wouldn’t get dressed. I found out why. Her back was bruised. And she wouldn’t say who’d done it.’

'Report it,' said Susan curtly. 'And toughen up. You soon won't notice it. It's just normal. All part of their education.'

'Cruelty is *normal*? One just accepts it?'

'Human nature.' Lynne shrugged. 'Dog eat dog. Can't afford to be over-sensitive in this hole. One does what one can, of course, to keep the little bastards from doing each other in.'

An ache passed through Issie, and stayed; a long, dull pang which perhaps would always be there; perhaps had always been there, submerged.

'But they'll never be the same again.' She spoke to herself, and it came out oddly, like a lament. She replaced her cake untasted on her plate; her eyes wandered shoals of pale faces, blanched by unsympathetic light, at angles to one another. Several hundred mouths were chewing, chattering, squealing, creating a barrage of sound that rolled across the room in meaningless waves.

Mutterseelenallein was the German word that broke the surface of her mind. It was a word in common usage, though it sounded so dramatic and drastic in English. It perhaps denoted a normal condition. If you said it to any one of these children, in the desolation of this forested beauty up here amongst the lakes, or even to one of these jocose adults in a quiet moment abstracted from the herd, each would pause and be pierced by this word. *Mother's-soul-alone.*

Her face worked and a few tears slid down her cheeks, hot and big. It wasn't just Denis but some loss that lay behind Denis, which his slight frame had somehow or other managed to cover, so that she'd been unconscious of it for the duration of that abortive spring. The forbidden tenderness which was theft really, was not legitimately hers, had still brought a sense of healing, bonding her into the tissue of human belonging.

There was a sense of having been thrown away. A fist seemed roughly to grasp her heart and screw it round in her breast. Tears filmed her eyes. In a sudden snapshot of memory, she was a little girl, being hoisted out of Renate's lap. A strange, cold tool was applied to her nape.

'Hayfever,' she managed to mutter. 'I must be allergic to something.'

'Doubt it. Not at this season,' Lynne replied.

Issie's spasming throat relaxed. She knew what she was allergic to. Not particularly this woman herself, who was no threat, just frivolous, shallow, bruised, one knew the type. No, it was her baby-soft, white-blonde hair that somehow or other repelled Issie, a ludicrous realisation that brought her eyes slewing round to study her neighbour. Lynne preened; acted as if she were modelling herself, soaking up admiration. She raised one hand to the precise slope of her hair. Sunlight revealed a shimmer of shades in the threads, from rosy to silver. 'Of course,' she reflected, with a narcissism that could not offend because it was so honest, 'I've been lucky in my hair. Crowning glory and all that.'

'Were your parents fair too?'

'Not so's you'd notice. I'm a throwback, I expect.'

'It's gorgeous,' sighed Susan. 'So unfair you should be so fair. Why can't it be shared about a bit? I mean, you are essence of blonde. It's pure elitism.'

'Everyone wants to be a blonde,' Lynne admitted. 'Blonde is fashionable. But,' she said, tossing a sop to the envious mousy and red heads surrounding hers, 'brunette is coming back in – or so I read,' she concluded, with a note of judicious scepticism.

'If Lynne is a recessive gene on the Mendelian principle,' put in Pugh the geographer next to her, 'give me recessive genes any old time.'

'When I first saw Lynne,' Susan said, 'I thought it was dyed.'

'She kept studying my roots.'

Hair dyed. Studying roots. Wants to be blonde. Metallic echoes like wind in telegraph wires set up a whining resonance in Issie's mind. It must be tiredness that caused these nervous stirrings. So disagreeable and it made every face look hostile. Nobody seemed to sleep in this place; the whole night had been confused by disturbances – scuffles, muffled sobbings. Surely it would all calm down? She would settle and get her bearings. She would, she assured herself. *You will be fine, you are a strong, adaptable, rebellious woman. You will not give in to irrational fears.* Yawning, she stretched her arms. But as she did so, that uncanny sensation recurred, as it had intermittently since her arrival at Plön, of getting into a bed whose sheets were still warm. Repeating some action already long completed by a person unknown. Seating oneself in a chair whose seat held the dying body-warmth of some previous, vanished occupant.

'What's the trouble?' asked Mr Pugh. 'Admiral Dönitz got to you?'

'I was just wondering when I'd hear from home.'

Perhaps there'd be a letter soon. For sure Owen wouldn't write. He never did. He'd never trusted his pen to spell or punctuate correctly, let alone express his innermost thoughts. Words fled before his shy pen. *You are my own*, he had said. *My one ewe-lamb. I have loved you as my own.*

The memory cooled and soothed, like a long draught of water to deep thirst.

'How long does post take to come?' she asked Susan.

'How long's a piece of string?'

'Roughly.'

'Three, four days – though I once got a letter that had been all round BAOR via Rheindahlen and Mönchen Gladbach; it had taken literally years to arrive. The chap had moved and I couldn't trace him when it got to me. Message from the grave. Well, he wasn't dead exactly, but he might as well have been.'

'Does Mr Quantz live in?' Issie heard herself asking. She blushed; her heart rose.

'No. Jerry can't live in. Except Mr Poppendick, he's so old they probably think he's harmless. Which he is; he's a sweetie-pie, he just came in from the road at the end of the war, he was a refugee, and they kept him on, he was a professor of something-or-other, somewhere-or-other. Patterson will tell you all about it. Which Mr Quantz are you interested in anyway, Taf? Shouldn't bother with the son, he's queer as a coot.'

'Just because he's impervious to your charms, Lynne,' objected Susan.

Lynne shrugged. Tired of their sparring, Issie walked back to her room across the spongy give of years of leaf mould. The scent of new-mown grass hung on the air. She looked down through the pines to the lake. A dusky sheen lay on the water, under a sky which ran an artery of bloody orange over darkening turquoise. *Queer as a Coot*... that was worse than Married with Three Kids... he looked nice, anyway. *A flower opening*.

5

Lake Plön, 1958, May 1945; Minsk, 1941

Michael read the morning news over his morning egg. A case going on and on in a Schleswig-Holstein court brought by a Jewish dentist against a well-respected teacher, who had indignantly defended in a restaurant the right of Modern Youth to paint swastikas on synagogues. Suez was proof, said the teacher, that the British lion had lost its roar; France was rotting in disorder; the Arabs would smash Israel; the US was too fat and lazy and stupid to become a soldier nation again. That left the Fatherland, which within a decade would be ready again to confront its Hour of Destiny. *Far too few Jews went into the gas chambers*, the teacher informed the dentist. *They forgot to gas you too. Those were the days. They will come again. Remember I told you so.* And the waiters put down their plates to applaud.

Is this a free country or is it not? demanded the teacher in court. *Does freedom of speech mean something or doesn't it?* The judge allowed him to rant on. The court wept at the teacher's noble sentiments: he would rather cleanse the streets, lick them clean with his tongue, than go crawling to a Jew. The race laws had been based on sound reasoning, he claimed. The court erupted in prolonged applause.

Adenauer ignored filth, protected rats. And here in Schleswig-Holstein, where the rats had found haven, Michael read today of the election of SS General Heinz Reinefarth to the State Assembly – 'the butcher of Warsaw', no less. He eyed the picture, which was small and indistinct, but the face was memorable. Only when he brought his eyes close to the page, obeying an instinct to stare into the depths of the rehabilitated butcher, did the bland face disintegrate into a random rash of dots. There were no depths. Where could you look these days without recognising some *Gauleiter*, Hitler Youth leader, Propaganda Ministry bigwig, strutting high in office, a face you knew? Fatter now, plusher, older, oleaginous, but the same brazen face.

Isolde Dahl: some such Wagnerian name had adorned the child his one-time friend disowned. The name churned up depths; it dredged him, bringing up filthy matter. The woman was a beauty, opulently made, with a strikingly oval, open face. He had seen his son hover over her as she sat by the lake, her skirts spread out around her in a blue flare, as if she had a lapful of gentians. He had seen Wolfi not daring to approach. *Keep it like that, Wolfi.*

The coffee Wolfi had left percolating on the stove gave out an aroma of the deliciously mundane. That steadied him. He poured and drank.

Michael cycled to Ruhleben, since the weather was so fine. He freewheeled past Lake Suhr, looking over to 'The Trout' camp. Old Dönitz and the final frenzy. He came in to the music room with his usual brisk step; set down his briefcase and hung his coat on the peg. The pair bending over the piano moved back, embarrassed.

'Miss Dahl. Good morning.'

'*Guten Morgen*. Your son found me playing... Chopsticks, I'm afraid, on your piano, and... he's shown me a few notes.'

She looked up briefly and caught Wolfi's eye; Michael registered the shy intensity of his son's rare smile. Wolfi said, 'Miss Dahl should learn properly. She has a natural feel for... Chopsticks,' and the young people burst out laughing, then quenched it.

'Well, I must get down to work,' said Michael, feeling hollow.

The young woman nodded and left. Wolfi picked up a cello by the neck of its case and followed her out. Michael looked through his list of pupils and set out the sheet music he would need that day. The girl was disturbing. And the room felt queasy, disorientated.

The two of them there, she in that bilberry-coloured soft dress, leaning over the piano, he in the blue shirt Quantz had ironed for him the night before: they seemed dressed to match, as if in uniform, their heads close, collusive. Sex undoubtedly played its moonshine tune across the gap between them. He sat down on the double piano stool and flexed his fingers to play; but failed to play. He looked at the backs of his hands, then laid his palms on his knees, rubbing them to and fro in mental inertia. He turned slightly, scanning the room over his shoulder. Everything was the same. Tall windows with blinds admitting flying buttresses of dusty light; that bare table at the centre. Captain Pauckstadt's operations table, where nicotined fingers had reached to fiddle with counters on an hourly shrinking map. It was the same colossally empty room.

***

Kube whispered: *bodenlose Schweinerei*. Bottomless bestiality. He had complained to HQ, Kube hissed, he was prostrate, he was helpless, Kube said, what could he do? At Lvov the pit was covered but blood kept gushing out, 'how shall I say it . . . like a geyser.' Kube said burying alive or half-dead was common. Wounded Jews worked their way out of their graves. The ground heaved, they were reborn, only to be shot and buried again.

Don't tell me, prayed Quantz. *Spare me this*.

Up they came. Up however hard you worked to pack them back down. The earth had lost its stability and turned into a churning sea. The people climbed down into the pit with gentleness and dignity. Naked, families soothed their children with calm, and lay down in the interstices between bodies to be machine-pistoled by the SS task forces.

Quantz was to report to Canaris.

'Spare me another trip,' he pleaded. 'Spare me.'

'But we must know.' The admiral had splashes of coffee on his tunic; his white hair was unkempt. He looked past Michael at the dachshunds. 'You will kindly execute commands. I am asking you only to observe; it is necessary.'

'Send someone else,' begged Michael. 'I'll be no good to you.'

Quantz was a witness, a travelling eye without the comfort of an eyelid.

Dahl had boasted. Boasted how he suffered from no pity, no ruth, no insomnia. 'Hard work, you have to be hard, work for men, real men, hard men, hard on us, cream of the cream, best blood.' On and on. He bragged how he took care of his kit even in the most foul of circumstances, not a hair out of place. Brayed a hee-haw laugh like a donkey. It appeared to be an acquired laugh, for Quantz had not heard it before: a Heydrich whinney.

Dahl's immaculate boot seemed a thing possessed of a will of its own, as it kicked the elderly man down into the pit. He had seemed to poise on the edge of that pit full of his people, hands clasped over his genitals. He had peered in, then turned to stare Dahl in the eyes. His hands left the vulnerable genitals and opened at his sides in a gesture of . . . not beseeching but as if professing the most profound bafflement. He screwed up his eyes like a person who needs spectacles. Perhaps he did. The victims had been relieved of their watches and glasses a short distance back, leaving time and space a blur.

The old man, suddenly a figure not of pathos but of judgment, opened his mouth to speak. Whereupon Dahl reached over, tweaked his beard, said something like, 'Get a move on, Israel, we haven't got all day,' and booted him into the pit . . . and shot, shot over and over again, shot regularly, as if measuring time like a clock. Michael reeled down a path into the woods, retching, vomiting. He could still hear the firing, getting fainter as he stumbled on.

Later, under the spell of drink, Dahl waxed lachrymose.

'You lads are lucky to have us to do your dirty work for you,' he bragged. 'Where would you be without us? And we have families of our own, you know. We are not without tender feelings. But our weakness we have overcome, rooted out.'

He had a new wife, he told Michael with pride, and showed a photograph. Two blond sons, and another on the way. Kissed the photograph devoutly. Said how he missed them; asked after Effi and Wolfi.

'Cat got your tongue? What's up? Got to you, hasn't it? This is nothing. Have a swig. What you've seen is nothing, man, compared with some of it. Toughen up – you have to be iron. We have overcome,' he added heroically, 'all effeminate feeling.'

Michael had begged Canaris to allow him to return to the navy, preferably on ship-board. The admiral must have realised his insides had gone to mush; he could be little further use. Canaris himself appeared less and less convincing as he became a stooped, haggard valetudinarian, living on reputation as an archaic god dangles by a mere thread of myth.

'Spare me,' Michael had pleaded. But memory did not spare him, for in what he was forced to witness and made no effort to stop, he must be accounted complicit. The venerable Jew surfaced, broke through the soil, got up and followed him like a hound. He was always there, observing Quantz.

But the Little Admiral was hanged, relieved of his memories.

***

There was no Kiel left. He came upon the smashed city as if dreaming awake. No Kiel. And Effi, Effi had died six weeks before in an air raid. Wolfi scavenged from the cellar of the ruined house. He did not recognise his father. His father scarcely recognised him.

'Will you come with me?' asked Michael.

His son acquiesced. Wherever there was food and shelter, the lanky, pragmatic ex-child would go. They returned together to Plön.

Dönitz and his government were said to be nicely set up in a castle owned by the Duke of Mecklenburg and Holstein, overlooking the picturesque waters of Kiel Bay, whence they proceeded by limousine to Flensburg for council meetings at ten prompt each morning, to discuss the government of a state garrisoned by four foreign conquerors. Michael heard that the admiral wore his dress uniform and grew more imperial by the day. But Michael had metamorphosed into his own double, in mimesis of a cultured Englishman: quiet, reliable, a musician and interpreter. He pronounced his Christian name the English way, and blessed his parents for supplying such an ambivalent label.

Michael and his son walked by the lake, the young man tagging behind, a dumb animal on an invisible leash. The compass of Michael's consciousness had shrunk to the life of the rediscovered boy; Wolfi could not help but seem like a minor destiny. What Michael had neglected, he had been permitted to redeem and he pledged himself to care for him. He watched how warily the lad walked, putting his feet down as if the nerves of the soles were tender.

'What is it, Wolfi?'

The boy shook his head. He was dry-eyed, sombre. He walked like someone whose roots hurt, that was it. This was the feeling Michael had when he looked at the strange way he walked. The boy had been torn up, bombed out and suffered mother-loss, and though the roots would heal and he was already adapting, the endings must tingle, like phantom nerve-pains from lost limbs.

***

The English girls and boys came and went. Michael forgot the view over his shoulder. He chatted to a new child, who showed real musicianship. Rachel's touch was fine, her sense of tone-colouring unusual. She had seemed less than promising when she sat down on her half of the piano stool, monosyllabic, crouched in to herself.

'How far have you got?' he asked her.

'Schubert,' she mumbled, which was not an answer. He asked her to show him what she could do, expecting little.

Her frozen gaze melted at the keyboard. She stretched her arms and, relaxing her hands over the keys, let her fingers ripple. She played from memory, fluently, magnanimously, without show or artifice.

'Well,' he said. 'Who taught you?'

'Our mam.'

He began a dialogue at the bass end of the piano and they improvised against one another. As the bell went, she turned up to him a soulful face with dark, liquid eyes that were dragged back reluctantly from far away and seemed to ask where the time had gone; why the one good thing had to be over?

'You will do well, Rachel. Have you enjoyed it?'

She nodded miserably. The music had perished with the magical hour.

He walked back across the quadrangle, past the flagpole and its rigging, behind a group of matrons, teetering on their high heels. He watched their calves, straightening the seams of their nylons with his eye. Their heels clicked on the tarmac. They cast a common shadow, with hydra heads and spider legs, which seemed to clamber down the shadow of the rigging in the late afternoon sunlight. Their tongues wagged. He caught a wisp of their hugger-mugger conversation, which was, *A kike Hitler forgot to gas.*

6

Lake Plön, 1958; Brandy Cove, Gower

Issie's eyes browsed the bodies of young men, poised on the jetty and high diving board. She waited, hugging herself, all gooseflesh in her bathing suit. The instructor had overrun his time with the seniors, teaching them a dive which began on tiptoe, raising the arms in the air in a V. They perched like a flock of birds before take-off and held the pose like statues.

The first wave leaped and disappeared. Their places were taken by a second wave. A pause and then a third. The pool churned with a shoal of bodies tussling in white water as they burst up from the depths.

Issie, planted on a rung halfway down the wooden ladder, shivered. Light gusts whipped in from the open lake, whose surface ruffled and shuddered. Her head was now beneath the level of the jetty. She peered out through a triangle between struts, to register the lake's disturbance by obscure contradictory forces above and below. Choppy and bitter-looking, a barren waste of waters. There was never, even in the most halcyon weather, she thought, a time when the lake lay at rest. At its most still, it would be a great creature asleep, the rhythm of currents its troubled unconscious breathing. Odd, the sour tang in the air, mingled with resin. The remains of all that had ever been there persisted, rotting and recreated; yet nothing in the seething crucible could ever be exactly as it had been.

A barrage of wolf whistles echoed around Isolde. She was conscious of the soft quiver of her breasts gathered in the bathing suit as she moved down a rung, thighs entering the water; the roundness of the tops of her arms as she reached hand over hand. Embarrassment trembled on the edge of nervy pleasure in being seen and liked.

Young bodies heaved themselves from the water and trotted single file back along the jetty. Their soles slapped along the rumbling boards, and Issie was aware of the cabled muscle in their thighs, their slicked-back hair. Come the new year, they'd be in uniform, these lads. Be conscripted when they got home. Call-up papers, medical inspection, short back and sides. Patterson fostered his babes on the parade ground, in fond concern for their about-turns, their sideways-wheel, their ability to salute as their fathers had saluted. So by the time they got to their first barracks, dreamed Patterson, the other blokes would be green as grass but Patterson's cadets would reflect credit on his discipline as a plebeian elite, half-trained already. One or two of the boys moved with careless authority, which went with a drawling accent that told Issie they belonged to the leaven of officers' children whose presence so warmed Patterson's heart.

Issie glided into the shouting cold of the water and powered off, up and down the length. She thrust forward with such attack that the end rushed up to greet her and she touched home at the same time as pushing off. She made the pool seem limited, its boundaries there for others, not for her.

As she rested, breathing fast, she allowed her body to float on the drag of tide. Beyond, through the lattice of struts, she took in the forbidden expanse of the lake beyond the section set aside as sport space. She would get out there, for sure, not submit to being hemmed in, barred out.

Denis fleeting across her mind struck her as an insignificant figure, his timid posture awakening impatience at that mild acquiescence in laws of other people's making. She belonged to a new generation... there was more to life, God, there was much more. The physiques of the young men diving, their virility, aroused her but it was more than that; something she had too, which meant one exploded from a diving board and somersaulted crazily, smashing into the water; it meant being young, young enough to make new starts, do the unauthorised thing and take off for somewhere, rather than quiver helplessly homeward.

'Mind if I join you?'

Wolfi's light, lithe figure slid off the jetty. He was such a sudden presence as to take her off guard, yet he arrived as if he had been expected. The exact person she wanted, on whom she had mused and brooded, until he seemed familiar, intimate – far more so than he actually was. Issie was intensely aware of his long shapeliness, rather delicate than brawny, the skin tanned a pale golden brown. The closeness. His laughing shiver, white teeth. Long eyelashes, the beautiful soft tawny eyes.

'I couldn't resist,' he said, and smiled as if shocked at himself. Her face was within inches of his face. 'I saw you in and . . .' A convulsive shiver shook him. She saw his skin was gooseflesh. 'Not my style at all,' he said. Green-grey swells of water washed over their chins.

'Your teeth are chattering. Better take the plunge,' she said.

'Actually, I'm not much of a swimmer.'

He proved it by thrashing a path up and down. His crawl was graceless, without economy. Reaching the opposite end, he gripped a spar, gasped for breath and looked back. Against the geometry of struts, Wolfi seemed oddly defenceless, disquieted.

A swell billowed him up and a blink of an eye later washed her up, letting them subside one after the other.

Then he smiled across the pool, and she smiled back, her heart tumbling over. There was a shyness in the smiles that made the meeting of their wet eyes, their chaste near-nakedness, intensely conscious. Then he raised his hand in a hesitant wave before pushing off again, into the loud palaver of his awful crawl.

She yelled to Wolfi that they'd better get out, the kids were coming, but had he heard? She didn't look round to see whether he was following. The costume was riding up over her haunches; she felt exposed, out of the water, heavy and cumbersome. Her thighs were numb, leg muscles gone to jelly. A squealing mass of little girls came pouring out of a hut and headed for the boards leading up to the pool. She jostled her way through the tadpole swarm of black-costumed bodies.

Those wolf whistles... piercing her, with the certainty of being well-made, meant as flattery, but bearing a mocking edge of predation. She heard them in retrospect, and her puckered flesh shuddered as if the wind on her skin was their male breath on her nakedness. What did Wolfi see when he looked at her?

Queer as a coot, she had heard Lynne sneer lightly.

She had seen him with Heini in the quad, the two of them leaning back to laugh. *Like a flower opening*.

Wolfi now came bounding out of the water. Too late. Issie watched him try to slip past the games mistress. She, however, sturdy and fifty, with a peremptory whistle on a ribbon round her neck, held her ground and reproached the young foreigner for trespassing into the pool at times set aside for pupils.

'You know the rules, surely, Mr Quantz, by now?' Pause. Embarrassed cough. A rising note. 'And when we swim, we deem it modest to wear the appropriate trunks or costume.'

The girls squirmed and tittered, for the young man was wearing navy underpants. Being soaked, they clung to his private parts. He murmured an apology, but Issie couldn't catch what he said. Wolfi had an abnormally soft voice, which he seemed disinclined to exercise. Was it odd, Issie vaguely wondered, in this day and age, to stay at home with your father and even work with him at the same job? She felt the slackening of her own bonds with home as a pleasurable emancipation. Things had been difficult so far, she had felt riddled with dreamlike sensations of dismay. But at least she wasn't a stay-at-home who would achieve nothing other than to marry one of the Vaughan cousins in Sketty and breed; and fester mentally; and enjoy no horizon larger than the sight of Ilfracombe from Bracelet Bay, sitting on a towel with grit in your ice cream.

But Wolfi was lovely. She watched him lope past her, head down, flashing her a sideways grin, as his eyes combed her ripe figure. She caught his sweeping glance and flushed. His clothes lay in a heap beneath a tree where he had discarded them on impulse.

Nothing here was ever done on impulse. Time and space were set aside for everything. Set hours for girls to darn socks on red wooden mushrooms; times for serious pursuit of recreation; hiking afternoons. To jump in the lake on impulse was unheard of. Presumably he'd have no towel; have to dry himself on his vest.

'I've got a spare towel if you need one, Wolfi,' she called. And saying his name like a conspirator seemed to unite them. Deliciously. *We are on the same side. No one knows but us.*

He had wonderful eyes, brown with lighter flecks in them, diffident but ironic. As she passed out the towel, marked 'Property of BAOR', their bodies, still streaming lake water seemed peculiarly nude. He stood back as if to avoid encroaching on her modesty and reached across to accept it. The pads of his fingers were puckered.

'Thanks, Isolde.'

'Issie. What did she say?'

'Oh, that it wasn't done. There are certain rules and codes. You know.' His English had that exquisite articulation nearly unknown amongst native speakers. 'You swim so marvellously well,' he added. 'As if you were born in the water. I'll leave the towel where you can see it.'

There was a flawed mirror in the hut, fixed at the height of a juvenile figure. Bending her legs, Issie slicked back her soaked hair with a comb and towelled off surplus water. She hoped he would be out there, waiting for her. They could walk back together. She saw his supple body in her mind's eye, its pale tan, the fleck or birthmark or whatever it was, above his breastbone. *Wolfi, you are gorgeous*, she thought. And the shyness, that was touching too. And she felt she knew him, but what did she know?

You are the most frightful know-all, said Renate in her mind's ear. *And really you know nothing. And look at your hair. Your hair, Isolde.* As if that said it all.

Renate would keep popping up in her mind,

forbidding things. Casting doubt. That wagging finger. *You will always go too far. It is in your nature.*

Issie hurried to dress. When she came out, carrying her wet things in a shoulder bag, the little girls were all scampering back out again, as if running from some extremity in exhilarated panic. The extremity being rain, which could be seen sweeping in across the lake, in a low dark cloud bank emptying its load over the far trees and offering a prelude in a shower of drops, which Isolde shared on her upturned face. A softly thrilling pulse beat up in her chest as she looked round. But Wolfi was nowhere to be seen; the wet towel was draped over a branch like a white flag.

It's raining! It's raining! The scurrying girls tumbled into the hut, before the storm could hit. How absurd to bother about a bit of wet coming from above, when you're immersed up to your nose beneath. As Issie returned on the shortcut through the woods, pine boughs broke the drench and slid the water down their arms, offering corridors of comparative shelter.

***

The compliment: *born in the water*. Isolde liked that. But she missed the salt of sea-swimming; the keen danger.

Renate had taught her that lust. On Issie's last weekend they had ambled through the woodlands to Brandy Cove – their special, secret place. Renate's very footsteps, sinking into spongy leaf mould, had reproached her: *How could you bear to leave this sanctuary?* and each step of Issie's replied, *I'll come back, you know I will.*

There had been no one in the cove, sheltered deep in wooded rock, with its planes of limestone tilted down to the triangle of sandy bay. They sped down and stripped off, two voluptuous women, the dark younger unable to match the athlete's physique of the blonde elder, though Isolde with wry amusement had noticed her mother clenching her belly, as if she must be not merely superb but perfect.

When they went bathing with the aunties and uncles, it

was to Renate's brown body that the elders' eyes were drawn; the men's in homage, the women's in censorious envy. Such brazen glamour seemed heathen to the chapel Welsh. Lennie, Issie's favourite auntie, was tall and lovely, but came from North Wales – virtually a foreigner – and was careful to avoid getting her fluffy hairdo wet. Her queenly head would ride above the waves in stately watchfulness, eyebrows raised as if in fixed surprise. Hence Lennie failed to exhibit the bouncing physicality which raised eyebrows when Renate Jenkins played beach-ball with the youngsters and swam far out to sea with the menfolk, flaunting a stylish crawl. And if it hadn't been cold and deep as the grave out there, the aunties would have been tempted to fear for the virtue of the uncles.

Why then her disapproval of Issie?

Because Issie was 'sexy': so said Renate. Renate stated that she herself was not 'sexy'. The aunties were wrong. Renate was just athletic. But Issie had an unconscious quality that needed watching.

You can't help it, Renate had observed with grave worry. *But men will automatically think you are... that sort of female.*

It all came back, the alienating love her mother had for her. The devotion mingled with grave apprehension of nameless disasters. Did Wolfi read in her this 'sexiness', Issie wondered, showering. She half hoped he did.

That day at Brandy Cove kept resurfacing. Issie and Renate had charged into the sea and hit the cold with a duet of shrieks; then struck out.

Her mother's mastery was effortless. She had surged forward, arm over arm, head down, so streamlined as to raise scarcely a splash. They had floated on their backs companionably side by side, beyond the breakers.

'Well now,' Renate had said, her warm, solid body crowding suddenly up against her daughter's breathless tranquillity, 'what could be better than this? Go on, what?'

Renate had flipped over, face bobbing next to Issie's as she lay on her back, hair a streaming anemone.

'Nothing at all. If you happen to be a seal.'

They had swum round the point to Three Cliffs and back to the bay. Breast stroking into the shallows, there arose that murmur of anxiety: would your clothes still be there? Towels? Thermos?

Cocooned in beachrobes, Isolde and Renate had shared the metal flask of coffee and dunked biscuits.

'Now,' Renate had insisted. 'Where would you rather be?'

'Nowhere.' Issie had tingled with well-being, satiated to the lazy core of her senses. She lay back on the warmed limestone and let the memory of light spangling on water play drowsily in her mind.

'Well then.'

'Well what?'

'Don't go. Don't.'

'I'll come back. Don't spoil it, Mama.'

'It's you who is spoiling it.'

'I can't spend my whole life in the water swimming up and down the Gower with my mam.'

'Whyever not?' Renate had expostulated, as if her womanly child could not hope to do better in life.

Because I want to live, Issie didn't say.

'Whatever you do, do not go looking for your father,' said Renate, as if winkling out unsavoury fathers was an unfortunate habit girls were prone to, a kind of dirtiness.

'If you go on about it all the time, you'll make me *want* to look for the bloody man.'

Renate looked scared. Opened her mouth and shut it again. Then she had stripped off, right there and then, without the embarrassed and embarrassing modesty screens within which Sunday bathers would struggle, hopping on one foot, sand in damp pants. Flinging off her costume she had stood in all her fierce nudity, nipples erect and pointed, seeming to outstare any prurient viewer as she towelled her flanks and back. Isolde had looked round, from beneath her more demure tent of towel, at the soughing peace of the bay. It was all hopelessly beautiful and there to go home to.

***

Homesickness turned the block into a place of torment. Issie patrolled as the children settled or resisted settling for sleep. Hullaballoos broke out in dormitories at opposite ends, so that she had to pace in wearied exasperation between the two. At her approach, the inhabitants of the last pocket of resistance whirled into bed in a flurry of spring twanging, which ceased as she snapped on the light.

Isolde surprised a raid on a child's bed; they had waited until their victim slept before mobbing her. She had shot shrieking into a nightmare of universal rejection, whose logic dictated that people hate and hit you for no other reason than that you exist.

'Why, why are you doing this to Rachel?' Issie demanded of the five pyjamaed girls. 'How would you like it?'

She perched on Rachel's bed, seeking to meet them on the human level. 'Why would you want to harm her? She's alone and far from home.'

Nobody spoke; nobody looked Issie in the eye. All that could be heard was quick breathing from the exertion, and a medley of sniggers.

'Well, go on, somebody speak. At least say sorry to Rachel.'

'She stinks,' said one. 'Look in her drawer if you don't believe me. She's got STs in there and mouldy tights.'

Rachel's look of dull bale said to Issie, *Go away. You can't help me. You're making it worse.*

'How can you bear to talk like that?' Issie lost her temper. 'It's vile. You're vile to talk to her like that. Now leave her alone and go to sleep.'

'I'll tell Sir you said I'm vile.'

'Do. You just do that, you little shit.'

There was silence. Isolde rose, stunned. Her own brutal tongue confounded her. She stood with folded arms at the door until they had squirmed down into bed, including the little shit. She switched off the light.

A subdued chant of 'Kampong! Stinky village!' arose. These children had picked up on their travels to Singapore a language to anathematise 'lower races'. It grew in volume until they were leaping on their beds, hollering. A window shot open and the contents of a drawer was tumbled into the dark quadrangle. The victim began to wail. Her keening spiralled above the chant of her tormentors.

Every time Issie intervened, she would make it worse for the girl; she recognised the cycle. Each time the reject would become more conspicuous, further distanced from the collective identity, more identified with the enemy. Yet one could not just leave her to sink or swim; pretend one had no eyes and ears, no heart or responsibility.

Up clicked Fräulein, on stilettos. She was carrying detritus on a shoebox lid, which she held out before her, her face set in disgust.

'Whose are these?' the matron asked. 'These most nasty, most offensive and smelling of objects?'

The shameful contents of Rachel's drawer were displayed to the room. Isolde stared, and looked away, hot with embarrassment on the child's behalf. Used sanitary towels were rolled in balls; the youngster had not known how to dispose of them. Bloodied green knickers and soiled tights. Isolde could smell them from where she stood.

'I didn't know...what to do...nobody told me, my mam didn't tell me...,' Rachel stammered, blushing crimson.

'Didn't *know*? It is disgusting. A matter of hygiene... germs. Dirty, dirty girl – to throw intimate things out of the window...in the quad...where *men and boys* might see?'

'Fräulein,' said Issie. 'It isn't the poor child's fault. She's new and can't cope. Please take these things away. The other girls threw them out.'

The Fräulein murmured in German observations designed as soliloquistic, on degenerate girls, lack of discipline in their upbringing. 'And this one,' she confided in a whisper, drawing closer to Isolde, 'with the hair like a mat and the dirty habits, is certainly a Jew.'

'What the *hell* has that got to do with it?'

'No, no, you mistake me, Miss Dahl,' the Fräulein

instantly backtracked. 'This is *why* they are setting upon her. *Because* she is a Jew. Do not imagine for a moment that *I* am an anti-Semite...it's just that I can smell it when it's around. I have experience.'

I bet you have. Issie wrenched the box lid away, distraught.

Susan Brierley appeared. 'Up!' she yelled. 'Out! Dressing gowns on!'

The six clambered out of bed, sluggishly, as if suddenly wearied. They spilt blinking into the jaded light of the long corridor.

'On your knees. Down. In line. Crawl.'

They moved forward on all fours, at first displaying a remnant of defiance but soon a common dismay set in. They dragged tails of dressing-gown cords, and in the smeary light one saw how frayed and dingy their clothes were. When the first child reached the end of the corridor, she began to get to her feet.

'Down!'

'Miss, we're sorry, miss, we won't pick on her no more.'

'You stop crawling when I say you stop. Which might be in half an hour. Or, if your crawling speed doesn't satisfy me, it might be tomorrow morning.'

Issie laid a light hand on Susan's arm. 'There must be a better way...than humiliating them...like animals.'

'Isolde,' her colleague enlightened her, arms folded, the brooch at her neat neck catching the light like a winking eye, 'that is precisely what they are, most of them. Animals.'

Issie stared. Susan was a ladylike, civilised woman of around thirty. Conventional. Her beige brogues told you of decent respectability; her fawn cardigan and tartan skirt reinforced the message. There was nothing peculiar about her. She had been kind to the newcomer Isolde; had gone out of her way (not far, but with a ready smile) to make her feel at ease. But she had a row of homesick girls down on their knees and crawling. *Animals*, she had called them, *animals*. Barked at them like a sergeant major.

Jew, that woman called Rachel.

The caravan of children crawled back, with a swishing sound.

'Better,' commented Susan. 'Pity your excess energies can't be put to some socially beneficial use. Harnessed to a plough or something.'

'I think that's enough.' Issie found her voice. Butterflies whirled in her stomach. 'Okay, girls, you can get up now.' She reinforced her authority by clapping her hands. 'Go back to bed, be quiet and – straight off to sleep.'

'Oh no. Get back down again. You, Nadine – down. Crawl. And when you have crawled, crawl again.'

Some were staggering to their feet, others lumbering back down to their knees, others dithering.

'I am the senior teacher here, Miss Persil, and take it from me, this is the language they understand. Strength is all they respect. Ask any teacher here, they'll tell you the same.'

The melancholy carnival began again.

'No!' Issie protested. 'This is barbaric. I shall go... I shall go to Patterson. I'm sure he... '

'Are you? Are you really?'

No, she was not sure. She faltered. The memory of the Dönitzing recurred; his contempt for the inferiority of the spawn of the other ranks; their imputed need for stern British discipline. Drill under the Union Jack.

'So – how long are you going to keep them here?'

'As long as it takes. As long as I can be bothered. And I don't want to be off with you but it's meant to be your duty. My evening off. And it was chaos under your supposedly liberal regime. Wasn't it? It's Okay, I was like you when I first got here. Wet behind the ears. Sentimental. But I learned.'

'Learned what?'

There lurked in Susan's now mild eyes a secret knowledge Isolde would prefer to live without. But in order to avoid it, she must assess it. And somehow she had been here before, craning for detestable knowledge.

Mir wird schlect, she had bleated to her mother, clutching her belly, bile rising, having eaten something dodgy. *I feel nasty*. Tasting her sour self.

'Learned what?'

All Susan would reply was, 'Reality.'

'Why did you make Rachel crawl? She did nothing. She was the victim.'

'Use your loaf. What would they have done to her afterwards if she'd been let off? If one crawls, all crawl. Collective blame. Fosters group bonding and discipline at the same time.'

'Can't we move her to some other dorm?'

'What's the point? She'd be in the same boat. Look, she'll get over it. She'll get as hard as the rest.'

No hope, then. Enemies everywhere and all that child could do was wait, endure, and graduate from victim to bully. Issie watched their tail ends creep down to the far end of the corridor. She could hear a subdued weeping.

'*Fräulein* said Rachel was a Jew.'

'I wouldn't know.'

'But doesn't that mean . . . that *Fräulein* was a . . . Nazi?'

'Weren't they all?'

'Well, no, I don't think so, at all.'

'In any case, she'd have been checked out. They all had to fill in questionnaires after the war. They all say they knew nothing about the camps and so on,' said Susan and then she blared, 'Hey! Keep going! What do you mean, your knees are hurting? You should have thought of that, shouldn't you?' She turned back to Issie, retuning her voice to a collusive murmur, picking a stray hair off Issie's cream sweater. 'Yes, they all said, "Oh no, I wasn't in the Party, I had nothing to do with it." Three Wise Monkeys wasn't in it. The whole bunch were in it up to their necks. Yes, I'm sure *Fräulein* was in ecstasies when they smashed the synagogues. Probably got a free fur coat out of the forced sales. A very cruel bunch, the Krauts.'

Issie looked down at the flecks in the marble floor, her eye registering their random scatter, some white, some khaki, forming arbitrary patterns, flukes plucked out by the invention of the onlooker. She scuffed the toe of her light shoe over the pointless code, her mind in an unfocused daze, as if she were running a temperature.

A cruel bunch, the Krauts, Issie reiterated inwardly, as though this distillation of her colleague's wisdom were proposed as a subject for an essay. 'Like us?' she queried, glancing up.

'Pardon?'

'Not unlike ourselves, the "Krauts"?'

'Worlds away. We are a free democracy. With standards.'

'So are they, aren't they?'

'Well... on the surface perhaps. Pick up the stone and you find black beetles. National character. Individually,' Susan conceded with some condescension, 'they can be quite decent. The chaps we fraternise with at Malente – not a bad lot to lark about with. Are you coming on Friday?'

'Can we put a stop to this crawling business now, Susan?' Issie heard her voice implore. Shame flushed her cheeks, at her flabbiness in the face of a regime so flagrantly unkind; a newcomer's embarrassment in a world which stood monolithically against those norms Tada had raised her to respect. 'Some of them are crying.'

'Yes, might as well put the little dears to bed. Have we tired you out, darlings? Have your pea-brains got the message? Okay, one more length then, just for luck.'

Back the weeping girls crept on all fours in the dingy light, heads low, the upturned soles of worn slippers showing behind the dragging skirts of dressing gowns. Up they got. Into bed they scampered. Not a peep out of them.

'That's how it's done,' said Susan. 'You'll know next time.' Her voice was placidly reassuring. 'Are you coming then, on Friday? Chaps in their *Lederhosen*. Bit of a hoot. Knobbly knees and all that. Do. It's about the only social life we get in this godforsaken dump.'

'I may come. Yes. Thanks.'

'Wear your glad rags. We all get dressed up to the nines.'

***

Sleep delayed. Issie asked herself large, uncomfortable questions and got no answers. The questions trooped nose-to-tail through her mind like a wretched convoy of children crawling down an ill-lit corridor.

What kind of people are we to punish the children with such inhumanity? How are we different from our predecessors in this barrack? Perhaps we aren't, except in degree. We just stop at a certain point. Perhaps this is all there is to it, power and rottenness?

She humped over in the bed, catching a pillow to her middle like a friendly body. There was a squalid taste in her mouth. She should have acted. It should have been stopped, decisively. That kind of thing could not be tolerated. Kids crawling up and down a corridor. It was sick.

If so, it was a sickness they all carried. Not just contagious but compulsory.

I've never been like that, thought Isolde. *I've never allowed myself to stand by and see other people gratuitously abused.*

But this time I did.

Come on, she said to herself, *you spoke up. You tried. You didn't just stand by and accept it.*

Was that true? Partly. She had protested; threatened to report it to Patterson. And it was just the jarring suspicion that the cruelty was built into the system that took the wind out of her sails.

Well, she could still go to Patterson, if such a thing happened again. Sitting up, Issie switched on the lamp and squinted blearily at the clock. Quarter past two. She took a few sips of water, feeling hagridden. What would she say to Patterson? A new, subsidiary question crawled in the wake of this: if she were known as someone who went behind people's backs, sneaking and tale-bearing, how would she make or keep any friends? She squirmed.

I need friends, Issie thought. *How can I manage without friends?* If she didn't have any, if she were a pariah among the English, how would she survive? Wolfi Quantz was the only person with whom she had felt a connection and he was, she intuited, somehow off-limits. Amongst her own people she would be an outcast, if she stayed true to herself.

She had no heart to fail again. To limp home to Wales carrying two failures in as many years, sole trophies of her teaching career, seemed out of the question. No, there must be some third and more supple way, not to comply but not to stick one's neck out either. A kind of compromise that didn't compromise you.

That was it. The dying embers of the day crumbled the equivocal word into its two distinct meanings. The word lay there in pieces, like the clinker at the bottom of the coke-boiler at home. *Compromise.*

And in any case, how bad was it to put a gang of incorrigibles through an unpleasant experience of limited duration, when they were so manifestly asking for it? And so cruel to the weaker among them.

Riff-raff, said Patterson.

Scum of the earth, dregs... someone said.

Still her tired spirit churned, full of ill-digested matter. *If I start thinking like that, I shan't be myself any more*, thought Issie, sagging back on to the pillow. *I'll have descended to their level.*

Who were 'they' though? Who were 'they'?

Do not go looking for your father, Isolde, I forbid it.

Chopsticks. Kampong. Gentle Jesus. Jerry.

As her mind fogged over with the slow descent into sleep, a mystifying and nebulous recognition formed and repeated itself tiresomely like doggerel – *we are them and they are us* – which became ever more meaningless and then dissolved.

7

Eutin, Malente, Fegetasche, 1958

Michael stood at the brow of the wooded hill, leaning on his stick, above Lake Eutin. His eye tracked the pearl-grey stasis of clouds over a lake that lay as still as milk in a bowl.

He frequently found himself paralysed in this unwilled immobility, while wandering the lakeside or even while rowing his boat, lapsed on the oars, and coming to with a start as if from the shallowest of sleeps. A sense of strandedness would provoke anxiety, the smooth-worn oars in his hands like some strange clubs he had been constrained to hold. For a moment he would look down, confused, at the polished grain of the wood: what am I supposed to do with these? What have I already done?

He was waiting, with customary patience, for Wolfi to say whether he was or wasn't coming on the walk.

Wolfi arrived, the arms of his sweater tied round his neck. His hair flopped in a soft wing over his forehead and his fingers gently stroked it in a self-caressive gesture.

'Your mane,' said Michael, and reached out a hand to rumple it in a friendly way. The young man winced back but said nothing. The nothing that was said between them seemed to have spread to a vast ocean of withholdings. Michael was stirred for the thousandth time by unease, looking at the quiet son who tagged at his heels. And not so young either. Wolfi, at an age when men are settling down with a family of their own, or perhaps branching out, seeing something of the world, appeared unwilling either to quit his father or to make any genuine approach to him. They lived alongside each other but not together, going about their lives like a staid, steady old pair. Yet Michael was sensible of being watched. There was little eye contact, only flickerings of gaze and banal chat over meals. Michael was alert, as soon as his back was turned, to the fact that his son was keeping vigil. Wolfi knew where he was at any given moment. He tracked him; kept track of him. Occasionally, the father turned sharply to snare the vigilant gaze of the son, whose eyes darted away.

Sometimes he could rest in the silence between them and was proud of Wolfi's willowy tallness, his musical talents and apparent self-sufficiency. At other times, his throat constricted as he tried to speak, about Effi, about the things that kept them mute. Six weeks the child had lived by her corpse in the ruins: how could he ever get over that? Michael feared to stir the silt that kept his son's pain safely unfathomable.

It was not my fault, he tried to convince Wolfi through actions more proper to a mother than a father. *It was the times' fault. I care for you*, he tried to say. He cowered from his son's reproach. *Yes, I let her down, I let you down, I was a shambles as a husband and father, and worse*, he silently acknowledged. *But tell me you love me*, he besought him.

Wolfi did not oblige. Asking nothing, he offered no confidences. He slouched. He wavered along, his rare smiles equivocal as a book with facing texts mistranslating one another.

And there were Wolfi's nervous dreads: his fear of water, for instance. His disdain for boats and yachting, Michael's passions. He had tried to teach him to swim. Hopeless. That stiff body, void of trust, flailing its arms in shameful panic. He doubted whether Wolfi could swim, even now, to save his life. Indeed, he was sure he could not.

They climbed in a silence Michael chose to consider companionable along the ridge above Lake Eutin. Two sailing boats were out, becalmed on the inertia of wind and water.

'Not good weather for it,' observed Michael.

'No.'

'I'm out of puff. Give me a moment.'

Wolfi sprang up the bank and lounged against a tree.

Beneath the young man, Michael saw, with an unaccountable twinge, that the roots were exposed. The twisted mesh on the collapsed bank of the road affected him with unease; thick brown coils, that should by rights be buried securely underground. All along the ridge it was the same, the bolus of each tree eroded out, so that one could pry into the viscera of what was never intended to be shown. The hillside shelved with irregular steepness above the track, and this enforced intimacy with the roots took place at eye level. Michael's finicky mind found itself seeking to correct the problem by mentally reconstructing the eroded bank, so that the insides could be packed decently back out of sight.

The qualm subsided. His eye accepted the lie of the askew hillside, the perspective down upon the lake. His mind steadied itself by browsing the fruiting boughs of a stand of wild apple trees; a whisper of autumnal redness in the maples.

'Not much of a companion for you, am I, Wolfi?'

'It's okay. I'm not bothered.' He sounded bored. Michael's own father would have beaten him for taking such a tone. He never would have dared to address his father with less than respect. The nervous negations to which Wolfi was given, and which Michael uncomfortably accepted, seemed something that belonged to the times. It wasn't just Wolfi; it was normal. Michael tried to embrace a narcotic ordinariness; a prosaic chap in shabby corduroys going about a palimpsest of limited activities, deviating neither into dream nor trauma.

Then Wolfi broke a decade's silence, speaking down to his father from the ridge.

'Hansi says his dad just escaped the rope.'

Michael blenched. The elder Hans Saur had been an eminent butcher. The younger had been bent on going to the dogs since the age of thirteen. 'Yes, well,' he said. 'We know...', and aborted his sentence, hoisting his small pack over one shoulder, to indicate that they would continue their ramble.

'What do we know?' asked Wolfi, in that breathy voice that was next door to a whisper.

'Well, Saur is not my cup of tea,' said Michael in English.

'Hansi says one of those bastards from Malente dropped by, and his dad was out; and this old fart said, Your father is a great man, Hansi. And Hansi said, No, he's not a great man. Just a fat man.'

'Very witty,' said Michael. 'Pity your friend dropped out of school so early.'

'He was slung out.'

'Yes, well. He was a bright lad, as I remember. Could have made something of himself.'

'Hansi says . . . ', Wolfi continued remorselessly.

Inwardly, Michael quailed. He had felt for so long the imminence of a blow, a stunning blow. That it would be dealt by Wolfi was inevitable, since Wolfi was the sole living person with the power to hurt him. He licked his lips, looked up at where Wolfi was lounging against the tree. 'Well?' he asked, staring him in the eyes. Wolfi would back off. It was Wolfi's nature to back off. The blow would be deflected, deferred.

'Hansi says it's a problem being the son of a mass murderer.'

'It would be.'

'Is that all you've got to say?'

'What do you want me to say?'

'There's nothing you can say really, is there?'

'What do you mean, nothing I can say?' Michael found himself severely rattled. Wolfi held his eyes. 'I hope you're not comparing me with that lump of shit?'

'But you were, weren't you?'

'I was *what*?'

'Never mind,' Wolfi dismissed him, but his hushed voice was on the wobble.

'I was never a National Socialist. Never. You know that.'

'Of course not,' said Wolfi quietly, with an irony of which Quantz would never have imagined him capable.

***

Two young female teachers headed a snake of bottle-green girls, putting on a hearty, wayfaring air: the blonde girl and the majestic-figured Isolde. She walked with an easy stride, breasts bouncing pleasingly, cheeks ruddy, a mass of hair tied up at the back of her head in a pony tail. A fine animal, Michael reflected, though ursine beside the gazelle elegance of the slighter woman. Yet she was trouble.

'Oh, look Issie, it's the two Mr Quantzes.'

To Michael's amazement, Wolfi had shrugged off his lethargy, run down the slope to meet them and seemed to be greeting them as old friends.

'Your German is excellent, Miss Dahl,' said Michael, drawing level. 'I had meant to congratulate you on it.'

'I teach it so I'd better be able to speak it passably.'

'Few of your compatriots speak our language. I was surprised.'

'Ah, but you speak such *super* English,' frothed Lynne, 'we don't need to *Sprecken Zee* the *Doytsh*, do we?' She wore a lemon cardigan draped like a shawl; a wide white belt was notched in tight round a tiny waist. Both women wore the American bobby socks, self-consciously cute on womanly legs. The dark 'Issie' struck Michael's senses as uncorseted, frank in her just-ripe fleshliness, a body that awed his imagination, as no wonder it did his son's.

The party of girls fanned out and began to disintegrate. Some flopped on the grass at the roadside or veered into the woods.

'Are you going to walk with us?' asked the anaemic blonde. 'Do, Mr Quantz. Help us keep discipline among this rabble.'

Quantz thought he could bear to abstain from this pleasure. Lynne pouted, caressed him with her eyes without particular conviction. Any man was better than no man at all, her eyes confessed, even Jerry.

'Oh, go on,' she wheedled.

'A middle-aged man must amble and rest.'

'And women must be sent on forced marches, in charge of a bunch of morons.'

Isolde flinched; turned the conversation.

'I'd have loved a chance to learn piano. Really loved it. We hadn't a piano when I was a child and I think you have to learn young, don't you?'

'Well – if you aspire beyond Chopsticks, to be a concert pianist, no doubt that is the case,' Michael told her. His son scowled. 'But no age is too old for music, *gnädiges* Fräulein. And you are young.'

How old was she exactly? The Dahl name seemed to fist him with its monosyllable. He dismissed a fugitive likeness to his one-time friend, in the straight gaze, the full mouth. To accept a coincidence like this would be tantamount to accepting destiny, or ghosts.

'But, Issie, I've said, I've already said I'll teach you,' Wolfi put in. 'Or the flute, or the cello, whatever you feel like.'

Issie now, was it?

'Fair exchange, after all,' Wolfi went on. 'You show me a proper crawl, I'll help you out with Mozart.'

'Swimming?' Michael coughed the word out, choking on a laugh, which he did and did not intend to humiliate Wolfi. 'That'll be the day. Wolfi hates the water, Miss Dahl. Always has done.'

'Oh,' said Isolde. 'Really?'

She threw Wolfi a knowing look. Wolfi angled himself away from his father. The set of his shoulders gave Michael to understand that he was a crippling source of embarrassment. *Old*, his son's posture said. *You are unforgivably past it. Get out of my sight, you corrupt old bastard.*

'I thought he was rather a water baby,' Isolde said, and again the two of them convulsed. Michael was tired of them, tired of it all.

As the column reformed and continued on its way, with Wolfi between the women at its head, Michael watched the tail of the snake attempt to thrash free of an alien element: Rachel, his pupil, acting as scapegoat for the wandering tribe's relentless misery. He caught from the corner of his eye a blow, as a girl in the rear of the group thrust her back.

He could see how Rachel might appear fair game. Her hangdog expression told you she had given up the struggle before she'd begun. Yet how hypocritical the English were, Michael thought, to present this ambush of the weak by the strong as a purely German turpitude. How had those people colonised the world? Through cricket and fair play? After all, he thought, we were indebted to the Anglo-Saxons for their Raj, with its racial categories – whites, Anglo-Indians, coloureds – all graded in meticulous filing systems with specified rights and privileges, or few, or none.

Trifle! Effi had exclaimed, her thin face glowing. *English trifle! It's all the rage. Penny's going back to see her gynaecologist and bring me back a tin of Bird's custard from Fortnum's so we can make some.*

This had been the short idyll of Effi's life, when she had thought herself beloved, setting up house in cosmopolitan Munich, pregnant with Wolfi, and with money for fads and frivols. The vaunted Anglo-Saxon treat had flopped into his bowl, a dollop of jelly topped by a yellow blob like baby's pap, tasting of nothing much. No, its flavour was, in point of fact, distinct: a special quality of English blandness, tasting of hypocrisy, cant and class snobbery. If hypocrisy had a taste, it was that slop of trifle.

Back hared Miss Williams, past the bullying in the rear.

'Oh, Mr Quantz! We're having a get-together with some friends at Malente. Wolfi says he'll come and I've told Issie I'll make you come. You will, won't you?'

'Kind of you to ask. But . . . '

'How can I tempt you?'

She could have once, with that flaxen mop and pouty mouth, the posture of a film starlet, the flounces of her cotton skirt billowing. He could have taken her there and then, rushing her back against the quilt of needles, throwing up her skirts, holding her by the wrists, too hard, forcing himself into the narrow place, too roughly, watching the surprised pleasure–pain in her dilating pupils. He wouldn't mind hurting her, hearing her cry out. An instant was all it took to see the whole act in filmic imagination, sudden and vicious as an animal that fucks where and what it can get.

'I rarely go out in the evening,' he replied correctly, with the right tone of just-enough apology, to make it clear to any person of average acuity that the invitation was unwelcome. Her yellow cardigan, angled so as to slide off one bare shoulder, now reminded Michael less of primrose or lemon than that wretched custard of Effi's.

'Ah, but you will make an exception for Issie and me? We never have enough men,' she lamented. 'There just aren't the men about these days.'

He would be interested to see what the scoundrels at the *Blütehof* got up to these days. Amusing to think of the company the pure Patterson's flock was keeping.

He pointed out the bullying of Rachel.

'Dregs, they really are. Still they've stopped now.'

'They are far from home,' Michael heard himself say in a grave voice that remonstrated with her baseness and his own. 'And therefore troubled,' he went on, hooking her gaze with his. As if life could be solicited for second chances, and a succession of minor atonements might be offered for a people's delinquencies.

She shrugged one shoulder, further shedding the cardigan. The skin seemed to blush its sunburn, for she was the kind of girl whose paleness should not be permitted to tan, sunbathing by the Baltic, along with bronze-bodied women lolling like seals.

'We're going back on the boat from Malente,' she said. 'Come with us. Wolfi's coming.'

'Where does your Miss Dahl come from, Miss Williams? Her German is that of a native speaker.'

'She's Welsh. We call her Taf. But I think her mother was foreign.'

Wolfi's dark girl was a beautiful *Mischling*. The term rose in his mind like a revenant. *Mischling*: a person of compromised blood, an unstable racial quantity, mongrel, hybrid, one part *us* to one part *them*. What to do with the *Mischling* had been an awkward issue in the early days of purity.

She might be Dahl's. And that was as unbearable as it was unlikely. That idea at least he could jettison.

Wolfi's probing insinuations went through and through him. He was a glass man to be seen through. A glass man where the light bent crookedly. *What do we know?* Wolfi had queried, in that shushing voice. Michael parked his backside on the coarse grass of a copse; lay back and let the warmth of a masked sun filter through the cloud layer. The party of young people went on ahead.

***

He must have dozed off in the murmurous warmth, and surfaced to the buzzing of a fly around his open mouth. It reached his ears magnified by proximity and at the same time distanced by semi-consciousness as if a plane were droning high overhead.

Slapping the insect off, he sat up stiffly. His mind felt unsettled. Effi dead. Ages ago. But that was not it. He had the black apprehension that the worst that could happen had not only happened but been unearthed. And that this was dull. Stunningly dull; a great weight of dreariness. Something smelt: faeces, was it? Burnt flesh? He clambered to his feet and batted at the fly, which would not leave him alone.

But there was only the remnant of a fire, a weathered cigarette packet and a rusted can.

Once, bodies had burst up, buried as they were in too shallow a pit, skinning over the material below. The secrets were spilled. *And you want to know that, Wolfi, do you? Oh no. If you knew, you wouldn't want to know, but there's no going back when you know.* And Wolfi would say: *you, you were complicit. My father did that.*

Tomorrow he must go to the dentist.

The drill would grind into his cavities, skidding, filling his mouth with uproar and detritus. He would gaze up into the dentist's eyes in a paroxysm of appeasement. The dentist would invite Mr Quantz to swill. Fragments of decay would be spat into the basin. The exposed nerve would sing with pain.

'Wider, Mr Quantz. I cannot see to work.'

So it had gone on until two years ago, the long expedition round the corruption eating Michael's jaw.

'The work is well-nigh complete, Mr Quantz. Your

dental health is as good as I can make it. You will need to come for regular annual check-ups.'

Quantz had thanked him from his new mouth. But two gold crowns had fallen out. Several teeth pronounced cleansed sporadically hurt. The orifice knew its own vulnerability, skin so thin and moist in there, like a woman's sex. His tongue slid around its interior, interrogatively, but not wanting to know.

The two gold crowns could have been anyone's. This thought had disturbed him. There they had lain, bleeding a residue of water into tissue paper. He had wanted them restored to his mouth at once but had delayed. He had now delayed two years.

They must be put away out of sight, must not be seen, or known, or thought of, his gold teeth. Gold teeth turned to currency. Melted crowns and bridges in vaults. Hair bagged in potato sacks for use in lagging, mattresses, lining for winter uniforms – such hair as fell in clumps from barbers' shears working round the clock, two minutes per head – shush, shush, it swished down, swags of women's hair that fell dusty and lustreless, grey and silver, black, brown, chestnut and red – hair which mingled on the barbers' floors till it could be baled and bagged, and which his mind could never assort, though it seemed to go astray from time to time, attempting to disassemble the assembly line, reverse production, return hair to heads, teeth to jaws, husbands to wives, reverse the trains and return the human cargo home to source, intact.

This must be stopped. This attempt to stop what had not been stopped must be stopped. He must stop it. Now. Stop. He stopped.

But wasn't this the place where Speer's trailers had stood, his latter-day HQ? Speer and his daisy chain of loyal women staff, phone cables snaking through the lonely woods. It seemed the set for a half-remembered B film, with idiotic costumes and spectacular lighting. They had waited in their cramped hideout, isolated in that remote and operatic beauty, eating boiled potato and cabbage. Speer and Annemarie Kempf and Edith getting the phone call: *The Leader is no longer alive.*

Speer striding in to 'The Trout' to confer with Dönitz. Handsome face drained; belted mackintosh undone. And then, staying at 'The Trout', with its thin-walled narrow rooms; being heard sobbing in the night. *What is it, sir? Have you been attacked?* the adjutant had asked. *No, it's this – it's this – look, Annemarie packed it for me.* A red presentation case with Hitler's signed photo. *He gave it to me. On his fifty-sixth birthday. Shall I ever sleep again?*

Quantz had noted out of the corner of his eye that the loyal secretary crept back to the trailer camp, after the end, with her sick mother and family. He had seen her toiling on a local farm for thirty Pfennigs an hour. He remembered the prosaic dignity with which she looked up under the cotton scarf covering her greying hair; dirt on her overalls and boots. A woman whose soles had pressed thick pile carpets at the hub of one of the most powerful ministries in Germany.

Later the Kempfs built cottages on a plot of land like many frugal refugees. The clearing was overgrown with bracken, and ink-cap mushrooms had colonised a rotting log. He kicked at the fungal growth, scattering its fleshy substance. There was a clouded green bottle half-hidden in leaf mould. Unscrewing the cap, he sniffed the unmistakable fume of paraffin.

***

The Englishwomen and children, Wolfi in their midst, were waiting on the jetty at Malente-Gremsmühlen for the boat, to carry them across five interlinking lakes to Fegetasche. There was a boisterous sense of carnival, bursts of laughter coming from the teachers, while the youngsters licked ice creams. Michael, having expected them to have caught the previous boat, smiled stiffly. He joined German pensioners in the queue, who were there to take the 'cure', which they augmented with sips from miniature bottles of brandy.

The boat ground into the jetty and disgorged its passengers; the children, piling on, all made for the open rear of the boat. *Lake Diek, ladies and gentlemen,* the captain in his white cap told them over the tannoy, the *first of our lakes... on our right we see 'The Island of Love'... depth of water under our keel is over thirty-eight metres...* As the little craft chugged out, children and pensioners oohed and aahed, roared with laughter and sang. Isolde Dahl's hair streamed back from her face as she stood to watch the shore recede, and Michael watched his son's infatuated gaze that told not only the woman but everyone in the boat, *I want to touch her*. He looked away. A gull cruised in a long arc across the dark green ramparts of trees.

The captain dispensed information he had offered once an hour six times a day every week for years, with a zest so fresh that they all cheered at the news of eels being smoked at Niederkleveez, and the pensioners took a sip of spirits, the wake churned, and the blue, white and red striped flag flapped out behind. As the boat nosed through the narrow canal into the last lake, children leaned out to trail with their fingers overhanging fronds. A dreamy bliss had descended on the passengers, a transient fellowship, English with German, old with young. Michael looked on as if from a separate vessel, into a toy world, the captain playing at sailors in his white hat, the ticket collector dispensing bucolic jests. A violent wave of nostalgia hit him. What was to keep him here, in this backwater? Training days at Mürwik came back: hard graft, discipline, salty excitement, young men with young men; ropes scalding between your hands as you plied them out, hauled them in, seas running high, and yourself running cunningly both with and against the currents. Yet here he bobbed becalmed in a tame game of boats, with women and children and the old, anchored to a reluctant Wolfi, land bound.

How about getting hold of some decent yacht and making a one-man voyage down the coast of... America. The west coast of America, the hard ride.

A touch of eros in the idea. A tensing-up, blood beating high.

Something middle-aged and staid in Michael ridiculed

such a puerile whim. But why? Why vegetate here? At sea you could be oblivious, body and brain at full stretch, skimming, tacking, the friable boat hurdling the waves.

Fegetasche came gliding into view, with its chestnuts, tips tinged with yellow, the tiers of the garden dropping down from the hotel. White tables and chairs on the terraces were mottled with fallen leaves; a blur of chewing faces peered from picture windows. The keel ground in ponderously.

'Think I'll stay aboard,' Michael told Wolfi, who was standing in the gangway with Isolde. 'Make the round trip.'

'I'm going with Issie.' He looked relieved.

'Goodbye, Mr Quantz,' said the young woman. 'Good to see you.'

Her breast was at the level of his eyes. He was suddenly, painfully aware of her, shudderingly aroused. Her colour was high, with the outdoors and the adulation; she glowed, gloriously healthy. Her breasts would be opulent. He wrenched his gaze away from that statuesque softness but it flickered back. His mouth was at the level where he could have taken one nipple into it. She oozed sex, a woman with that kind of figure, that wide open face, couldn't help it. Invited, craved touch. He watched her breast under the white cotton rise and fall as she waited beside him for the gangway to clear. He was offended by her. Whenever she came into his line of vision, he was melted, disturbed. He crossed his legs, watched her disembark, his son taking her hand for a moment, eyes meeting eyes, brimming with coded messages.

Michael watched the gently tipsy pensioners clamber up to the hotel, eager for coffee and cakes. Hoped not to die in his bed. Hoped for women, horizons; keen, clean stress and tumbling asleep at night dog-tired, beyond caring.

***

The homeward walk, after several beers in a favourite Gremsmühlen pub, was solitary. The sky cleared; clouds rolled back and the indifferent divinity in the night sky scattered handfuls of calm stars as Michael wandered home. The rhythm of walking further soothed his mind and he thought that the Dahl girl would give Wolfi a chance to lose his virginity, but that her acquiescence would reveal her looseness; her ineligibility as a marriage partner. That buxom type of girl, full-lipped, asking to be kissed, handled, entered, did you a service. Not good for a man Wolfi's age to be a virgin, for God's sake. A laughing stock. Needed an initiation. Not a mate to breed by. Someone, let's face it, to fuck. A three-quarters moon hung steady over Lake Eutin, and its counterpart rested on mirror-still water. A good fuck would do Wolfi good, grow him up a bit. Some mellifluous lyric of Goethe's was called to mind by the moon, but would not quite come through, teasing Quantz with the paradox of remote proximity. He'd learned it once by heart. It was as if the learner-by-heart and he stood on opposite sides of some gulf and hailed each other.

8

Munich, 1934, Berlin, 1936

Michael fucked whenever and whoever he could, but tried to give whoever a good time too; fair was fair. It shocked Paul Dahl that his boyhood friend enjoyed a woman in a natural way, failing to enquire into her ancestry, as the purer brethren required. By the time one had assessed a girl under sixty-two different categories – thickness of lips, height, hair colour, eyes, nose shape and a brief craniological survey – the yen would have passed.

What was life for if not for fucking? Michael taunted his comrade. *What's youth for?* They were twenty-three, after all. Paul flushed red as a radish. Michael viewed his white-blond hair; no eyebrows to speak of and skin transparent as a girl's; eyes milky-blue.

'What about Effi?' asked Paul, straightening up. 'Effi and your son?'

'Oh, Effi. What she doesn't know can't hurt her.'

Paul looked pained. 'Poor girl.'

Michael was annoyed to find himself reddening. He changed tack. 'You're just jealous.'

'Certainly not.'

'I suppose she whips you,' said Michael.

'*Quantz*.' Pained, prudish, he spoke like his father the schoolmaster, a pretty funny impression for a twenty-three-year-old looking all of nineteen. 'I shall be true to Renate till the grave. It's not a joking matter, marriage.'

Paul fetched his boots from the bed-end and buffed them up, though he could already have seen his face in them. Michael predicted a swift rise by virtue of devout pusillanimity married to blondest narcissism.

At first he'd been glad to spot Paul at this gathering of *Schutzstaffel* and naval Intelligence. Michael with

Canaris; Paul with his chief. The childhood friends elected to share a billet.

'No, Michael, we're not schoolboys now, sniggering over smut,' said Dahl. 'It's all too important.'

Michael knew what he was about to say. Wait for it:

'Every sperm is sacred. Not to be sloshed about any-old-where. Every sperm has its destiny.'

'What about wet dreams though? How do they fit in to the Grand Plan? What a waste on the part of the Immanent Will. Chuck us a fag, will you.'

Wet dreams were irrelevant. Paul slicked his comb through his hair, head to one side, angling his blue gaze at the mirror, tapering chin thrust sideways.

'But how sad, how very sad to think,' mused Michael, lolling back with his arms behind his head, 'of all that sacred sperm going to waste night by night, from the loins of millions of Nordic youths. Couldn't a way be found to collect it all in a pool? A lake of soldierly semen! Tanks of the stuff. Could be doled out to the Band of German Maidens if suitable husbands can't be found.'

'What a good idea,' exclaimed Paul, kempt and booted now, and jerking down his tunic. Outside the rain soused down the dark pane. '*Yes*,' he bleated and he was serious. 'That is a real idea. With our scientists' amazing new discoveries, nothing is impossible, I do truly believe that.'

'Oh, please.'

'No, really. The task is . . . colossal. And we really do need the right children. I mean, two hundred million. That is one hell of a lot of children.'

Paul stood spruce in his uniform, smelling of *Kölnisch Wasser*. He took Michael's virile hairy chest as an ideological disaster; Aryans being the furthest possible remove from apes. 'What is funny?' he asked.

It had taken Michael a while to account for those miniscule puncture marks on his companion's chest and the unnerving absence of genital or underarm hair. His friend was depilating on a regular basis with a clandestine pair of tweezers. Mortified when caught at it. He was worried, he explained, about his *fundamental* blemishes, which could not be tweezered or trimmed away. 'My face is too broad,' he mourned, 'I know it is. One of my ancestors way back must have married a Slav woman. You don't think it's too broad? Really?'

He let Michael into other cosmetic secrets. It turned out he shaved his hair above the ears to narrow the appearance of his forehead, a trick learned from Himmler himself. It made Michael weak to think about the hours the fellow had spent in front of the mirror. Narcissus at the pool.

Paul tapped his watch, despite knowing Michael would vault out of his pit at the last moment, stub out the fag and make himself presentable, all within a fraction of the time it took him.

'Look at it this way,' Michael suggested, propped on one elbow, ash on his pillow. 'Here am I, a living factory producing high calibre spermatozoa. And randy as hell. Wife martyrishly available once a month if you're lucky. Mother Nature says to me: get out there. Who am I to oppose Mother Nature? What am I supposed to do? Conserve the stock, wanking away my most fruitful years, or be generous?'

Out of bed; shaved and was into his uniform quick-sharp. His companion's eyes trawled him as he emerged smartish in naval blue. Somehow Paul's black uniform, with its chevrons and collar patches, seemed brighter. If black could be said to shine, Paul's black shone.

'But there are laws about these things, Michael,' he kept repeating, genuinely pained. His fussy admonitions were a lisped echo of Himmler's sermons. 'If you and I don't respect them, how can we expect others to do so? And some of those women you go after are... honestly... from what you say', he lowered his voice betraying fascination, 'filth, Michael, I wish you'd be more careful.'

The two of them chewed ham in the mess, swilled coffee. They spoke of Lübeck and Travemünde; singing round the campfire on the beach, potatoes cooked in the embers, and how good they tasted. No humble spud since then had been tastier, at least they could agree on that.

***

There was a trip south into Bavaria after the joint meeting, in a fleet of limousines. Himmler made his chauffeur stop as they passed a flaxen-haired urchin playing by the lakeside; the whole fleet was brought to a halt, Dahl and Quantz being in the last car but one.

Michael, unused to outrageous pantomimes of this order, was intrigued to observe Greatness stepping down with tears in its eyes to fondle the head of Futurity, scooping him up in his arms with many an edifying utterance not audible to the obsequious retinue.

He felt for the poor little fart peering aghast into the specs of his patron. An aide was sent to dig out a sacred Teutonic Mother, stuttering an impenetrable dialect of Bavarian, and now forced to endure torture by congratulation on having risked her life to produce this perfect little specimen, whose mouth was being crammed with chocolate. Hens squawked and pecked around at their feet.

A camera crew appeared on cue to record the moment, though the Chief's winsome behaviour was in point of fact not hypocritical. He meant it. He loved the boy.

'Fine hens you have here,' Himmler congratulated the child's father. 'Westphalian pure-bred pullets, if I'm not mistaken?'

'Right, sir. Yes, sir.'

'I know a good hen when I see one. A good plump, corn-fed German hen is a credit to Party and nation,' pronounced the Chinless One. The entourage nodded agreement.

'And your cocks?' Himmler enquired.

'Oh yes, sir, we have cocks.'

No one laughed. Heroic restraint was shown on the road between Munich and Berchtesgaden, amid the sublimity of the encompassing mountains. Impeccable black-uniformed figures, with a scattering of army grey and naval blue, ringed round the silent three-year-old with a snotty nose and a thumb that recurrently crept toward a moist, chocolate-stained mouth. It was as if a superior firm of undertakers had descended from hearses to view a future client.

'I have gone into the principles of breeding,' confided the Chinless One.

Still no one laughed.

'You are doing an invaluable job for Germany,' he finished, turning on his heel.

Re-embarking, they swept off south.

'The *Reichsführer* has explained to me personally,' Paul breathlessly informed Michael, 'the Mendelian principles of poultry breeding. It was honestly eye-opening.'

Already Paul was up to the wrists in blood. At the Röhm Putsch, he had been one of the elite boys poised on the running boards, agile, faceless assassins disciplined to the second – so he later bragged, *sotto voce*. This had been his blooding.

Yes, I was there. Yes, I was one of those.

Paul appeared eager to impart secrets to his friend; they came away like ripe fruit nudged into an outstretched palm. Michael was puzzled at such garrulous credulity. Insensible of having transgressed taboos, Paul seemed blithe about his wet red palms.

He'd not killed before, he confessed radiantly – well, not to speak of; he'd beaten criminals up, of course, roughed up Yids. But this was historic. Here they'd been shooting comrades. That took guts, and total commitment. Michael remembered the altar boy, wearing that same devout expression; and all the mothers cooing to Mrs Dahl, *Oh, the little angel*. Same look. Same lad. They all envied her this perfect child, with a sprinkle of freckles over his nose, his milky innocence.

Paul saw his killing duties as the necessary dark side of his mission to procreate. Get rid of the trash; replace it with perfect SS specimens. Lovely inseminations of his loins, ejaculations of blondness.

'I'm going to have a son,' he crooned. 'A son.'

'How do you know it's a boy?'

'Got to be. A man knows. Didn't you know, Quantz? With your Wolfi? There's nothing like it, is there, absolutely nothing in this world?' Tears in his eyes. 'It all fits together, Quantz. Those criminals being cleared away and our tiny baby coming to take their place.'

Paul got a daughter. Michael commiserated: 'Better luck next time.'

But the fellow was besotted. 'No, no, I wouldn't swap my little one for anything in the world,' he raved. 'Come and see her, Michael. I wish you would. She has the most ravishing violet eyes.'

He mentioned that they had thoughtfully returned the ashes of their executed Party comrades to their womenfolk in pasteboard cartons.

***

Michael would have lost track of Paul, had it not been for the Little Admiral. At Intelligence HQ at Tirpitz-Ufer, aghast briefings in the *sanctum sanctorum* of Canaris' office voiced what was hushed up outside.

'I hear you have a pal in the SS, Quantz.'

The admiral sat behind his desk, looking less than legendary. Michael was conscious of the scruffiness of his chief, his round-shouldered unmilitary bearing.

'You must mean Paul Dahl, sir. I'm not sure if I'd care to call him a friend, exactly. We were close as boys.'

'Uh-huh. Still . . .'

Across the sleek, dark wood of the desk sailed a scale model of the light cruiser *Dresden*. A trio of bronze monkeys, picked up on Canaris' exotic Japanese excursion, conveyed the triple injunction: see all, hear all, say nothing. Quantz, having come over with him from service on the *Schlesien*, Canaris' last command, felt he occupied a position in the master-dissimulator's consciousness somewhere between man and dachshund. Conversations in French and Spanish evidently brought comfort to an agitated spirit worn out by scheming to destroy with one hand what it upheld with the other: the *Führer* Canaris adored and deplored, Heydrich, his own lethal protegé. Quantz's presence in the background as a minor functionary reminded the admiral of an abdicated world of maverick marine adventure, pursued with effervescent guile, out of doors, travelling south under cover to Spain and South America.

'Keep in close touch. We gather he's a rising star. The leadership thinks highly of your friend.'

'To be honest, he's not that brainy. His father was the village schoolmaster: used to call him "my regrettable progeny".'

Canaris yawned, eyes pouched with fatigue, sick with tense boredom. From the battered leather couch, as if on cue, Sabine the dachshund plopped down and scampered over the carpet. Down the admiral dived, chortling, and allowed his hands to be wetted by the creature's tongue.

'There's my darling.'

Seppel, her mate and companion, yapped enviously.

'Come on then, daddy's other darling.'

The festival of licking and petting continued with both dogs – scraggy little scraps, thought Michael, hoping that neither would cock a leg or sit straining on the carpet to 'do a poop' as the admiral genially described his pets' anarchic excretions. Odour of doggy urine pervaded the office, camouflaged in disinfectant.

'Nobody who dislikth or maltreatth animalth can be a good thort,' stated the admiral, lisping on his sibilants in his passion. 'Get yourthelf a dog, Quantz, a true companion.'

'I was thinking of doing so, as a matter of fact, sir.'

'Were you indeed? What breed had you in mind?'

'Would you advise a Schnauzer, sir?'

'Patriotic sort of dog. Good choice, yes, I'd certainly say so.'

Michael's sole feeling in relation to the crapping, rolling, guzzling sausage dogs was a desire to kick them. This was the only lie you would risk telling to Canaris, the lie about animals. He would always fall for it. In the aqueous interior of his mind, where you viewed (if anything at all) refractions of refractions, cunningly or pointlessly multiplied, only his love of dogs was uncomplicated. He simply could not understand how others might not similarly dote.

'Dear little fellows,' ventured Quantz.

'Too right,' agreed the admiral. 'An animal is your

friend forever. One must be prepared to offer complete devotion in return. Hey, I'm glad you see it that way.'

The dog hairs on the admiral's tunic-breast were tokens of his after-lunch romp with his little friends, after which he and they had snuggled down on the leather couch for an hour's siesta. Michael supposed he rose from these joys pleasantly enervated (for he would still be yawning), a benefit Michael could only derive from a violent fuck. And, these days, the fucks had to be violent, to be felt at all. His nerve endings seemed to have numbed, so that he fingered life through gloves, peered out through a mask and fucked through thick rubber.

'But about your SS friend. Foster the friendship. You say he's no intellectual. Well, I can't say that comes as a surprise, and it's no bad thing from our point of view. After all, you're not expected to discuss Kant's *Critique of Pure Reason* with the chap. His wife . . .'

Michael blenched.

'Yes indeed. I have met the young lady. A person of a certain . . . what shall we say . . . forceful character. A notable swimmer, I believe. Happily the lady is not our problem. Feed him morsels I'll supply. And then milk him. You can toddle off down to our Munich office and make contact from there. You'll find he's come up in the world, by the way.'

He got himself invited to Paul's wife's 'At Homes'. He had begun to suffer migraines. Left and right lobes parted company; the world spun into a vortex in his left eye, a prelude to the sensation of being shot in the temple. Words failed in their function as if they had translated themselves into arbitrary cipher, hiding not meaning but void; a void with its own appalling agenda. Before occasions such as Renate's At Homes, Michael begged a friendly migraine to incapacitate him, but of course they struck only in the aftermath.

Perhaps migraine was an instrument of truthful perception. It magnified the crackle of a newspaper into an inner thunder from whose transmission he shrank. It reflected light into the eyeball as a lance into the brain.

He switched off the casuistical wireless, drew the curtains, took ergot and lay in the candour of the dark.

Quantz was surprised at the amount of truth he was required to pass across, in solution with disinformation. At least, he supposed it to be the truth, and often wondered blankly, *Why would Canaris give such-and-such away?* Wandering the labyrinth of the admiral's mental processes, he would stray into areas of divagation where wiles seemed to double back on themselves in self-defeating loops, a Byzantine legerdemain which brought to light – nothing, nothing at all, save the suspicion that Canaris practised, like conjuring, a specious magic.

He lay and suffered his migraine. A little girl played two-ball against the wall, on and on, without getting tired of it.

Push-pull, stroke-strike, retreat-advance; in this habitual dubiety everyone in Quantz's office was implicated. Nobody thought twice about their double-thinking.

***

A servant opened the door of a rather swish apartment, relieved Michael of his coat and directed him into a living room, all red carpets and subdued golden light, with suede settees and armchairs, presided over by Renate in a yellow dress and long gloves. Her face was powdered and lipsticked more than was considered consonant with the virtue of Teutonic womanhood.

'Heil Hitler!' Her arm shot up. A palaver of salutes exposed Renate's shaven armpit. A fleeting hope, bred more of curiosity than of concupiscence, since she was definitely not his type, that her bosom might pop out of her corsage, was disappointed. Whalebone did an efficient job. She stood to her full height beside her husband, a richer, redder shade of blonde – a cornfield next to a wheatfield.

'So, Michael. What do you think of the new me? I had those rustic braids all cut off. Don't you remember my earphones? Of course you do. Plaits in a knot round my ears. Lovely, patriotic style for the peasants, but perhaps less becoming in people of our standing. How do you like our apartment?'

'Very fine.' How young she was for all this: scarcely eighteen, he guessed, and acting like a hectic schoolgirl who cannot believe her crazy luck in landing a part in some film. He viewed her lacquered helmet with distaste.

'Everybody adores it. And I can't get used to the fact that it's all mine! Little me! Got it for a song from those Levis . . . had to sell up and clear out . . . sad for them but she should have made the best of it, instead of all that wringing of hands. I say, do you really like my hair? I brought the plaits home with me in a box, so I can pin them on if I feel like it.'

In his mind's eye Michael saw a pair of dead plaits in a box.

As her yacking mouth moved, he sized her up. That kind of regulation female left him cold. Gushing about seeing her *Führer* in the *Osteria*, and how he passed only inches from her table, with his dog whip, think of that . . . and he looked her directly in the eyes, she felt quite weak, she really did . . . had she mentioned the *Führer* was wearing a raincoat?

Michael enquired, since some response seemed indicated, whether it had been raining.

'No. It was a fine day.' She looked at Michael baffled.

Her talk passed to lemon chiffon and apricot moire. Swallowing brandy, he looked her over to see what Dahl fucked. Athlete's body under silk. The muscular bicep in the nude arm desexualised the image. And underneath the froth, a will to dominance. The lemon chiffon and apricot whatnot were a sweet, fruity and unconvincing coating to this.

Baby was brought in by the proud father. The guests gathered round to praise Baby. Baby had a square face, red cheeks and the look of Renate. Michael felt at once embarrassed and fascinated by Paul's effeminate behaviour.

After some communal cooing, Renate seemed to tire of adoring Baby. Her sights were clearly on higher things than the Mother's Cross. 'Watch out, Paul, she's dribbling. Give her to Trude – Trude, clean her up.'

Paul continued with his public act of worship. He sat his darling on his black lap, vowing to add at least nine more children to his quiver. He smiled into the child's eyes and received with rapture her babbled hymns of love.

'All in good time, Paul. Michael and Effi have only got one squeaker. Haven't you, Michael?'

'That's right.'

Michael noticed that Paul glowed with less bright a ray. It seemed she wanted to swim, not breed. Swim for her *Führer*. Her sights were set on the Olympic team, no less. Paul shot his wife a look of chagrin. Michael's antennae registered the access of tension between the pair.

He escaped only after the cake in the shape of a swastika. Renate had enquired of the baker whether they couldn't have swastikas in black icing to adorn it: totalise the cake, so to speak. The baker replied that, in her opinion, black icing was not appetising. People did not want to eat black flags. As a traditional baker, she did not go in for novelties, an ideology which struck Michael's hostess as reactionary. For how could a swastika be seen as a 'novelty'? Weren't runes as old as . . . how old were runes, anyway? Ancient. Prehistoric. She would seek out another, politically sound baker. At their wedding they had had a swastika cake, and wasn't it lovely, darling?

Michael bolted for the door as soon as was seemly after the cake. He kept his runes separate from his eating. Besides, the need to relieve himself in a good guffaw had become almost unbearable. He had made an arrangement to ride with Paul, *sans* Baby and Valkyrie, on Wednesday.

***

Paul confided his wife's reluctance to breed. He bet she was seeing some Jewish gynaecologist.

'Are there any Jewish doctors left?'

Paul said he must be a Jew if he was giving out contraceptives to Nazi ladies.

Michael admired the *non sequiturs* of his puritanical SS brethren. He shrugged: 'Come off it, she's only – what – eighteen? Plenty of time for sprogs. After all, your chief's only got one girl, hasn't he? Wolff's got what? A couple of daughters. There can't possibly be any shame.'

'Not for the big men, no. But for those of us on the lower rungs of the ladder, it does matter – and,' he murmured confessionally, 'I want to do my bit. How can the Fatherland revive as it's destined to do, if we of the right sort don't procreate?'

'If it's destined, it will happen anyway,' Michael clarified pithily.

Paul shook his head at this intellectual teaser.

'It's not that simple. There is our Heroic Destiny. But we must co-operate with it. I want more Isoldes. More. I don't want luxury, Michael, not for its own sake. I want to use it to bring at least four or five more little ones into the world. It's the very least I can do.'

'And such pleasant work. At least your part. All you have to do is shoot your bolt and wait.'

'Whereas she, yes I know, risks her life with every child. Of course.' His resentment was softened, but then he blurted, 'But it's natural for women to want children. So if it's natural, why doesn't she want them? Know what I think?'

Michael shook his head. They sat forward in a conspiratorial huddle. But Paul at the last minute changed his mind; sagged back in his seat, sweating, his eyes averted. Michael helped him out:

'She prefers swimming? Proud to think she might swim for Germany?'

'How do we know what she's doing all those hours at the swimming pool?' Paul burst out. 'Or who she's doing it with?'

'You could always have her followed,' Michael jested.

'Do you think I haven't thought of that? I've been taken for a ride, Michael. Every time I look at the child, I wonder... I mean, I'm not blind. At least she's blonde. She's blonde, at least.'

In the cold space beneath the marble pillars and the

black, white and red flags, Paul struggled with unmanly tears. All the Tristans and Siegfrieds his wife denied him filed through his brain.

'Do you want my honest opinion, Paul?'

'Of course.' In his flushed face, the pale eyebrows had almost disappeared, leaving lashless blue eyes staring as if pleading for mercy.

'I've been about a bit. Your wife's a bit too exemplary for my tastes. She wants to swim for Hitler – well, good. She's given him a baby – good again. She's a thoroughly decent girl. What more do you want?'

Oh the gratitude! Oh the failure to query Michael's malicious use of the deathsheads' watchword, *decent*! Remorse rocked his friend.

'Then I've wronged her,' Paul lamented. 'And my Isolde. I've wronged them both.'

He had hit his wife in a quarrel; struck her across the mouth with his leather glove.

'What can I do to make amends, Michael? What a jealous bastard I've been, what a shit, my Isolde . . . '

Michael was staggered at these people. They throve in a pathological atmosphere of cynical distrust on the one hand and milksop sentiment on the other. They murdered and they doted.

***

'No,' said Effi, with the kind of stubbornness she could show when scared, 'I don't want to go. I've got nothing to wear.'

'Sorry, we've got no choice. How much do you need?'

He handed her a wad of notes. She dug her fists in the pockets of her apron, head down.

'Get yourself something nice. Come on, buck up. Treat yourself to a hairdo while you're at it.'

She put one hand up to her mousy hair. How meagre she was, how shabby. There was absolutely no need for her to look like that. Worse looking women were dolling themselves up nowadays and learning to act the part. Why Effi needed to maintain that lacklustre image, he could not imagine. She could hardly be surprised that he spent so little time with her.

'Wolfi's got a cold, anyhow,' she said. 'I can't leave him.' Relief flooded Effi's face, before she subdued the gush behind her habitually hard-done-by mask.

'That's nothing, a cold is nothing,' said Michael with irritation.

'A cold is nothing? In a child prone to ear infections?'

'Look, if I'm ordered to bring my wife to one of these functions, I bring my wife. It's as simple as that.'

Effi took a step back and offered no mutiny. She did not ask him where he was when he was not with her; why in his infrequent stays he took so little interest in his son.

'Come on, take the money, get yourself something decent to wear, do, dear.' He thought, *Scrawny chicken.* Then he thought, *I ought to be ashamed.* Then, *Why did I marry her?* and remembered why: Wolfi.

'I honestly don't want to leave Wolfi,' she bleated. 'Don't make me. I'll be worrying about him all evening. And I can't talk to those high-ups, Michael, you know I can't. I'll let you down.'

'Of course you won't. Just sit quietly with the other ladies and agree with everything that's said to you. That's just about all any of us do.'

Effi reached out her hand reluctantly and took the money. Wolfi upstairs began to grizzle. Michael took his wife in his arms, pulling her slight body against him, sensible of its strain as she strove to answer the call of the sick child.

'Don't bother about him,' he said. 'You'll spoil him, Effi, if you pander to his every whim.'

The straining body in his arms asked, *Is your little boy's earache a whim?*

'Come on then, we'll both go up and see him. I'll call the doctor if necessary.'

Wolfi stared with wide, dark eyes from his fat featherbed. He greeted his father with anxious silence and denied that there was anything wrong with his ears.

***

The get-together of *Abwehr* with SS high-ups was leavened with underlings and their wives – *chez* Heydrich – to 'cement relations' between chameleons and serpents. All were dressed in civvies, which somehow resembled fancy dress, vaguely embarrassing; a bleak, chilly affair.

King Heinrich, on top form, beamed seraphically, as he set the conversational tone by enlarging to the womenfolk on the subtleties of racial categories.

Effi, in a brown costume, sat in a row of opulent spouses on a sofa the exact colour of her outfit. Michael could see his shabby little wife's terror of being singled out in this glittering company. His heart squeezed as the *Reichsführer*, proceeding by way of boastful flattery, commended his own ability to detect origins at a glance.

'For instance, you, my dear lady,' he said to Wolff's wife, 'I would have you down as Phalic or Dinaric. But Mrs Quantz, I would detect in you a touch of Alpine. One gains an eye for the structure of a face after long study.'

Effi, cringing, squeaked: 'Is that good, or... not?'

'That will do nicely, *gnädige Frau*, for where Phalic predominates, the little touch of Alpine dissolves away in no time.'

Michael's other half patted her forehead with a handkerchief. The row of wives, hailed by Heinrich as blossoms on a bough, sat on the monumental sofa in such a way that the failure of Effi's feet to meet the ground made her look like a child. Michael grinned over to give her courage. She was so pale that he feared she would pass out or burst into tears. Poor little thing, he should have left her at home with the boy.

'There will come a day, ladies, in just a few years from now, when all important posts in the state will be occupied by blond men. All thanks to you ladies.'

Through Michael's mind flashed the sarcastic verse:

Blond as Hitler,
Tall as Goebbels
Thin as Goering
Sober as Ley.

He took in the permanently blue six o'clock shadow on the orator's chin; what there was of chin.

Talk swivelled round to German culture. Dürer was brought out, dusted and put away again; a galaxy of poets minus Heine and Zweig were slapped down like winning cards; Mendelssohn ignored as a Yid but Bach and Beethoven given an airing, like a music box whose lid is shut as soon as it's opened. All the toys in their toybox. Michael kept his mouth shut. Though he didn't care for Jews, to abuse their magnificent art was sheer buffoonery.

'Come on now, Reinhard, play for us.'

'What shall it be?'

Heydrich was ready, as ever, to strut his fiddle. Michael was requested to accompany him. He sat at the grand piano. The friendless, unnerving man beside him lodged his violin beneath his chin. He was sensitive to an exquisite extreme, like a sniffer dog. A nose for men but an ear for music too, with a delicate susceptibility to cadencing and nuance, a lightness of touch and virtuosity of fingering – guaranteed to melt hearts. Effi's eyes were resting on Michael, with a frank sympathy rarely shown between them. He sent her a complex, momentary message, forehead wrinkling with apology, mouth ruefully smiling.

Heydrich turned to check Quantz's readiness. The pianist's fingers suspended over the keys felt like a bunch of sausages. Stiff, fleshy, caggy fingers. Ready, yes, he signalled.

He began. Hobbled along, clodhopping through the exposition, ham-fisted. Heydrich raked his bow across the open strings in protest.

'Tuning up, Quantz?' he asked with saturnine bonhomie.

'I am not a competent accompanist for you.'

'I've heard you before. You're perfectly adequate. Play.'

There was something so insulting about the accusation of *adequacy* that it put Quantz on his mettle. He began again, more easily this time, concentrating attention on the score. He took leave of absence from present company, in a world whose language was coded in notations going beyond all languages understood by the company being entertained.

Yet as he played, his mind was penetrated by his partner's. Heydrich was a profound musician; no stridor – almost too tender. Good range too, only the power was controlled. Quantz was aware of a residue untapped, even in *fortissimo* passages. As Heydrich joined Quantz, Quantz opened to Heydrich, thesis and antithesis, addressing to one another contrary pleas and pledges whose conflict struggled in the one harmony. Soul to soul with the rat-eyed inquisitor, Michael's piano entered into a synthesis of beauty with his interrogator's violin.

They ended; re-emerged. The reverberations died. While Michael raised his eyes slowly from the keys, Heydrich removed the fiddle from under his chin. Tears stood brimming on his eyes; one or two spilt. The audience watched in silent awe at the musician's emotion. Michael swept his gaze over the company, which regrouped in his consciousness like a shallow fresco on a stone wall. His glance was arrested by the face of Paul's wife, eyes streaming tears.

I've just been made love to by a ghoul, he thought. Could there be an aesthetic, pure in itself, alien to ethics, innocent of human sympathy?

***

'My whole career, Michael, my whole career's in jeopardy.' Paul showed him a handwritten note from Himmler:

> I request that you discipline your wife and curb her voicing of opinions in the most improbable places concerning this and that political occurrence. In general, I have the impression that in your marriage you fail to exert sufficient control and that you have not educated your young wife in the manner which I have a right to expect.
>
> I had received reports of your wife's ebullitions, but, supposing these outbursts to proceed from excess of laudable zeal, had refrained from drawing them to your attention. I

enclose for your perusal a copy of a letter she has visited upon my office. I am assuming your ignorance of your wife's folly and rely upon you to enlighten her on what is and is not expected of the wife of an SS officer. I need hardly inform you that your wife's chances of being included in the German Olympic team are slim.

I trust you will remedy this situation, by whatever means lie in your power.

Reichsführer SS

Paul, livid with anger, was scared shitless. He showed Michael the letter with a suspicious look, as though he resented him for reading it. Renate's 'ebullitions' he kept to himself. Michael was curious, having never heard her utter anything but ultra-correct platitudes.

'Have you shown her the letter?'

'Of course I've shown her.'

'What did she say?'

'She says he should be shot.'

Michael was silent. No wonder the fellow was wound up. She could be the death of the pair of them. Renate extorted a grudging respect.

'If I can't shut her up,' Paul said finally, 'I'll have to get rid of her. I've found all sorts of stuff. A Dutch cap. A douche,' he whispered, flushed. The cosmopolitan contents of Mrs Dahl's sponge bag seemed to elate him, black misgivings substantiating themselves as incriminating trophies. Quantz imagined him pruriently turning them over in his hands, sniffing at them, secreting them in some secret place, whence he could abstract them at will and charge himself with the same thrill of revulsion.

'Will you come round? Give me an honest opinion?'

***

'Did you know I'd been left out of the team, Michael? For political reasons. Yes, it's because I speak my mind. Things have got beyond a joke. Look, I don't like Jews, I never have liked them and I never shall. I mean, they came here from... wherever it was they came from

...didn't they, and made a fat profit out of us. I know that. I don't want them in our swimming pools or cinemas, of course I don't, who does? Of course they ought to be stripped of wealth and so on. I mean, I have a lovely silver fox dirt cheap, from one family who moved on – not to mention this apartment. But my friend – Elisabeth – I didn't know she was a Jew, she doesn't practise their revolting rites or anything, has just been...taken away. In her nightgown. With her feet bare. Her feet bare on the pavement; she could have cut herself and it was cold. I saw. They just came and dragged her out of bed – Paul's lot. I shouted out of the window – she lives in the flat two along "Hey, you, what are you doing to Mrs Reiter?" and I ran out in my slippers and said, "You've made a mistake, you've got the wrong person, there must have been a mix-up." But they insisted she was the right person. They were quite courteous and respectful – but that's not on, is it? That's the kind of thing you can't go doing to people.'

'What I've been trying to din into my wife's head is that they're not "people like us".'

'Elisabeth is. You know Elisabeth, Paul. You liked her. If she is a Jew – if she is, and I don't believe she is – then...there must be decent Jews.'

'Well of course there are, woman,' he exploded. 'But you can't judge the tribe by a few outstanding individuals. A civilised country has to make laws for everyone.'

'Is it civilised to drive people out of their houses and through the streets with dog whips, barefoot in their night things? Is it? Is it, Effi?' Now Renate in her turn tendered an appeal to her guests. She seemed to grope for difficult light through invincibly thick blinds.

'I'm not political,' wavered Effi. She wrung a handkerchief between her hands, as if it had just come out of the wash. 'I don't know about those things.' Effi left politics to menfolk. She had always accepted without demur, and indeed with some relief, her sphere. About laundry and cooking she had strong opinions; on the Jewish question none. Tentatively, she suggested, 'But this Elisabeth sounds such a nice... perhaps it *was* a mistake? Michael, don't you think... it might have been a mistake?'

Paul assured her courteously that if his people picked someone up, there was always a good reason for it. They just didn't make that kind of mistake. His wife must get it into her head that she couldn't change anything. In intervening, she had probably made it worse for this woman. It was raining, he observed, what dreadful weather.

'How? How did I make it worse for her?'

Paul made no reply. He stood moodily at the window, looking down into the street at passing cars, the hats of women, bobbing umbrellas. Renate stood up and tapped him on the back, so that he swung round, with the evident urge to strike her.

'What do you do to people, Paul, in those cellars? What? Do you do it too? Do you join in? Do you?'

She measured herself against her husband's physique; matched him eye to eye. He dwarfed her. Ignoring her taboo question, he called peremptorily to the nurse: 'Bring in the child, Trude.'

The girl shrank from her father. She was a sturdy, ruddy-cheeked child, her head covered by a blue silk scarf.

'Ah, the dear little mite,' crowed Effi.

Paul gripped the child's cheeks between finger and thumb, its mouth was pinched out, showing the moistly delicate inner lip. Then he whipped off the scarf, to reveal a stubble of dark hair. The girl was quiet and did not cry.

'Oh the poor little thing, whatever are you doing?' Effi cried in a shocked, husky voice.

'Bleached!' he shrieked. 'Bleached! I'll be a laughing stock.'

'What does he mean?' asked Effi.

'I bottle-blonded her,' said Renate, dead-eyed. 'He says she isn't his. Because she isn't really blonde.'

Now Effi came into her own. She could see nothing political whatever about the question. It lay fair and square within her province.

'Yes but children's hair isn't always the same colour as their parents,' she explained, to Paul's fury, and having started on the theme in which she felt herself to be expert, she did not let up. 'It's a known fact, no, it really is, Paul. I mean, look at our Wolfi. He was fair at first but now his hair's a sort of light brown, all fluffy and sweet. You're hurting her, Paul . . . come and sit by Auntie Effi, my lovely.' She put out her arms to the child. 'No, really, I'm sure you mean it all for the best, and I can't pretend to understand the science – I know Michael thinks I'm dense – but there are some things a mother knows. My sister's children all have different colours of hair; it's quite striking when you see them. I'll show you a photo. There are five, three boys and two girls, and she's expecting another any time, and of course no one knows what it will look like, because you can't know, can you, beforehand? That's the mystery of it.'

Everyone in the room, including Effi's husband, was dumbfounded by her tirade, which showed no sign of concluding, so Michael spoke over her.

'No doubt your wife was trying to save your feelings,' he said smoothly. He understood that the thought of being derided by his fellow butchers was a determining principle in Dahl's psyche. Incapable of guilt, he was controllable by shame. 'Everyone wants a flaxen angel these days. My God, if you arrested all the bottle-blonds in Munich, you'd lose a quarter of the population.'

A double expression of relief and balked suspicion flickered on the milky-pink face that had swallowed doctrine as a monkey gobbles peanuts. He was clearly itching to get rid of Renate. Probably he'd got thoroughly tired of the harpy and had some other girl lined up. Effi was still wittering, this time addressing words of consolation to the icily silent Renate.

Michael went on, 'Didn't you say something about some Slavic ancestor in your own family? Your wife was probably covering up for you.'

He exulted in telling lily-pure Paul Dahl he was a bit of a *Mischling*. Effi plucked the child from Renate's knee, where she was furiously sucking her thumb, with hectic cheeks, and hoisted her onto her own lap.

'Would you like a sweetie? I brought some red and green bonbons along for you. Now what have I done with them?'

She pretended to search in her bag, smiling into the eyes of the child, who cheered up and joined her in rifling the handbag's fascinating innards. A paper cone full of bonbons was swiftly found and extracted. Isolde twiddled open the wrapper and, having briefly admired the bright, striped sweet, popped it in her mouth.

'Is it good?' asked Effi. 'My little boy loves them. Don't cry,' she advised Renate. 'They're not worth it,' she whispered.

Michael caught the whisper. Effi had seldom answered back, rarely advanced criticism. She operated in a sphere of stillness, sealed off in a bubble from the life beyond her. So this was the substratum of her thought: *They're not worth it*. This axiom sustained her through his absences and when she scooped up his shirt from the floor, soiled with smoke, sex and alien perfume.

'Do you knit at all?' she now asked Renate.

'No,' replied Renate faintly, as though the preposterous ordinariness of the question made her want to swoon.

'You should. It's so calming, I find, the rhythm you know, and the way the needles click. It's soothing.'

Renate had not the ghost of an idea that Effi was offering her limited all in the way of comfort. She smoothed the expensive material of her slacks with trembling fingers. As they left, he kissed the child's cheek; a ticklish aftermath of the contact remained on his lips, which nicotined, inky fingers couldn't immediately rub away.

Effi passed no verbal comment on the drama they had witnessed. But she hurried up the stairs to Wolfi's bedroom without removing her coat and pored over the boy's sleeping face. Later, when Michael came upstairs, he found her cuddled up in bed with her son.

'Isn't he getting a bit old for that kind of... lark?' he asked from the doorway.

'I shan't have him for ever,' she replied.

Michael crouched at the bedside. The boy's milky breathings sighed from the pillow. She had plunged under the feather quilt; a cream island in the surrounding darkness. She had come to drink peace of the child's sleep, the security of his innocence.

'Look . . . ,' he said lamely, 'it'll be all right.'

***

He saw his wife and child less and less; and Renate Dahl only once more before she and the child vanished. This was at the Berlin Olympics. Not in the stadium, dizzy with applause, under the adoration of Leica cameras, but in the Olympic underbelly, amongst the mishaps and disgraces. The girl who sank in the butterfly; the dropper of Germany's relay baton.

Michael had been invited to the party at the Goerings' palace on the Leipziger Platz. A fairground with beer on tap; *Bratkartoffeln*, *Sauerkraut*, game and champagne. He strayed here and there: had a go on the roundabout; jostled amongst SS men winning novelities at the shooting gallery; tipsily endured both ballet and the 'sky-ballet' – Ernst Udet in a biplane, skimming the lawns. The jovial host seemed omnipresent, a mountain of swaggering flesh in leather shorts and frilly shirt; a folksy edelweiss in his hat. Replete with oddities, Michael sneaked in to reconnoitre the house. He found himself beside an indoor pool, where, to his pleased surprise, two silent, naked girls swam between bottles of champagne, placed at either end.

One he recognised as the disgraced American swimmer, Eleanor Jarrett, suspended for some act of flamboyant drunkenness; the other was Renate Dahl. He sucked in his breath at the luscious body of the American, lazily backstroking in the wash of yellow light. The swimmers passed one another in the centre, uncommunicating: *hail and farewell*, *hail and farewell*. At either end, as if synchronised, each reached up for the bottle and took a swig. Neither noticed Quantz. They swam as if in a dream.

9

Lake Plön, Malente, 1958

The autumn trees rained gifts. A chestnut at Fegetasche exploded a conker at Issie's feet. She rubbed it against her skirt to gloss it up. 'Did you play with these at school?' she asked Wolfi. 'On strings?'

He shook his head. 'I didn't get much school. Somehow or other, I never did the ordinary things.'

As they herded the last of the weary children in through the school gates, a sycamore seed spiralled down slowly. They watched the seed spin on its axle, till it came to rest at the verge of the path. Wolfi bent to pick it up. 'Twins,' he said. 'Miracle of engineering. See how far it manages to land from the parent tree.' He let it fall again, and they watched as its well-designed imbalance carried it crookedly askance.

He asked about her parents.

'I don't know about my first father. I think he was . . .' and the word came exploding out from between her teeth, '. . . a rat. I think he was . . . such a crook that even my mother couldn't stand it.'

She stood aghast. Had she said that out loud? But Wolfi didn't look fazed. He nodded, as though this were only to be expected.

'They were,' he agreed. 'That's what they were, all of them.'

'But not your dad.' It was not meant as a question.

Wolfi said, 'I go around with this idea . . . of being a bad seed. I should try to spit myself out. Try to un-be me. Hansi, my friend, says . . .' He seemed to be clasping himself in his own arms, so that as he opened himself to her, he simultaneously shielded himself.

'I don't think biology kind of works like that,' she said,

though the same fear crouched in her. 'And anyway, I like you as you are. Don't you dare un-be you, Wolfi.'

'All right, I won't,' he capitulated, and his eyes looked enchanted.

***

They were getting ready to go 'on the razzle' at the *Blütehof*. Isolde fizzed with anticipation; felt she had hardly been living in Germany at all, apart from Wolfi, but stranded on a solipsistic island of Englishness, or aboard a ship whose insular, rule-bound crew hove high-prowed through foreign seas. They had no wish to get wet. She dragged a brush through her hair. None of Renate's strivings with Kirbigrips and potions had ever tamed the mutinous curls for long. No Jenkins cousin had such an unruly head; theirs was calm hair, neat and straight or amenable to regimentation with pipe cleaners, which rolled the hem under in a sausage-like arrangement. *Decent hair*, they had apparently. She had grown up feeling vaguely ashamed of the luxuriance of her own.

Yet Denis had asked, *May I touch? Touch your hair?* with such tender longing. And once he laughed and asked, *Tell me truly, is that natural? Or do you wind it up in rollers?*

And she had a vision of his wife's on the conjugal pillow, stuck with curlers in a brown net.

He brushed her hair from her face and watched fascinated as the curls sprang back.

So you don't spend hours under the dryer, in a row of ladies, with their heads baking in ovens?

I couldn't be bothered.

And you don't wear any make-up.

Neither do you but I don't go on about it.

And Denis had laughed at her waywardness, for perhaps he was inwardly convinced of the womanliness of artifice, and was guiltily on holiday in a realm of anarchy, and said, *Oh how lovely you are.*

She now examined the person in the mirror, holding her head at a provocative angle. She tied a belt round her pale coat, pulled on a beret. Issie had changed from the person who came here, so grieved by Denis, a reject of the English system which had stated categorically, *You have sullied your womanly honour*. In those very words.

Had they really said that? Sullied? As if a woman's modesty were a sort of apron which couldn't be laundered? As if poor Denis could have left his handprints all over her body for ever. Whatever the thing with Denis had been, dirty it was not. Yet it had been in its own way a lethal form of folly. Had Doreen found out? Perhaps she knew all along? Knew, and thought, *Well, men are like that*, or sobbed at night at his turned back, finding his externally malleable inoffensiveness the worst kind of cruelty. Isolde squirmed inwardly. Still she was the one who'd got kicked out.

She had paid. So it could go into the past, all the hurt to the woman, whose name she could hardly bear to remember. She was cleared of her debt; Denis would have to pay off his in instalments, year by year, in small acts of contrition, and lie, and repeat like a credo, *I love you, dear*. Yet even as she reassured herself, Isolde didn't feel quite clean.

And they had all looked her body up and down, as if its voluptuousness constituted an affront to genteel morality. Her tallness and bearing and the turmoil of her hair. And Renate, confiding in Mrs James, *Her hair is my despair. It gets so greasy, you would not believe, and when I try to do anything with it, such as a nice slide or a bow of ribbon, she runs off and loses it 'accidentally on purpose' in a puddle.*

She had taken the bristly brush to Issie's topknot as if something demonic might be trounced out of the scalp. And Issie yelped and ran away. One hundred times her scalp would be scraped, and then denounced as a greasy nest.

As if I were guilty of myself. And Wolfi saying, *Bad seed*, bending to pick up the sycamore crescent, from where it had spun away from the mother tree. Arcane memories filtered from a prior time when her hair had been a matter of great account. They had become lost souls hunted from shore to shore, all for this dark, shadowy thatch. It made no sense; but the memories had become, since Issie arrived at Plön, insistent. She had been an object of shame to herself and to everybody, and the blond man had hurt her, putting something cold on the nape of her neck.

Had he worn an iron helmet like the one Patterson had clamped on her head in her Dönitzing? Cold and void. Was he one of those?

Was the blond man dead? Slowly she turned from the mirror to the window. Someone out there. Near at hand. In the lake, under a mound, screened by these huge skies that marched impersonally overhead?

Or alive, out there, anonymous among millions?

Dwarfed and whimpering she seemed to rush wildly around in a room so out of proportion to her stature that no wall could be reached, wherever you ran. There was no sense in this. It was a distorted echo of some bad dream. Forget it.

***

Issie, Lynne and several Fräuleins arrived early at the *Blütehof*, the estate above Malente where hospitality and menfolk abounded. Its gardens were overgrown, a romantic wilderness in which the house's timbers recalled their rooted origins. Against the haze of greenish light amongst evergreen and birch, the scarlet jacket worn by one of the women glowed like a berry. Monumental wrought-iron gates, hinges rusted away, leaned spreadeagled against walls eaten with ivy. Isolde registered their magnificent scale and symmetries. Each bore the sign of what looked like a double fork of lightning.

'Aha,' said a young man introduced as Werner. 'You're studying the runes.'

'Is that what they are? Runes? What do they mean?'

'Just decorative, I think.'

'What is this place then?'

'Nowadays it's an orphanage, run by a philanthropic organisation. And the great hall is used for meetings. It used to be a home for mothers and babies. There's a statue of a Madonna and child somewhere or other.'

Issie attended to the Madonna, and tried not to look round for Wolfi. This was not the icon you were used to seeing in homely wayside Calvaries or pietàs. She was a mother of stone, suckling her stone son with her hard breast, her lidless gaze keeping vigil over the nervous unease of the woodland. Her heroic motherhood was qualified only by a film of lichen that crept across forehead and nose, promising a more complete defacement in process of time, and stains from weather and the droppings of birds and animals. Isolde reached up to touch the cold breast.

The *Blütehof* was a beehive of orderly activity. The young ones (the orphans, presumably) were humping great feather quilts which had been hung to air up the staircase, while kneeling women polished floors. How cheerfully corporate it all seemed, each one dedicated to the whole honey-making enterprise.

'What goes on?' Lynne asked a startled-looking young man, who rolled up a list he was checking and stuck it in his pocket.

'We're getting ready for a reunion. You're early. I'm afraid we're not ready for you.'

'Who is being reunited?'

'Brotherhood of Ex-Marines, no less. Come through – I'll call Karl. Make yourselves at home, do.'

Despite the warmth of the season, a log fire blazed in the room in which he left them. Oil lamps gave out low luminosity against wood panelling. The melancholy eyes of stags' heads reflected the glow, their antlers casting a tangle of shadows back against the panels. The guns that had presumably shot them were displayed crosswise between the heads.

'Aren't they sad?' Issie tried to avoid the mild eyes' steady reproach.

'Oh my giddy aunt, not old Doughnut.' Lynne pointed to a wall empty of wildlife, opposite the fire. A huge portrait dominated it, placed centrally.

Issie went up to the portrait. Here indeed was Grand Admiral Dönitz in full dress uniform, his chest, neck and hat boasting as many silver and gold decorations as a single person's outfit could hold, his face staring bleakly to the left. In the flapping light of the fire, Dönitz's face bore a fugitive resemblance to that of Patterson, something mouse-like in the pointed chin and nose, the large ears, some quality, or negation, that failed to answer to the heroic model. So that must have been Patterson's meaning when, during her ritual Dönitzing, he had asked her what she thought of the admiral. Every time the chap looked in the shaving mirror, he saw Dönitz; whenever he confronted Dönitz's picture in his private shrine he saw his own double. How each visitor's failure to spot the likeness must have balked his *amour propre*.

'What's he doing here?' wondered Issie. 'And look, here are his memoirs – *Ten Years and Twenty Days*.' She leafed through the table of contents: *Threat of Bolshevism – I am Hitler's successor – My policy – Showdown with Himmler*. There was an odd sensation of a play of unholy symmetries; the one face opposing its reflection in the Little England of the school and the Old Germany of Malente. For coming here was like entering the past. The splendid comfort of the room seemed archaic.

'Miss Dahl, Miss Williams.' Their host entered with his Alsatian. 'I see you've found our Good Admiral's personal testament. Came out only this year; we've eagerly awaited it, for he was a man much wronged, you should know. A great naval officer and patriot! Condemned as a war criminal! Madness. See how he ends his book: *Let no man besmirch the fighting men of this last war. To do so is to besmirch the honour of those who gave their lives in the execution of their duty*.'

'What a lot of besmirching,' yawned Lynne. 'Anyhow, we're here but where's everyone else?'

Issie prickled with dislike; their host's chivalry was so immaculate as to constitute a form of sarcasm, and his opinions bored her. The Alsatian embarrassingly thrust its nose into her lap, sniffing lewdly.

'Warm yourselves, do. You look so charming together

in the firelight. A portrait by one of the Old Masters, one so fair and one so dark.'

Lynne accepted a glass of white wine, archly. 'Only if you come down and sit with us. We don't want to be lonely.' Issie scrambled up as soon as their host had squatted on the fur rug, the sleeves of a cream polo-neck sweater rolled, showing muscular forearms. He was a good-looking man, lean, clean-cut, conscious of his own charm. She sat back in the recesses of a leather armchair. The air was narcotic with resinous pine logs and burning oil.

'It's an impressive house,' she said. 'Has it much history?'

'There's the vestige of a stone circle in the grounds. It has always been associated with the care of children.'

Issie watched him talk; felt how he gratified himself with the sound of his own voice. Superficially expansive, Karl pleasured himself by dominating his listeners – not that Lynne could count as a listener. She yawned uninhibitedly as she waited for the monologue to end.

'And what about the statue in the grounds. The mother and child?'

'We're having her cleaned and restored. In fact, the whole place is due for a facelift.'

Only later did Issie register a sidestepping of her query.

'And we have illustrious visitors this year,' said Karl. 'Everything must be spruce for them. What would you say in English: shipshape and Bristol fashion? Is that correct? Do not laugh at my poor efforts, Miss Williams – you see how hard I try with your colourful turns of phrase!' he said gallantly. 'Drink up, young ladies. *Prost!*'

'Would we have heard of your illustrious visitors?'

'I doubt it – Dr Globke, one of Adenauer's big white chiefs, commodores, captains, a trinity of admirals. There will be nautical chat, sea shanties and so on. The usual shindig.'

'Oh glory, don't talk to me about admirals,' begged Lynne. 'We have Admiral Halston. He comes for Founder's Day and the sea cadets parade up and down for him. Then he grants us all a half-day and we have to cheer. And then there's torture by Gordon Highlanders.

Pipes and drums! Kilts and sporrans! Playing their stirring national melodies up and down, till you think you'll scream – don't talk to me about admirals.'

'Since you feel so deeply, I shall defer to your wishes by avoiding all ranks above corvet-captain.' He rubbed his Alsatian's fluffy belly as it lay panting in the warmth of the fire and favoured Lynne with a smile of playful homage. Issie watched Lynne bask in his admiration. Watched him take amiable refuge in Lynne's bantering narcissism.

'Haven't I heard the name Globke?' Issie persisted. 'I'm sure that's familiar.'

'You interest yourself in local affairs, Miss Dahl?'

He leaned on the mantelpiece, looking down. Something in him plucked at her nerves, kindling resistance. His arrogant smoothness, so unendearingly polite. She thought, *The blond man*, though Karl was not blond. He was dark, thinning, the hair oiled close to his head. But the thought, *The blond man* made her rise and confront him, chin jutting.

'I read the *Spiegel* actually – and cut out bits for my sixth-formers. Isn't he quite . . . notorious?'

'Oh, Issie, what are you on about?' demanded Lynne, dismayed. She too stood up, smiling into Karl's face, as if to reassure this Kraut that he was considered to have overcome his unfortunate Krautishness so as to become a pet amongst his betters.

Their host spoke over Lynne's head. 'An awful lot of nonsense gets talked in the papers – generates copy, I suppose. We have a little saying: *Was vorbei ist, ist schon vorbei* – the past is the past. That is why these friendly get-togethers are so frightfully important for us here.'

'Absolutely,' breathed Lynne, her cheeks pink from the firelight. Isolde silently observed his manipulative contempt for the gossamer web Lynne spun round him. She was clearly after him. Thought him a prize. Assumed he would prove as indulgent a husband as he was courteous a host. Was he old enough to have served in the war? He must be in his late thirties: so, yes. A possible past belled out behind him, a hinterland of shadow.

'This Globke,' said Issie, with a persistent truculence

she had learned at her mother's knee. 'This Globke was a Nazi. Wasn't he?'

'Oh, honestly, Issie. What are you on about? That's all done with. Honestly.' Lynne was blushing furiously. 'Who cares about all that now?'

'What, you don't care that the Secretary of State was a top dog in the Jewish Affairs office? Helped make up the Nuremberg Laws?'

'Possibly, Miss Dahl, in your zeal, you have overlooked the fact that men of real merit are rare. Dr Globke is a true democrat.'

'*Now.*' He seemed to swell, his face far too close. Issie flushed to the roots of her hair, mortified that she could not control her gauche blushing. For he mockingly saw it, and it weakened her. Still she faced him out: 'Yes, *now*,' she said. 'Anyone can be a model citizen *now*.'

'Precisely. Now. And now is what matters.'

'And that man Gehlen. And Dr Blankenhorn. And . . . ', she had run out of names, 'hundreds of them. It doesn't matter that they helped murder millions of . . . ?'

He cut in icily, and with a grammar of pedantic literariness, 'To a young lady, Miss Dahl, and a charming young lady at that, nobody will deny the privilege of exaggeration. But this, if I may say so, *gnädiges Fräulein*, is the purest fantasy. You are living in the world of English war films, where the jolly old British save the world for democracy. Where you are all Dam Busters. And we are all mass murderers. Your hands are not so clean,' he said in German. Involuntarily, Issie glanced down at her hands, balled into fists against her skirt. 'Look around you at our children here. They are orphans of the war. Millions died, Miss Dahl. Millions. Of Germans.'

'You mean air raids?'

'Your war ended in May of 1945 but Germany's did not. Perhaps they didn't teach you that at school? Two, three million Germans were starved to death. By the British and Americans. Our youngsters are casualties of evil.'

Karl's abrasive manner seemed to implicate her personally. Thirteen million refugees, he said, should be on the West's conscience. Sold down the river at Potsdam.

German children were starved out, looted, Red Cross food sent back, while the Amis ate cucumbers and fried potatoes in front of German children. Yes, cucumber and potatoes. What had she to say to the cucumber and potatoes, he appeared to demand. And the milk. He made it seem as if she personally had poured away gallons of milk rather than give it to German children. 'Oh yes, the occupation was generous; it killed us slowly, slowly.'

She didn't believe it. We wouldn't behave like that. Would we? But the rush of defiance had dwindled; she could think of nothing to say. Because it sounded true.

Karl pushed the sleeves of his creamy sweater up his arms. One half of his face grinned. 'Well, we're all on the same side now. I like a young lady who speaks her mind,' he patronised her, and she could see it was a lie; he liked a woman who lay on her back like the Alsatian bitch and panted for attention, silking around his legs.

'Don't mind Taf,' Lynne advised their host. 'She gets bees in her bonnet. Takes *everything* to heart. You should have seen her with the wasps the other day.'

Both Issie and Karl looked glazed.

'Wasps?'

'The boys were cutting up wasps for a lark. Issie worked herself up into a tizz about it. Cruelty to animals, apparently. Report them to the RSPCA.'

Karl looked gravely down at Lynne and shook his head, chiding her like a child. 'Now there, Miss Dahl was right to protest. I have to praise her there. We must be tender to animals. The creatures cannot speak for themselves. No, I really do believe that. We have a sacred obligation to them.'

'Even wasps?'

'Even wasps. I myself am a vegetarian.'

Lynne floundered, at a total loss. Checked any quip that might have risen to her tongue about the dangers of wasp eating. 'Blimey,' was all she managed. She stared in her bafflement at the stags' heads on the wall but offered no observation.

'That is a different matter. That is in the nature of a cull.'

A cull, thought Issie. *That is in the nature of a cull.* Her knees went to water. Her fingers gripped the high mantelpiece.

'But now,' Karl said, 'it is time for our get-together on the lawn.'

Issie tried to peer into the main hall, as he ushered them out to the lawn.

'Another time. We're all at sixes and sevens. Is that your correct English phrase, Miss Williams? Sixes and sevens?'

Among the guests on the lawn he stood out, phosphorescent in his cream sweater.

'He's gorgeous though, don't you think so? He's a dish, isn't he? He's so juicy I could eat him.'

'He's scary.'

'You put his back up. You have to know how to treat these people – stroke them, humour them a bit. Then they'll eat out of your hand.'

'More like eat the hand, and crunch up the arm with it.' How he had loomed at her, so that the room seemed full of threat.

***

On the lawns, two long tables with benches stood at right angles, overhung with looped lamps, which altered the aspect of the evening, deepening the twilight. Beer and wine flowed. Men dressed in leather shorts with embroidered shirts drank from heavy *Steins*; girls with coiled plaits and dirndls brought platters of sausage and cheeses. Isolde sat amazed, wine glass between her hands, as if she had blundered into another Germany, which held its festivals sacrosanct, timeless simulacra of olden days.

And they sang. Swaying on the benches, they crashed their *Steins* to the rhythm of the chorus. Squealing hilarity broke out among the English women who joined in the stomping refrain, arms linked and swaying to and fro in conspicuous parody of its perpetrators.

Humba humba humba
Tä tä rä...

'You don't sing, Mr Quantz?' Issie asked.

'I am a musician. I bear it as best I can,' said Wolfi's father.

Whenever she passed the piano room and heard him play Mozart or Bach, she would pause, listening through every pore. And when he smiled his teeth were lovely, almost perfect. But Wolfi had said, *Bad seed*. And the tension between father and son scraped like nails on a blackboard. Wolfi quietly slid in beside her.

'No,' said his father, 'this kind of folksy music does not appeal.'

'In the pub down the road from us at home, you *can* hear real music, Mr Quantz,' she said. 'Popular music but real. Part-singing so perfect it brings tears to your eyes. *Bryn Calvaria, Myfanwy* – do you know those songs?'

'Oh, are you going to sing, Taf? Hush, everyone, Taf's going to sing.'

'Don't be daft, Lynne.'

'Go on, Issie. Everyone's agog.'

'No, stop it.'

But she did, she lifted up her voice, a powerful contralto, chapel-born, and arrestingly sure of itself. *Myfanwy*. The men around Isolde stared, went quiet to listen, and she herself seemed to listen, as if some other person sang. At the points of most passionate longing, instead of increasing volume, the voice reined itself in. Face lit from above by a lamp, centred by the attention of those around her, she brought the party to spellbound silence, until moments after the final note.

'Is this one of your English songs?'

'Welsh,' she said. 'I come from Wales. It's a country with its own language.'

They asked her to translate and while in translation the text failed lamely, the mood altered. The company gave voice again, replying to her *hiraeth* with their *Heimweh*. *Ein' feste Burg* was built as a tower of voices, and folk songs in the minor key were sung until the choir waxed (as happened at home, upstairs in the Oystercatcher) lachrymose.

'Your voice is exceptional,' said Mr Quantz quietly.

'Not where I come from, Mr Quantz. Singing is normal. It's just something you do.'

'You sing so beautifully,' said Wolfi. 'You do everything beautifully.' He spoke as if they were alone. Surrounded by trees rather than people.

Issie was stilled by Wolfi's nearness. Her bare arm, not quite touching his, lay resting on the table a fraction of an inch away. The hairs on her skin rose. She shivered and almost withdrew, aware of his body's lean hardness beside hers, and how his arm was downed with fair hair under the light. If he edged across, ever so slightly, the partition would be down, the threshold crossed and their arms would be touching.

Touching.

Issie's heart turned slowly over, a sensual pang brought the skin of her forearms out in gooseflesh. The unpleasantness with Karl rolled up in a dirty little ball; it had no meaning. Touching Wolfi was the only thing that mattered. She edged her arm a shade nearer.

Everything around them had darkened. The nocturnal party now revelled at the centre of an immense, tight-fitting blackness. Insects sparked as they butted the lamps. Lynne was singing the school song:

We carry as ambassadors
Proud banners of our land:
To blazon wide our history,
As one four kingdoms stand.

'You didn't know we were jolly old ambassadors, did you? We're supposed to be setting you Doytchers a good example.'

Issie marvelled at Lynne's cocksure manner of address, as if to persons of substandard intelligence. The victims of these undiplomatic 'ambassadors' seemed to dismiss it as the froth of women's blether.

An accordion was produced. Couples got up to dance, in and out of the arcs of light. Lynne made for Karl.

'So, here you see our two nations fraternising in peace and harmony,' observed the man opposite. 'Just as God meant us to be. I used to be a proud member of the

German–English Fellowship – did you ever hear of that? Now, what about you?' he went on. 'Dahl. That sounds, if I'm not mistaken, like a good old German name.'

She was conscious of Mr Quantz's sudden, avid stare into her eyes.

'We have people from all extractions in our country. In Cardiff and Swansea there are communities of Poles and Italians – and a large Jewish community, of course.' She threw the latter in their faces, as she often had in Renate's.

'You have not yet gone as far in that direction as your transatlantic cousins.'

'In what direction?'

'The racial melting pot. It's good to keep national characteristics, customs and so forth. And we Germans and English share so much in common. We are of the same stem. In my opinion, you English and we Germans will move forward hand in hand.'

'But in what direction?'

'Forward,' put in a sozzled Werner, as his contribution to the *entente cordiale*. His arm was hooked round Susan's neck. 'Forward together,' he announced heroically. 'Comrades and brothers! We and you, you and we! Never more to be sundered. Forward indeed,' exclaimed the tactile fraterniser, thumping a beer pot with his free hand, beaming. 'Forward against common enemies.'

One of the *Fräuleins*, the gentle young woman from a boys' block, asked Wolfi to dance. Issie was left with his father.

'How do you like the school?' he asked her.

It welled up in her to confide in him, this gravely listening man who seemed to distance himself from every group.

'I find it difficult,' she said. 'I don't see eye to eye with people about the harsh discipline. And the kids' bullying. It's as if the youngsters were daring . . . someone over there . . .' she gestured across the invisible lake ' . . . to take notice – to stop it all. But there isn't anyone over there. There's only us, trying to do our best, or giving up, or just not trying. Or worse.'

‘Of course, we can’t take everything on our own shoulders.’

‘But I don’t want to be part of a machine. Do you?’ she burst out. ‘A machine for producing human beings with the human bit missing. There’s this child Rachel Goldman; she gets horribly picked on. You teach her, don’t you?’

Under the chiaroscuro of the swinging string of lights, Mr Quantz’s shadow was tossed around over the strewn table. He wore his watchful face like a rubber mask, which you might peel off and find other, more mobile features looking out from beneath.

But he spoke with calm disinterest. ‘I will keep my eye out for our young Rachel.’ He took off his spectacles, yawned and rubbed his eyes. The half-moon lenses on the table showed specks of dust in the light. She resisted an urge to give them a good clean as she would have done for Tada at home, chiding, *I don’t know how you think you can see out of them.*

Instead, she drank. Dancers whirled round the dark lawn, clapping and hopping in some vertiginous communal folk dance. She held out her glass for a refill. The tables tilted till they lay at an angle like a keeling ship.

Issie and Wolfi enjoyed a complex, tacit, intimate conversation with their eyes; soft, feathery touches of their arms. She hoped he might kiss her. Wolfi’s father, glancing at his watch, rose to leave. Overhead a propeller-driven plane stammering past, winked a red eye. Looking up at the house, Issie saw windows full of fair-haired children’s faces. Christmas angels came to mind, in the boxes of an Advent calender, opened all at once in a fit of impatience.

When she looked up again, the children had vanished. She was skew-whiff; wondered if they’d been there in the first place. Someone filled her glass with burning liquid that smelt of almonds and insisted she down it in one. Should she neglect to drink, this stranger would be heartbroken. All hospitality would be profaned for ever. She obeyed, eyes level with the waistband of an ample pair of leather shorts, which creaked as the wearer moved.

'Brown sauce,' said Wolfi distinctly. 'Cold gravy. Watch out.'

She was scooped up and borne away, over the plunging lawn. In a pair of powerful arms, she whirled clockwise. Susan's yellow dress rippled past her. Faster and faster. Her partner crushed her against his broad body, his hand pressing the small of her back. He danced nimbly for one so stout. Then all changed partners. Issie staggered back to Wolfi. 'I need to go home. I'm not used to wine.'

'That's not wine you've been drinking. It's cherry brandy, Issie.'

He helped her to water.

'Hey, you rotter,' came a woman's voice, mingling levity with affected indignation. 'Cut it out. Enough's enough.'

Susan and her swain approached the table. 'Taking liberties.' Susan deplored lax continental morality. 'You go for an innocent dance on the lawn and liberties are taken.' She fluffed out her hair and reached for a glass.

'It is nature,' explained Werner philosophically. 'What can one do?'

'Now, I warn you, Taf, watch out,' said the injured party and slapped Werner's fingers teasingly. 'Never let Jerry get beyond a certain point with your virtue.'

Werner beamed. Issie choked. The uproar began again, pounding beer pots and songs of homeland, deserted maidens and yesteryear. The festive noise swelled, seeming to know no limits, a hullaballoo of *Humba humba humba*... The upper windows of the house were uniformly dark. All the children's lights were out.

> *In München steht ein Hofbräuhaus*
> *Ein – zwei – suffa*

'Hey, Issie, it's your duty tomorrow,' said Susan. 'I helped you out the other night and you agreed to do my Saturday for me, don't forget.'

A queue of young creatures in faded dressing gowns shuffled down the corridor of Issie's mind, weeping.

***

The statue of the nursing mother stood in shadow. Issie swayed in the lee of her silhouette. So many fair children gathered here. No black lambs among the pale tribe. Karl had really not wanted her to see the main hall; had chivvied them along.

A horse whinneyed. The sound brought a memory of the stables, at the farm where they took the youngsters for riding lessons; the smell of hay and droppings, the breath of clopping horses led out into frosty air. The farm was also a stud. Exquisite animals were reared there for future sale. Issie had been waiting by a rick at the stables where Persian cats had hollowed a tunnel for their kittens, when two foals walked by with their mothers, and the farmer's wife said, 'Now, there's breeding for you.'

Pure-bred stock. She looked up at the statue, with the square-headed child at the breast, taking its stony drink of eternity.

Wolfi walked at her side, down the track. She reached for his hand.

'Wolfi, what is that place all about? Do you know?'

'Old-fashioned people,' said Wolfi. 'Boring, horrible people. Living in the past. I only went because of you.'

And they were all abolished, the 'Brown Sauce' men, the 'Cold Gravy', whatever that meant; as Wolfi opened his arms to her. Globke was nothing, Karl was nothing; the blond man was nothing, because Wolfi's lips brushed against her lips, and then withdrew, and he immersed his hands in her hair, tenderly stroking her cheeks with his thumbs. For that reason the old ones were vanquished, squeezed out as Issie and Wolfi held one another beneath the trees. Walking, murmuring, kissing again.

Wolfi kissed her goodbye shyly, tongue hesitant in her mouth, as if to flutter-tongue a flute. She felt his willowy tallness, the warmth of his body through his cotton shirt. Her heart leapt electric in her breast.

***

'You're late tonight, Miss Dahl.'

Did he never sleep, Herr Poppendick, the fragile old

man with silver hair on duty at the school gates? She felt delirious. The kiss made her golden, as if glory must be visibly scattered from her. 'I've been to a party – up at the *Blütehof* – the others are still there but I felt I'd had enough.'

Pop's face, in the yellow rectangle of the porters' window, expressed distaste.

'Very wise, Miss Dahl. You've written your name in the time column. Shall we just rub it out and start again?'

'It's the cherry brandy. Not used to spirits.'

'Potent stuff, but tastes like cough syrup.'

He had been a professor of ancient history in his prior life, she knew: lost his position; fled Hitler; fled the Soviets. He seemed to have stepped from some antique world, for which the modern world had no appropriate place. Veering away, Issie looked back to where Pop remained enclosed in his brightly lit box. There he sat in his narrow home, with a pile of abstruse tomes, a remnant of Weimar, camouflaged as a doorkeeper, seeing them out, seeing them in.

In München steht ein Hofbräuhaus
Ein – zwei – suffa –

She crossed the parade ground, past the flagpole and its rigging, a black net against the starry sky. Most of the lights were extinguished in the buildings flanking the quadrangle. Wolfi's kiss was still on her lips, tender and fading.

They were of the future, not the past, she and Wolfi; young and modern. They could shake off the burdens that made the older generation crooked, stumbling forward whilst peering back over their shoulders, sly-eyed, hagridden, concealing their shames and stigmas. Each carried his secret like a suitcase, kidding himself that it was invisible to others. Superciliously, they dared you to demand, *Open up that case. Let's see what you've got in there.* Renate. Karl. Mr Quantz even. Patterson. The Fräuleins with their smut about Jews. Admirals. Issie and Wolfi, Wolfi and she, would live in a new world, free of all that.

The kiss said so. She could see for miles through the clarified air of her requited desire. It took only one kiss to generate a film-like certainty of joy to come with Wolfi. His mouth tasted novel, the strange tongue tenderly entering between her lips. She returned the kiss with equal shyness. He was tall, so beautiful. Soft hair, falling across his forehead. Saying, *Oh, they're old-fashioned. I only went because of you.*

She waltzed up to the darkened block and let herself in; began to mount the stairs. The fizz went on in her head. A future without boundaries. With Wolfi. Bubbles in her mind popped one by one. On the landing of the stairs, sat a figure in a chair. Nadine, in a thin dressing gown, her feet naked on the marble floor.

'What the heck are you doing here?'

'Please, miss, I've been forgotten.'

'But why are you sitting on the stairs?'

'It's a punishment like, miss, I didn't do nothing, but we've all been put to sit in different parts of the house because of the noise,' she bleated.

'Who put you here?'

'Mrs Boothby, and my feet are froz.'

Issie sent her back to bed. She found Rachel in an unlit cloakroom. When Issie snapped on the light, the child's eyes screwed up. She cowered against the coats hanging from hooks. Across her cheeks fingernails had raked, leaving smears of dried blood.

'Who did this, love? Who did this to you?'

The girl shrank from Issie. 'Mrs Boothby made us . . . '

'Yes, but these scratches?'

Rachel hung her head and muttered, 'I done them myself.'

'Or was someone bullying you?' Issie spoke softly, crouching beside the child, trying to take hold of one of her hands. 'You can tell me.'

Rachel held her head down and shook it. She bunched her hands into fists, clutching them to her chest.

'But why? Why would you do such a thing to yourself?'

No reply. The girl's body twisted away from Issie. The

windowless cloakroom, with its many hooks, smelt of plimsoles and gym pants. Issie wanted to gag. Wished she weren't so sloshed.

'Run along,' she said, straightening up. 'Go to bed now. Get some rest... Well, go on then.'

'No, miss. I like it in here. I'd rather be in here.'

'Don't talk daft. Come on. I said: *Move*.'

She located the girls one by one, behind open doors, in the dark; one claiming to have seen a ghost and so panicked that she refused to sleep with the light off. Issie, exasperated, left the light on and the door open.

'I will not have my discipline interfered with.' Eyes bulging (some kind of thyroid trouble), Mrs Boothby stood and fumed with folded arms, to her full height, which was inconsiderable.

'That's not discipline. It's bloody sadism, you old battle-axe.'

Issie elbowed her aside, to gain access to her own room.

A litany of accusations followed her in. Issie was guilty not only of obstructing justice, but of setting a poor example through swearing, drunkenness and rudery. Her attitude was that of an anarchist. Where was her respect for senior staff? Should she fail to apologise when she had sobered up, Mrs Boothby would have no option but to report her.

'Nuts,' said Issie succinctly, turning the key, stepping in and slamming the door in one nimble motion.

'I can smell your breath,' stated the voice on the other side of the door. 'I can still smell it, Miss Dahl, from here. It smells like a brewery.'

Issie left her colleague to her execrations, shutting the inner door. She sat down on the edge of the bed and, slipping off her dress, stood in her petticoat, taking off her nylons and laying them over the back of the chair. Her stomach felt queasy and her palate dry. The trace of the kiss had faded from her lips. She'd never drunk so much in her life. In the yellow light everything in the room bore signs of jaundice, and shifted out of true, blurred and bilious.

10

Lake Plön, 1945, 1958

Heini stopped raking leaves at the school entrance when Michael confirmed the rumour that the British were packing up and giving Ruhleben back to the German Navy.

'No. Surely not. We'll be out of a job. No one's said anything. When?'

'Next year. I'm sure they'll re-employ you, Heini. You're a bargain.'

Heini looked devastated. 'I hope you're wrong, Michael. I really do. I could hardly bear to leave it here, and uproot my youngsters. I want them to grow up near to nature. Don't smile, it's our only hope. Every year we can look up in the sky and say to one another, "The wild geese are leaving, and they'll be back."'

Heini's passionate earnestness simultaneously tweaked at Michael's sympathies and at his sense of humour, for Heini did not have one, never had, though he would courteously smile when a joke was pointed out. How youthful Heini still seemed, despite the fact that he was thinning on top.

'A stationary appraisal. The gentler way,' said Heini.

Michael's throat constricted. He looked away, to the chestnuts on the other side of the road, their great hands ginger and ochre at the fingertips. Heini's science was a form of mysticism. Michael envied him his remoteness from the pulse of the human clock.

'You are a lucky man,' he said, half in jest. 'You have your birds. We have to make do with each other or, worse, ourselves.'

Heini shot Michael a complex glance; then gestured up into the branches, where the oak, one of the Methuselahs of the area, fabled to be over six hundred years old, splayed maternal arms that branched crosswise. 'Do you ever remember this tree?' he asked Michael.

'No,' said Michael. 'Should I?'

But at the moment of denial, recognition rushed in on him. From this tree the young rating, Heini's friend, had been strung one sunrise that late April. Günther. Nervous as hell, he'd bolted, his mind on the turn.

Michael said, 'Yes, of course.' There was a pause. 'Günther,' he said. 'The idiot.'

Günther had deserted straight into the hands of Dönitz's naval police and been summarily hanged, a cardboard message attached to his neck:

I am a traitor who by my low cowardice allowed German women and children to die instead of protecting them like a man.

Dew had darkened the corpse's clothes. Petals had showered down in spring winds that rocked the body softly, mottling his jacket with flecks of pink.

'He wasn't an idiot,' said Heini. 'Just clumsy.'

'Well, that's what I meant. He was a good person, Heini. He was your friend.'

'I'm glad you remember.'

Death had been prosaic, on a landscape where unburied bodies bloomed. But Heini had come rushing to Michael, his glasses held together by sticky tape, weeping frantic tears.

'My pal – that's my Günther they've hanged, Michael.' Michael had been visited by a distraught sense of affliction, which punched through all his defences. 'They can't have, they can't,' Heini had cried, tears streaming down his face. 'It can't be him. It is him, Michael.'

'Get a grip. Grow up.'

'You've got to help me.'

'Keep your head low. Or you'll end up beside him.'

'And leave him there? Up there?'

Michael had looked up to where the lad was hanging, jacket riding up his wrists, patched with blossom.

'He's out of it, Heini, he doesn't feel a thing.'

'Please, Michael. Help me cut him down. I can't just leave him there.'

Michael had taken the corpse by the legs and held it steady, Heini sawing through the rope. The poor chap had shat himself; he remembered the sad reek and the soiled trousers.

Looking at the shaking Heini, he had thought, *We'll be lucky to see you alive again, my lad.*

'I never thought you'd make it through.'

'No, I didn't either. Not when Günther went.'

Heini took off his glasses, rubbed his eyes with the ball of his hand and blinked. 'Pure luck. Not exactly the military type, was I?' They both laughed, palely. Michael resisted the urge to take the chap by the shoulders and hug him; to say, *I'm glad you're here; you made it*. How much more easily flowed comradeship than family love.

'So what are those ghouls doing up there?' asked Heini.

'Where?'

'At the *Blütehof*.'

'God knows. Some filthy stunt, you can be sure. Dinosaurs. All marching forwards looking backwards. The future lies with refrigerators,' Michael said with a brittle laugh. 'Fridges and Coca Cola. I'm not sure if our Old Guard has quite grasped that.'

'Know what they remind me of?' asked Heini. 'Last year when the *Heerwurm* migrated. Remember that?'

Michael laughed. No one had ever seen anything remotely like last August's mass migration of larvae in the woodland along Lake Plön. *Hey, come and see this*, someone had called. *It's the worm army*. Michael, off-duty, had strolled into the woods and watched with disbelief and revulsion, as the mass of worms had flowed down the sandy path between the trees, filling it from edge to edge. As if planning a takeover. There'd been something of the comedic, something of the apocalyptic, about the way this blind mass travelled the man-made path, in cohorts, phalanxes, multitudes of maggoty selves, all marching as one.

Photographers had followed the march, snapping busily: 'Epic mass emigration in Schleswig-Holstein!' the radio announced.

'Old Müller and his wormy army,' said Heini. Then he went on, without a pause, 'Where did we bury him exactly? Günther. I was never sure, afterwards.'

'It was over there, wasn't it?' said Michael carefully, pointing up to the wooded mound overlooking the guard post.

'Yes, yes, I think it was,' said Heini, with equal care. 'Do you remember the bells?'

Michael and Heini had stood by the shallow grave. And then the bells of the Nikolaikirche had pealed across the water, from a remote and unseen source, so that their sound travelled like the outer ripples of some past peal, already concluded. *Lachrymae rerum*, the bells seemed to toll. *Lachrymae rerum*, the tears of things.

The sound had stilled Michael. The Brits were no more than a kilometre away. But the incessant firing had paused and the churchbells, so long silent, had created pools of tender sound in the inner ear. The landscape had been golden; the refugees along the Eutin road had passed bathed in sunlight.

'Don't you try running, for God's sake,' Michael had counselled. 'Just stay put. Give yourself up. Understood? When they come. When you see me move, you move.'

But Heini had been lucky enough to catch a British bullet in the thigh, and was safely laid up in the infirmary.

'That was Dönitz, did that to my Günther,' said Heini. He had laid down his rake and taken up a brush, for Mr Patterson liked the entrance kept immaculate. 'He could have been alive today if it hadn't been for that bloody clockwork sailor.'

'Yes.' Those hangings had been Dönitz's express order. The admiral had encouraged savage measures to keep the remnant fighting. Had been at Posen when Himmler had announced the secret of the Final Solution, bonding the hearers in blood-guilt one to the other. Tyranny, terror, loss of human values of all kinds, untying the bonds of nature; Dönitz had been part of all that.

I think I shall start a kindergarten when I get out, the admiral had been reported as proposing in Spandau gaol, *a mixed one for puppies as well as children.*

'I still dream of him, you know... Günther. He's always seventeen but I'm thirty. It's odd though, isn't it, when you hear drill going on in there, you sometimes think you're back.'

The fact that the place was reverting to the German Navy, as a training school for lower officers, coiled Michael's thoughts back in a loop. He passed Patterson drilling his cadets. Girls to the left, boys to the right; their chief's pride and joy, replica wooden guns over their shoulders. Right-wheeling, shunning, saluting, beneath the flagpole. The great bell that had called the barracks to parade stood in its quaint shelter, like a house for a gnome, quiet now.

Sea shanties. Quantz remembered sea shanties. The old comrades of the *Marinebund* had sung them for Dönitz, the day he came out of prison, two years back. Lived now in Hamburg, where he had written his memoirs, full of half- or quarter-truths, ever the upright naval officer, nervously disclaiming the honour of being Hitler's darling, despite the evidence of that five-ton armoured Mercedes, Adolf's personal gift, and his Gobelin tapestries. Dönitz had been up there with the *Blütehof* cronies only last May. Up there with the worm army. Did Herr Patterson the good scoutmaster know that? Hardly.

Günther. A lad not much more than a child, the age of the English manchildren now standing easy beneath the mast, callow faces impassive, as their chief addressed sterling words to them. They were to parade for Admiral Halston. And every parade from now on would have the heightened emotion of the valedictory.

On, then, on with tonic soh fah, the diatonic scale that was the foundation of harmony in European music.

'You are doing nicely, Rachel,' he commended his pupil, on whose behalf the Dahl daughter had petitioned him at the weekend, with those so soulful eyes. And the phrase broke through like the ticking of a clock. Dahl daughter. Daughter of Dahl. No evidence for that. None. Surely she would have changed her name? Must be coincidence. But last night at the *Blütehof* he had seen the father in the child, seen him looking straight out through those serious eyes. For Paul had been serious too, idealistic. Had had a sweetness once. A lovability. And she was lovable. In the flesh: lovable. Spurts of adrenalin made his guts spasm every time he thought about it but he kept his nerve as he'd always done, kept his mask up, spoke with characteristic control and civility to his pupil, Rachel Goldman. 'Good progress.'

Rachel said nothing. She sat bolt upright to play, her neck a graceful stem, but shrank into her own shoulders as soon as her hands left the keys, a sea anemone that flinches into a ball when touched. Fingernails chewed to the quick, she blossomed wildly at the keyboard. The hangdog look fled as she concentrated; listening to the score before she set her fingers to the keys, and committed herself to an interpretation. For she did have the sense of an interpretation, rather than the mechanical exercises one extracted from most younger pupils. It was beautiful to see. Yet in speech she was gawky, inept. Her tongue stumbled, powered by fright in fitful rushes of gabbling.

'You ought to play duets with Sonia,' he suggested. 'Really, you should. She's good too. Do you know Sonia Birch?'

Rachel shook her head, and instantly closed up; became impenetrable.

'Where do you come from, Rachel?' he asked, as she got up to go.

'Hildesheim. Army Air Corps.'

'No, I mean, originally.'

'Manchester.'

'Ah, the Hallé Orchestra!'

She looked baffled.

'They have a great orchestra in Manchester. A fine tradition of music. The Free Trade Hall. Sir John Barbirolli.'

'Oh.'

She looked fixedly at Michael's right shoulder, as he made these attempts at communication.

'Haven't you heard of the Hallé?'

'No, sir.'

'Well, when you go back...'

She shifted her gaze to the round face of the clock above the door. 'We don't go back. Sir.'

'You don't? Why is that?'

'We don't go nowhere twice, sir.'

'No, of course not. I'm sorry.'

'I liked it in Malta, sir,' she volunteered, and swooped into one of those flurries of talkativeness that were so hard to follow because the words seemed swallowed before they were fully formed, aborted to make way for the next. And she spoke with a northern dialect. 'It was lovely in Malta, with the sea, we were bathing all the year round practically, and my mam took us on picnics, and there's a castle, and we had a massive beachball. My mam said we'd landed in paradise.' Rachel skidded to a halt. 'I've got to go, sir.' She smiled. 'Thank you for the lesson and everything.'

'If you need to talk about anything, I hope you'll come to me.'

'Like what?' She stiffened.

'Oh, anything that's on your mind. Come in and have a chat.'

He could hear how false that word, *chat*, sounded. When she had gone, he could still hear himself inviting a damaged youngster for a *chat*. How very English of him. How did they usually put it, *a nice chat*? *A cosy chat?*

The little Jewess, he had heard the Fräulein call Rachel. The same woman with the dyed red hair showing grey at the roots who was given to that old chestnut of a jest, *We should have built bigger ovens while we had the chance.*

***

He took his sandwich and flask to the lakeside at lunchtime, hoping for some privacy but obtained instead a view of Wolfi and the Dahl girl, her skirt hitched up, paddling up to the knees in the lake.

The girl was a beauty. A person with a conscience. But a Dahl.

Wolfi was picking up Dahl's litter, knowing nothing of her origins. Waves lapped at her bare legs. Her shadow broke up on the perpetually fleeing surface. She skimmed her hands dreamily over the surface of the water. Michael watched Wolfi's eyes fondle the substantiality of her muscular thighs. The skirt looped up into its waistband displayed her right leg to the hip. The other side of the skirt dangled in the lake, soaking up wet.

Wolfi, who hated water, was larking with her as if he had made a sudden discovery of his own youth. Mr Patterson would hardly like his staff cavorting in the lake, making an exhibition of themselves, for all to see, thought Michael. The two of them would soon get their marching orders.

She was wearing a dark blouse of some soft material, a billowing skirt with blue flowers. Her sandals she had left with a bag on the shore. He looked through the birch trees at the little heap.

Worn, scuffed shoe leather shaped to the breadth of the foot; poignant leavings.

Empty shoes; a triangular bag, tied at the neck with a bootlace.

He looked at her shoes, which took the shape of a rather broad foot. No single individual had an identical foot shape. He remembered the way she walked, heavily, sandals slapping her soles. The sort of woman who would run to flab in later life. And her passionate temper would turn to carping and dominance.

The victims at Minsk had left their clothes in little heaps.

He had seen the leavings through the trees.

The father must be there, coiled in her, the mother.

She aroused him in a terrible way. The years of celibacy seemed, in the light of Isolde, impossible perversity. He was intimately aware of her long lashes, the curve of her eyelid, the gentle but unreposeful brown of her eyes.

She turned and saw him, pointed him out to Wolfi: 'Look, your father.'

Wolfi scowled. His glance said, *Keep your peeping-Tom eyes to yourself. This is my life, my person.*

Isolde waded back out, wringing out the soaked part of her skirt. Sitting down unselfconsciously on a fallen log, she took a hand towel from the linen bag, and began to dry her reddened feet and calves; Michael looked away, over the sheet of water, having to drag his eyes from the firmness of her flesh.

'What do you want?' demanded his son rudely.

He ignored Wolfi, addressing himself to the woman.

'Excuse my intrusion. Quite inadvertent. But while I'm here, I might as well tell you I had a word with my pupil, Rachel, this morning. Since you had mentioned her.'

'Do you think she's all right?'

'Oh yes, I would think so.'

'So I can stop worrying about her?'

'Well, they usually settle down, don't they? Takes a while.'

'Thank you.'

He told her about the excellence of the child's playing. 'You don't often come across it with these transients,' he said.

***

Resting on the veranda overlooking Lake Eutin, Michael heard Wolfi come in; called out to him but his son did not deign to answer. Wolfi bounded upstairs, three at a time.

Isolde and Wolfi would get kicked out. Then they would marry. He saw it now. Wolfi would be uxoriously faithful, offering his wife the devotion that had bound him to his mother. He would unite himself to that filth's child, that free spirit. She was odious to him, yet his heart went out to her. She let loose in Michael uproar, like some cacophonous modern composition in which horror and beauty had not only met but fused.

He went to the bottom of the stairs and called to his son.

'What?' asked Wolfi.

'I said, do you want to eat now or later?'

'Oh, I'm not eating. I'm going out.'

'But I've got a meal planned. You might give warning if you're going to be out,' Michael whined, and sounded in his own ears just like Effi, forlornly subject to his arbitrary visits, peremptory dismissals. Not really protesting, since she had given up hope long ago, but notching up a vain tally of offences.

No answer. Michael wearily climbed the stairs. Wolfi was standing in his vest, his jaw a meringue of shaving cream, razor in hand. He took the pressure of his father's eyes in the mirror.

'Where are you going?'

Wolfi did not turn round, as courtesy required. He merely carved a pathway through the shaving cream with the razor, which he rinsed under the tap.

'Out.'

The quiet was such that Michael could hear the blade rasp through the stubble. He felt exasperated shame at the possessive way he was behaving; bound to alienate. Absurd and womanish; it flashed through his mind that there had always been an element of effeminacy in his dealings with Wolfi. Cooking and cleaning for him, kowtowing, as if he knew how much was still outstanding of the debt he owed him. A mother.

'What's up?' Wolfi asked offhandedly.

'Nothing. Well, I've got our meal ready, that's all. I did not expect that you'd be out tonight.'

'Sorry.'

Michael lingered at the door. All those years of wondering about Wolfi: whether he was *like that*. The sort of chap the Navy had been full of, to whose furtive couplings aboard ship a blind eye was normally turned, despite their official designation as criminal perverts. But it seemed Wolfi was just a late developer. Had been unable to grow beyond the trauma. Clung, as it were, to his father's apron strings.

'Is it serious between you and this young lady?' enquired Michael. He was aware of sounding starched, like his own father in whose presence one stood to attention and, despite the compulsion to laugh, spoke humbly. Why could he not address Wolfi as he could Heini?

'That's my business,' retorted Wolfi. He reddened. Flipped a comb through the quiff. Michael bit back the urge to deride the Americanised hairstyle but Wolfi registered his downward glance at his tight trousers and pointed shoes, which were new. Michael had never before seen these winkle-picking absurdities.

'I wish you'd talk to me a bit. Confide in me,' he said, conciliatory. He bent to pluck the dirty shirt off the floor. 'Surely we can talk to one another. Man to man?'

'When did *you* ever talk to *me*?' his son burst out, there in the bathroom where his voice echoed, tinny in the enamel emptiness, holding the shaving brush in his raised hand. 'Come on, when?'

'There's no need to shout.'

Michael turned sharp about and went downstairs, his son at his heels, the shaving brush still absurdly gripped in his hand, like some effete weapon snatched up in emergency.

'I'm not shouting,' Wolfi shouted. 'I'm asking you, when did you ever tell me anything?'

'When did you ask?' He looked down at the discarded shirt in his hands and the broken line of dirt around the collar coded something inexpressibly dear, an intimacy he could not bear to lose. A tenderness that was the best thing he had ever had, although – no, because – it had only ever flowed one way, from Michael to Wolfi. A kind of grace. He shivered inwardly, aware that the more he said, the further he alienated Wolfi. And he feared Wolfi, as the prey fears the hound.

'I'm asking now.'

'I'm sorry, Wolfi. Of course if you want to go out, go. Sorry.'

'About my mother,' said the son hoarsely.

'What about her?'

'About you and the National Socialists.'

'We've had all this.'

'All these years,' Wolfi sneered, 'I've been pussyfooting

around you, afraid to ask you anything, in case I actually find out something. Well that's over now. And don't muscle in on my personal life. Mind your own business, will you? Leave us alone.'

So they were *us* now. Wolfi's eyes blazed at Michael with the confused rage of two decades. The face that accused him was the same as that of the unnerving adolescent salvaged from the bombed-out house in Kiel. It was the same as had peered out from the mound of the goosedown feather bed, eyes echoing his mother's in their eternal conspiracy.

'I don't know why you're saying all this,' said Michael steadily. 'I presume it's something to do with this girl.'

Wolfi charged on. 'I've seen the way you look at Issie. I saw what you did to my mother, with your...carrying on. Don't think I didn't know. I saw her crying. I was the one who had to comfort her while you went whoring around.' Big tears overflowed Wolfi's eyes. He made no effort to wipe them away. 'You killed her. You. You brown shit.'

'I have told you once and I will tell you again. I was never a National Socialist. I admit I was not the best husband in the world. Not the best father. I've tried to make it up to you, Wolfi. I can't make it up to her.'

'That's right, you can't.'

'At the same time,' Michael went on, hand over his mouth as he gave small nervous coughs, 'I loved you both. In my way. You might not think much of that. But it was so. Things were different in those days, it was a different moral atmosphere. But I was not, absolutely not, a National Socialist.'

'Oh, no, I suppose you were a member of the Heroic Resistance, weren't you, the silent resistance that never existed? Or you knew nothing about it all? Come on, which of the two were you?'

Rarely in his life had Wolfi raised his voice to his father. Never once had he pointed down to the abyss at their feet. They had lived their lives doing all the routine things, pottering, fishing, reading books on the very edge of a sheer cliff. Pretending there was firm footing and no drop into the gulf of the unspoken, they had kept their balance. Sweat broke out on Wolfi's forehead. The area around his mouth went white, as if he might throw up.

'I've told you, Wolfi, I was with the *Abwehr*. Under Canaris. Intelligence work. You know about Canaris. You know he wasn't a Nazi. You know he was hanged. You know all that.'

Michael opened a cupboard and pulled out a pan. He laid it with care on the oven and began to peel and slice an onion. Let Wolfi get it out of his system. Yes. Obviously there was muck in there which needed clearing out. Yes. When the lad had had some childhood illness, Effi had urged him to vomit.

'What I know,' whispered Wolfi, 'is that you knew.'

'Certainly,' Michael replied evenly. 'I knew. I knew everything. I was paid to find out. But we were powerless, Wolfi, to change anything. You can believe it, or not believe it, as you choose. Your ability to believe does not change the facts. I survived. And because of me, you survived. Had I been what you call a brown shit, would we be living on hacks' wages in a dead end like this? I'd be in big business like the real shits – like your friend's father.'

'Like who?'

'Your young English friend who I'm not allowed to talk about, so low a form of life am I. Her father.'

'What do you mean, her father? Who do you mean?' Wolfi had come over and was standing beside the oven, his shirtsleeves rolled up, unconsciously wringing his hands. He stared at the onion and mushrooms sizzling in the butter. 'Do you mean my Issie?'

'Look, forget it.'

'Tell me.'

'I am almost sure I knew this girl's father before the war. He was big in the SS. A very nasty specimen. Divorced his wife, and I gather the mother and child emigrated. He is now a big man in vacuum cleaners.'

Wolfi paled. He turned away; hesitated. Then he said, 'So what? What difference does it make who her father was?'

'I just thought you ought to know where she comes from. Are you eating, Wolfi, or not?' He put in the steak, turning up the flame. Blood spat in the hot butter and filled the kitchen with the scent of charring meat.

11

Kiel, April–May, 1945; Lake Plön, 1945–58

'Mummy!' he called into the rubble. 'Mummy!'

Wolfi and Effi had gone to bed; they slept together in the double bed, for neither could risk losing consciousness without the other's warm presence. Years ago, Father had wondered whether Wolfi wasn't too old for all this petting, did she want to turn him into a mother's boy? Together mother and son had stared at the father with solemn eyes. Strapping on his leather belt, he had gone away. And Effi was his life. Simply that, Wolfi's life. Frail and underfed, with the twiggy collar bones against which he nestled his head, she was sole guarantor of good. While she shushed him, cuddling round so as to enclose his lanky body, she hummed a tuneless lullaby which soothed them both. They slept fully dressed. He had nodded off when the raid struck; her presence grown remote as murmurous waves washing and blessing the sanctuary in which they lay.

Then the sound spiralled into a keening cry; the lament divided into the whine of a plane and the siren's ultimatum. As Wolfi came to, the bomb hit. The bed buckled, walls imploded, and Wolfi and Effi fell through the floor.

Wolfi crawled out from under a tent of thick timbers, into a bellowing night emptied of Effi.

'Mummy!' he howled into the hole from which he had just crawled. The whole square was alight. New waves of bombs struck. In that inferno, he could not have heard her voice.

But if he had survived, she must have too, must have. Wolfi's private logic told him his survival meant Effi's.

And it was so. When the planes had gone away, he

scoured the masonry, throwing off individual bricks and tiles. A doorknob came off in his hand. Chalky, choking powder clogged nostrils, ears, eyes and coated tongue and palate. He coughed till he was sick. Explosions shook the wilderness of ruins as fuel blew up. He burrowed back down into the hole from which he had delivered himself, reasoning that she must be near. And so it was.

Her voice, thin but strong, answered his call. 'Wolfi. I'm here. Are you all right?'

He had not wept. Now he shook with sobs of relief.

'Don't cry, lamb. Mummy's here. Get help.'

'I'll dig you out.'

'No, sweet, you get clear. It all might shift, we both might be crushed. Go and get help.'

How could Wolfi tell her, dawn rising, that there was no help to be got? He climbed out and saw the great, grey wasteland. A few headscarfed women wandered the ruins, in the rain, with a bewildered look too banal for the occasion. He clambered back into what he now saw as a shelter.

'Is someone coming?' quavered the invisible voice. She was caging her panic, but it thrashed its wings within her voice.

Later, she asked, 'Wolfi, have you any water?'

He was parched too. Found a can half full of rainwater and drank half of it. Sirens wailed. Gulls cruised the ruins. Craters pocked roads. He looked through the once-upon-a-time walls of his neighbours' houses. The poodle from next door whimpered somewhere underground. Three elderly men and a girl passed along the street. They walked like drunks. Rain sleeked their hair flat to their heads.

Wolfi shouted, 'Mister! Mister! My mum's buried in there.'

One made a shrugging gesture. Wolfi ran down to waylay them, to explain what was necessary, what must be done to bring Effi out.

'It's my mother,' he said. 'Please will you help me dig?'

They waved him away.

The dog's whimpering weakened.

Bombers came again. Wolfi cowered in his den. The earth shook with the onslaught. He crouched foetal. His mother wailed, 'Water.'

Wolfi pulled away spars and bricks with his bare hands. He set his intelligence to the task, working out which of the masonry was structural. He feared to crush her face or her dear, small hands.

'I'm coming,' he promised. 'I'll make a tunnel, I'll put water through.'

The load-bearing timber which joined her prison to his den shifted suddenly and the whole structure lurched. Effi gave a shriek and then lay moaning.

'My legs,' was all she would say. 'Oh Jesus, my legs.'

She seemed to fall asleep.

Wolfi ran off through the ruins, looking for help and bread. There didn't seem to be any firemen, just a queue of women at a standpipe, carrying buckets. One had a loaf under one arm. He took a rush at her and snatched the bread. She hardly had time to react before he was off, dashing through the mountain ranges of devastation on his long legs.

'Mummy, I've got us bread.'

Her voice was weaker. It spoke with the kind of resignation he didn't like but understood when, having tried to cajole his father, she gave up the fight and knuckled under. That voice of hangdog renunciation had always weakened them both. She said, 'My legs have gone to sleep.'

There was a nasty smell. It came from Effi, it oozed from the smashed sewers and the corpses in the ruins.

He pulled till his fingers bled at the stone that walled her in.

Something gave. He flinched back, working on hands and knees. There was a narrow gap. Close by in the ashen light lay her face, so pallid as to seem bleached.

'Mummy.'

'Wolfi. Darling. Beautiful.' He inserted his hand into the hole and reached through to Braille read the features of her face, smoothing her clammy cheeks and chin, dry lips, gently running bloodied fingers over her eyelids. Her tears came then, bathing the pouches under her eyes. Crouched in the hole, Wolfi dipped his fingers in water and she sucked them. He soaked the bread in the rainwater and fed her moist pellets.

'Be brave now for Mummy. You'll be all right. You're nearly grown up now, not a baby any more.'

She was telling him she would not survive. But this was impossible. After all, they could see one another, there was no partition. As long as he kept his eyes on her, mothering her, she could not ebb away. As long as he fed her. But how could he keep his gaze fixed on Effi when he needed to be away to find help? There must be help to find. She was the horizon of his world. There could be no other. All the night through the bombs fell.

'Have you got any pains, Mummy?'

She did not think so. He could no longer see her face. He was afraid of her smell. He was afraid of the strange things she claimed to see and the wildness of her waking dreams.

Next morning when he crawled out to get help, there was a bonfire over at the harbour. A sensational bonfire, with explosions spewing flames like a firework show. He could not help but pause to admire it before loping off to find aid, bread or milk.

There was a queue. He did not know what they were queuing for. He ran to the head of the queue. There was nothing there, only a closed door into the remains of what had used to be a baker's shop.

Nobody would come, though he dragged on strangers' hands and pleaded. Their eyes were far away.

Effi said nothing. She went on saying nothing.

He got used to the stink of her saying nothing. After all, that was all he had. She was where he belonged. He scavenged, filched food, collected cigarette ends and returned nightly to his lair.

***

The planes stopped coming. The stars came out, a sickle moon.

Wolfi looked at the clear pool of the bombless heavens. He felt tiny; a germ on a face. Walls still standing in the phosphorescent rubble cast black tongues of shadow.

When jeeps and lorries started to pour in, they disgorged British soldiers and marines. People began to swarm again, criss-crossing one another's paths, insects in a disordered hive. They ate what they could find: offal, dandelions, dogs, pigeons.

***

Wolfi slunk round the English soldiers' barracks. Jeeps roared in and out; the entrance was busy. A guard ordered him off. Wolfi disappeared behind a wall, hunkered down, then came back. The trick was to track soldiers as they sauntered off to survey the picturesque sepulchre that was the city, or the docks, a graveyard of scuppered subs, where ships' masts poked fingers from the oil-brown Baltic.

A sly shadow, Wolfi slipped after a khaki man wearing a webbing belt, jacket dangling over his shoulder in the warm spring air. He whistled; paused to light up, cupping his palm round the match. Wolfi drew nearer, taking the risk that the soldier would become aware of his presence. Urchins and women on the scavenge abounded. As you bent to your pickings, they darted out of nowhere, to snatch them from under your hand.

The corporal came out onto the harbour. Sunlight glittered on naval wreckage and demolished cranes and warehouses, making of havoc a fabulous dreamscape. Wolfi's prey perched on an oil-drum, yawned and stretched. Then he relaxed forward, leaning his forearms on spread legs, to take in the peaceful harbour. He finished his smoke.

Wolfi was onto the butt like a hawk. It was, yes, a good one. Longer than the usual mean British butt sucked down to the pinched fingertip and thumb. Fat with unconsumed tobacco.

He had a new lair now, where the kitchen had once stood. He could not stay beside Effi's corpse. The smell had made him gag. There had grown the feeling that the filthy thing in the ruins was not exactly his mother. But he had neither power nor wish to leave it permanently behind.

In the new lair he had fashioned from bricks and timbers, and a tarpaulin which kept out wind and rain, you could crouch but not stand. He had furnished it with a plywood fish-crate that preserved a vestigial fishiness and the cartoon of a Baltic cod, smiling with thick lips as it was trawled into a jolly fisherman's net. The cod was blue, the sea was blue, and the fisherman wore yellow oilskins. There was a league between fisherman and fish: the cod had always been dying to be caught, gutted and served up on a plate, and the fisherman obliged.

This box centred the den. Wolfi slept on a pile of sacks and hoarded his gleanings behind a brick in the wall. With exquisite care, Wolfi prised out the brick and removed five butts. Now he knelt, with the tackle of his trade before him on the fish-box altar. Opening a cigarette paper, he shook the tobacco into it; with skinflint concentration eked every speck. Then he rolled it and licked along the seal of the paper.

'Mister,' Wolfi said to the man with a trimmed moustache and greased hair. His satchel was stuffed with provisions. 'What'll you give me for a cigarette?'

'Let's see it. Give us a sniff. Seeing as it's you, a portion of cheese and a roll.' He held out his hand.

'Two rolls,' insisted Wolfi. 'And you give it me first, then I'll give you the cig.'

'Think I'm a charitable institution? Take it or leave it.'

Wolfi calculated. Knew, or thought he knew, he could do better. But Wolfi was only his hunger now, a walking stomach, empty and spasming. He dreamed in fitful sleeps of pork cutlets with onions and mushrooms; thick sausage; saw sauce ooze fat; dipped bread into gravy and filled the cavern of his stomach. Sometimes, among the stink of cadavers, the cruelty of imagined dinner scents came to him. And when he hung around the barrack, he got a glimpse into the mess where the English sergeants and warrant officers were tucking into ham, baked potato, and apple tart with custard. And he remembered custard. How

Effi had put out great dollops of yellow slop on to the plates saying *English custard, boys. A treat for you. Go on, eat up*. And how he tipped the basin up and drank it, liking the thick, hot comfort of the milky sweetness as it warmed his throat and sloshed in his tummy.

'All right then,' said Wolfi. 'But have you got a big one?'

'Big what?'

'Big roll. And a good slice of cheese. Please, mister. This one's a good ciggie, isn't it?'

'You'll have what you're given, and be grateful,' said the moustache with prim reproof.

The roll was stale. Hard. But it was a roll. The cheese, edged with green mould, smelt high. A week ago he could not have brought himself to eat it.

Don't gobble, darling, there's plenty, said her beloved remembered voice. And how she had stinted herself to feed him came back. How she said, taking off her pinafore and hanging it on the door, that she found she honestly wasn't all that hungry, so he could have her ration; and how, although he saw it was a lie and he should have refused, he stuffed his face with both portions of sausage, and suffered the famished generosity of her smile, because that was what mothers were for, and only when he got to the last two or three bites, and his pangs were partially assuaged, had he allowed himself to see her thin face staring at his plate, and pushed it across so that she could feed on the scraps.

He forced himself to cut the roll and cheese into three sections with his penknife, wrapping two of the portions in cheesecloth. He hid them behind the brick.

***

He had left himself behind, up there where open air gaped. An abdicated self hung suspended in his mother's arms, in the big lumpy bed with the bolsters, warm and remote. But Wolfi himself had suffered violent division. He had slipped out of his old self to become some animal, like a rat. A rat that must make its way in life, adapting to conditions in sewers and drains, slithering through narrow-waisted holes, into cellars, rooting among offal, garbage. The rat had leapt from his heart fully formed and nosed its way around the bowels of the city. It held its body heat in chill, dank places; gnawed with razor incisors, whiskers quivering, snout alert. It seemed normal to be the rat. The creature had always been hiding coiled in Wolfi's breast, ready for the emergency that would make its birth imperative. Yet the child he had been still hovered above in the salty air, tender and rocked, like a baby in a Moses basket.

Up the wrought-iron steps of a blasted house the rat crept, a staircase which seemed attached to the house on a thread, for it swung away terrifyingly, with a groan. Wolfi was glad; he kept on going. It meant the house had not been stripped.

Wolfi had the idea that he could not die now. His rat-self belonged to the tribe of survivors. At the same time, none of this was real. It was a kind of film. In the film there was a game, whose rules must be guessed, for they were arbitrary. It took instinct to guess, wit, luck.

The second floor seemed aerial. The staircase floated out in slow motion, its flimsy girder parting company with the house. The sight of the huge plunge beneath rolled Wolfi's stomach clean over; then the rat-brain spasmed into action. He took a floundering leap across the abyss, to land on the masonry at the edge of the floor. Just as it gave, with an evolving crash, he launched himself into the room, and scrambled to the back wall. There Wolfi lay, till the landslide subsided.

The staircase within no longer existed. There would be no way down on that side. Still. He ferreted. A baby's cot, lying askew, as if it had just tumbled the baby out, was veiled in a chintzy net, a chalk of plaster. A chest of drawers with piles of baby clothes, nappies, a dummy (he pocketed the dummy), and, what he was after, goods tucked beneath the clothing – three gold fobs, a bracelet, a locket containing a curl of hair. Good stuff, all good stuff.

He shimmied down the drainpipe at the back of the house, and fell ten foot as the pipe gave. But he had learned to fall softly, cat-relaxed. The pockets of his shorts bulged with loot.

***

Wolfi began to observe bands of vagabond boys slouching past. Cigarettes hanging from the corners of their mouths, they ran in packs, hands in pockets, jaunty and vivid, little men who had vaulted from childhood to manhood in one bound. They swaggered with a display of insolence, past the loneliness of Wolfi's lair. One group passed on bicycles, with perished tyres, ringing their bells, as if off on a picnic.

The urge to join them was visceral. His rat-mind pumped a strong message to his heart, he was shot through with the fierce compulsion to be with his fellow species, to quit the lonely competition.

Faltering at the border of his domain, he wondered whether to approach the next group with his spoils. Trade loot for the safety of numbers. But Wolfi had rarely had friends among boys. His father had helped him sidle past the youth oranisations. He lacked resources to deal with his equals.

And could he leave her?

The rat-brain insisted he leave. Pack up, move on. Over there.

Shoals of people came. Families with carts, dragged by old women and girls without shoes. He had shoes. Good that Wolfi had shoes. When they looked over at him, he looked back impassively, warning off all comers. Some pushed prams. He saw a slaughtered piglet in a pram.

More boys came past, and he made a mistake.

Grasped too late that the hulking lads were Werewolves trained for conflict. They laughed as they emptied his pockets; kicked him in the groin, split his nostril. Ransacked his little house. Filched his precious matchbox of lard. Wolfi crouched in the remains of his den and, his mouth squaring up like a baby's, sobbed. They had not discovered the cache behind the brick but the lair was wrecked; he must begin again, rebuild his home, knowing now its fragility. The rat had vanished into this snivelling ex-child, who buried himself in his sack-bed and sucked the rubber dummy. Remembered the honey Effi used to dab on the end when he woke at night with earache. His nose went on bleeding. The tender balls and penis stabbed with unbelievable pain where they had kicked him. No one had ever raised a hand to Wolfi in his life. Cruelty had never come near him.

***

The man was born from the sea mist. Wolfi heard him stagger around on the debris, pulling at bricks and masonry. He raised the edge of the tarpaulin and squinted round. Raincoat skirts dragged on bricks as the man pitched about. A drunk? Or one of the many madmen who had come from who knew or cared what hell, and spoke no German, but sang in melancholy, alien tongues of something else, somewhere else?

Wolfi's father seemed to be digging near Wolfi's mother.

He tossed out bricks and grunted as he levered off rafters Wolfi had been impotent to budge. Sea mist drifted in, muffling sound, veiling the crooked figure.

It gave out a cry, harsh, penetrating. Michael had got to Effi.

Wolfi emerged. He pattered over the ruin, nimbly.

'Wolfi, is it you, Wolfi?'

Wolfi took in the greasy, haggard but well-fed face that presented itself. Looked into eyes that could afford to weep; asked in a whisper if there was anything to eat?

He was caught up in a bear hug. The father was weeping uncontrollably into his neck; tears trickled down the boy's chest. Wolfi thought of Coca Cola while this was going on. He had seen a bottle on the carburettor of an Ami jeep. A whole bottle of fizzing ecstasy. He had never tasted Coca Cola but he hoped, prayed to do so. The very sight of that bottle had made Wolfi sick with desire. It had been an object of reverence. The Ami had prised off the cap with a coin and raised the precious liquid to his lips. He had chucked in a handful of what Wolfi took to be peanuts and washed them down with another swig.

'Your mother? Effi? In there, she's in there, isn't she?'

Wolfi, sat down at the father's side, nodded.

'How long?'

Wolfi shook his head. Questions of time foxed him. All he knew was that he must hang on to the father as his sole lifeline. This man must fend for him; must not be allowed to escape again.

'It's best if I take you back with me,' said the father. 'There's nothing for us here.'

Stealthily, Wolfi left his mother behind in the graveyard of rubble. He detached himself from her, without unpicking the knot, but stretching their bond into an infinite elasticity.

He did not look back.

Rather he kept his eyes on the father, walking close in his lee, against the torrent of paupers toiling up into Schleswig-Holstein. Father kept the miracle of smoked sausage and chocolate in his pockets. It was all Wolfi could do not to pick the father's pockets when they lay down for sleep in a ploughed field. Wedged between loamy furrows, Wolfi's mouth watered at the thought of foodstuffs his tastebuds seemed to invent, for it was so long since he had tasted good things that he had half-forgotten them.

The fields fled away to either side like polders, flat and expressionless, and the skies were vast. The father bathed the boy's pink eyes in salt water.

'My God, Wolfi, but you look scrofulous,' he said, awkwardly jesting away the child's damage, stripping him to the waist and washing him in a stream. Wolfi's watchful eyes besought, *Don't go*. The father's eyes promised never to abandon him, but Wolfi knew you could never be sure. The father got him an egg at a farm.

Wolfi looked at the egg in wonderment. He took it into his own hand and coddled it there.

It's an egg, he thought, amazed. *An actual egg*.

He could not get over how it was an egg. A brown speckled egg, straight from the hen that morning (*although who knew how old it was?* said the father, the farmers had got the whip-hand now, they cheated you left, right and centre).

'Aren't you going to eat it?' asked the father. 'Or are you waiting to hatch it?'

Wolfi nodded.

'You'll have a long wait. Aren't you going to talk to me, Wolfi? Just a little?'

Wolfi sat on a hummock of grass, holding the egg that was not going to hatch. He smelt manure in the fields around; heard sheep shift on the pasture, their lambs suckling. A tall shepherd-woman standing vigil in the field eyed him as if he were a whole gang of sheep rustlers. Wolfi nodded at his father, to show willingness to speak but his eyes explained that words were fugitive; always fled, like these flatlands, out of reach. The father hunkered beside him, in the posture that Effi had called 'coopying down'. Effi and he had baby words they exchanged like tokens of safety. The words had not worked.

'You're going to be all right now, Wolfi,' pleaded the father. 'Eat your egg. Fatten you up a bit. And I want to get you to a doctor. Those lungs don't sound right.'

When you crunched dandelion stalks, sticky milk came out.

If he ate this egg, the egg would be consumed.

The father seemed to be on a bed of pins whenever he looked at the enfeebled son, his conjunctival membranes bright pink, mouth a mass of cold sores. His eyes swivelled away and he said something cheerful about what they would do in the future, what they would see, how they would make a life, just the two of them together.

'I tell you what, if I get you another egg, will you eat that one?'

Wolfi nodded solemnly.

'Just a tick.'

He was gone. Gone. There was nobody with Wolfi, in the centre of wide plains where wind came sweeping, and the skies were so low and pale. The utter forlornness of the vista brought volts of panic. He stumbled up and rushed bereft toward the farmhouse door, where the father had disappeared.

'Daddy,' whispered Wolfi, and his eyes gushed tears. 'Don't go.'

The farmer's wife held a tin jug of milk. Pursed-lipped disdain flitted across her face for a gangling youth who galloped into her kitchen like a panicked colt.

Wolfi's father took his son's hand and squeezed.

***

They stood together by the lake. Its waves somersaulted in foamy lips at Wolfi's feet. The silence between himself and his father had deepened fathomlessly with the years. Occasionally the one waded out into the shallows of the other, with a nervous query. Now they skimmed pebbles: Wolfi's bounced in arcs bent on curving homewards; his father's were inventive, far-reaching, with rhythmic and riddling Morse-like skips.

Quantz's gaze chivvied his son; then roved away. He busied himself with earning their daily bread. And he had been in luck where so many millions vanished, or survived on starvation rations provided by the victors. The British felt confidence in Michael Quantz. Wolfi perceived that. He kept his eyes trained on his father, observing his adaptation to the likings, customs and bias of the occupiers. He discerned with relief the chameleon powers of this man. How suave he was, how self-deprecatingly sure in his skill to stay afloat. Father taught Wolfi how to pronounce the victorious tongue so as to speak better English than the English. Mastery of nuance is the key, he explained, for they judge you by your well-spokenness. That's how they tell which class you come from. Make yourself seem to lack an origin. Don't make the mistake of swallowing your words or talking down your nose, as their officers do, he instructed Wolfi: speak with a purity that expresses reverence for the tongue of Shakespeare. They will like that.

Don't kowtow: they are hypocritical enough to dislike the display of subservience.

Equally, don't strut about: bad form in foreigners.

Appeal to their sense of fair play. For their world is a cricket pitch. Be prepared to play the sporting loser.

Learn the subtleties of their untranslatable art of diffident irony.

Wolfi liked the cabin they had in the woods above Eutin. Later they built a cottage there, with their own hands. Those hands were sensitive, mobile. Wolfi learned the flute, cello and piano. At school he toed the line; made few friends and no enemies. History stopped in 1900. That was that. Henry I, Frederick the Great, Bismarck, then really nothing much. But the German people had suffered much, old Schmidt allowed it to be known. They had been sacrificed by, he whispered, *a certain hook-nosed race*. Our time might come again, if we did our duty. Many lies were told about atrocities; propaganda spawned by the victors. Boys should not believe aspersions. Nor should honourable children give up on ideals learned at their fathers' knees. He would say no more.

The lessons droned. Streams of tedious, encrypted garrulity poured from the little man's mouth. And Mr Schmidt, with his nicotined teeth, felt the youngsters' alienation as personal affront. It had not been like this in the past, he stated, the young people then had been disciplined, passionate about ideals.

'What ideals, brown shit Schmidt?' asked Hansi.

Mr Schmidt swung round, puce-faced. He held in his hand a wooden pointer, with which he had been indicating nineteenth-century boundaries on a map of Europe.

'Who spoke?' he screamed. 'Who spoke?'

Spittle shot out of his mouth on the sibilants.

'I said, what about that brown bit, Mr Schmidt? On the map. The brown bit on the east of the Oder. That bit, Mr Schmidt. Sir.'

In the pause while old Schmidt balanced the politic against the punitive course of action, boys tittered openly and nudged one another. Wolfi knew that in the past the old fascist, who like thousands of others had been reappointed, would have commenced a physical onslaught with the wooden pointer. Hansi would have been reported. Shamed. Expelled. One day he would have vanished into 'Night and Fog'. But now old Schmidt readjusted some inner machinery, cleared his throat and began a meandering excursus on the poor quality of Youth Today, with animadversions on the importance of respect for authority as the foundation of a democratic society.

Wolfi, lean, spare and seventeen, looked as though he must be an athletic youth, though he was not. He topped his father by half a head. Yet they were both aware of Wolfi's nightmares, under the still surface. He tucked in close to his father whenever possible, less on the principle of attraction than on some resistance to antipathy which he did not analyse. Anxieties seeped through the floor of his mind; nameless and irrational dread of open spaces, of skies across which a flight of geese passed in V formation, of an absence that stalked him.

Hansi ran his old banger round the villages, with his fist on the hooter. Blasted out jazz on a radio hung from his neck. Hansi said, tough-guy style, 'My dad gives me the habdabs. Old fart. In Poland, he was. What was he doing in Poland? Don't ask. They give me the pip, the old men. Yours was at Minsk.'

Wolfi mused on a back view of Michael Quantz, seated at the open piano without playing, hands on thighs, just staring at the dusty innards of the brown lid. No music on the stand. It came across Wolfi that he could plunge a kitchen knife into that broad back. This thought came and went calmly. It was just something you could do. What was father reading there, in that mindless impromptu of scratch marks and blemishes long in the making? Where had he been all those years when Wolfi and Effi were all in all to one another? What coldness came radiating from his father and even now numbed him, however conscientiously Quantz guarded his son from himself? Effi's stricken cries when her husband went out to his women found echoes in those of the water birds nesting round the lake, haunting and ghostly. The sedge rustled stormily in the wind. Sudden uproars discharged cannons of hail. The resinous woodlands seemed shaken to the roots. The stork picked her way upstream, alone.

I know you were in Russia, you were at Minsk, he thought, staring at his father's faded check shirt. Hansi could call his dad a shit. Outright, just like that. What could Wolfi call his?

His father turned slowly and met his gaze. 'I was miles away,' he said. 'Want to play something?'

They flicked through the sheet music: duets for flute and piano. Hansi was going to Canada, he bragged, or America, or Australia. Some time. He executed fancy footwork in the street, inspiring local people with a horror of terminal decadence. Whereas Hansi strummed an ill-tuned guitar and vituperated his father and uncle in public, Wolfi played the flute and edged dextrously around his parent. For theirs was a cooperative enterprise. They carried between them the invisible burden of Wolfi's terrors. If Wolfi shocked his father into dropping his half, where would be his balance?

He flexed his lips for the embouchure; set the flute to his ready mouth and spread supple fingers along the keys. He blew; and the beauty of his playing brought tears to the father's eyes, so he said afterwards, though Wolfi could see no evidence of tears, only the unnerving blueness of a gaze that seemed to see too much and confide too little.

But his teeth were rotten, thought Wolfi, he had lousy teeth.

Young men who came stumbling back from the east were practically toothless. They looked twice their age. Hundreds of miles they had slogged, holed boots packed with newspaper. Their uniforms were in rags, some lacked an arm or a leg, they saw things that weren't there and talked to the dead.

The new rulers marched past, swinging their arms, berets at a sloppy angle. The commanding officer took over the gentry house at the oil mill. Officers commandeered the best houses in Plön. In a small castle previously occupied by the SS elite, they set up a yachting club for their own caste. Their ladies came out to join them.

'Think they're in India or Kenya,' observed Father. 'Playing at pooja-sahibs, and we're the coolies.'

The two of them had been recruited to play at soirées.

High-pitched small talk outsang the tempered softness of Wolfi's flute. Father and son were treated with condescension and offered triangular sandwiches scattered with cress.

'No, please, do. Take two,' offered the hostess' turquoise-satin daughter. 'After all your efforts. So charming.'

Wolfi blushed and obliged.

'You are most kind,' said his father correctly. 'Delicious fare.'

'If only they knew,' he added, when the turquoise-satin one had melted away.

'Knew what?' Wolfi, stuffing a compartment of his flute case with triangles, in a brown paper bag brought for that purpose, got no answer.

Polite laughter eddied up and down, at some anecdote. Teacups clinked on saucers. Wolfi wondered how to get hold of sugar lumps.

Turquoise-satin was back. Her curls had an insane symmetry, to Wolfi's eye. Darkly regimental, they lined up as if the rollers had just been extracted sideways. Then lacquer had been applied to rigidify them in awful perfection. Wolfi could not take his eyes off these empty sausages.

'I say,' she said. 'My mother would like awfully to hear some Elgar. Do you happen to know any Elgar?'

Father nodded courteously. He and Wolfi, repressing smirks, led into a medley of the Elgar classics they had got together for colonial consumption.

Land of hope and glory,
Mother of the free...

The company rose in awkward ones and twos until all stood, chins high, patriotically moved, as they looked out of the windows over forests and lake. Their voices were raised, at first quavering with embarrassment, and then more confident. Booming basses and reedy sopranos joined forces:

Wider still and wider
Shall thy bounds be set...

Wolfi and his father conspired, eyes meeting eyes, as they unleashed against the herd of voices parodic descants of their own invention. To a flutter of applause, they responded with ironic bows of the head and accepted butterfly cakes which Wolfi felt bound to consume on the spot, since space in the flute case was limited.

***

But now the fragile coalition had been split. With one easy bound he had broken the unwholesome bond with Father. He shook him off, forsook him. Wolfi watched, jeering, from his new position of power, as Father staggered and shuddered where he stood, exposed on every side. Wolfi would be his own man, not that man's son. He turned away and walked down the ridge to meet his new freedom, seeing Issie's figure emerge in his mind's eye, through the flow of evening air. Seeing himself emerge. Wolfi's senses were so alive he shivered.

Slav, his father had said. They had wrangled in hectic dispute, Wolfi in a paroxysm of dismay at his own towering fury that threatened the fabric they had fostered over years.

Mind your own business, he had yelled. *What does it matter?*

I just thought you ought to know where she came from.

How do you know anyway?

Coincidence. It so happens that…

What's it to do with you? Haven't you done enough damage?

What damage am I supposed to have done?

Your generation – all of you.

I am not responsible for that madness.

Oh, really. Oh, is that right? Well, thanks a lot for the information. How can you people live with yourselves? How?

The smell of the fat in the pan had turned his stomach. Wolfi had stormed out of the house, and afterwards thought of what he should have said about Slavs. For Slavs had founded this place, hadn't they, on the peninsula in Lake Plön. He never thought of the right retort until hours after the event.

An SS father now big in vacuum cleaners.

Most of his life he had been paralysed in confrontations. Lately some spirit long quenched had begun to struggle free in him, voiced itself. Pent vitality surged, accompanied by a swarming trepidation. Sexual claims stormed through the anxious chastity of years.

Other women seemed to have been put together in a factory. He was aware in the girls he had kissed and petted of hidden fortifications, whalebone and elastic, pods that held up stockings and unnerved you by snapping open. He had always stopped at the hard conical contrivances like armature over the bosom which stuck into your chest when kissing. Issie's freedom from . . . apparatus, artifice . . . brought pangs of delight.

She came to meet him through the woods, padding on beechmast between bars of tree shadow. Her dress was green, with full skirts that swung, emerald when the sun caught their folds, then moss dark. They took hands.

When Wolfi touched her face, the fear dissolved into tender excitement, he saw how her underlip quivered, as if she might cry, although she smiled. He raised her chin to kiss her eyelids and brush his lips over her mouth. His tongue parted her lips and entered her mouth.

Just gently, just the tip of his tongue.

Her eyes were large and darkly liquid, with a strangeness that came of the fact that retina and pupil were hardly distinguishable.

If you had someone this beautiful, you would lose her. That was the law with which he had been early familiar. He had heard his mother call out to his father, *Leave us alone, I shan't have him for ever*. Loss saturated the heart of love, not the canker in the apple but the very juice of the fruit. But that was no reason not to take her hand. He melted; hardened and ached. Issie pressed the inside of her palm against his as they sauntered down no particular path in the green gloom, leaning inwards; then he laid his arm round her waist. Wolfi marvelled as his fingers moved with the sway of her firm body. He brimmed with her, as though she had entered him: how she moved, the flesh-and-blood reality of her, the swish of her skirt over strong legs. Her arm came round his waist, beneath the jacket.

He glanced down just as she glanced up. Both were flushed. Each smiled with conspiratorial rue, as if they tracked two other hesitant lovers walking ahead, embarrassed and unnerved, with whose feelings they sympathised.

Her eyes were slightly slanted; the lashes curved, giving a sense of exotic foreignness. Her tilted face was a broad oval.

'But how would my father have known your father?' he suddenly burst out. He was instantly mortified. This was his life. Nothing to do with Father, but Father was here, beside them, sullying it all, saying, *Slav. I don't mind about Slavs but you'd better know*. If this whole business could be got out of the way, he could live his own life. 'He seems to think he knew your parents... before the war.'

'Knew my parents? Which parents?'

***

They lay on his raincoat, their faces washed with one another's tears. The tears had dissolved all boundaries, equalising them. Issie's face was a whole world Wolfi had explored with his eyes and fingertips. *You cried*, he thought, *and I cried. That makes us one*. He hardly knew her, yet he would have rounded indignantly on anyone who said so; or cynically claimed that such beauty and balance could not go on at this intensity forever. Low sun tipped their faces with an obscure gold that dimmed from moment to moment. From so close, he was aware of each eyelash, the throb at her temple, the melt of her eyes.

And it was my hair, she sobbed. *My hair. It gave me away. He sheared it off with clippers.*

Your beautiful glorious hair. But why? Why would he? Was he mad?

He crooked his arm round her head, where they lay

face to face, lips lax and tender with kissing, and buried his hand in the shadows of her curls, massaging the scalp and brushing her forehead with his lips.

I don't know. They never said. No one ever said anything. Then we were refugees. Then when we were in Wales we became refugees again, we were in some kind of prison camp for enemy aliens. I don't remember clearly, it's all a blur – but I did overhear some things – whispering – about his shaving my head – I must have blocked it out.

Whoever would do that…was not worth a hair of your head.

Wolfi had seen pictures of the concentration camp victims: their shaven skulls. He had never asked his father until now, *Did you know? Did you know about that?* And Father did know. He knew everything. It was out in the open that he was a rat like all the others. And Wolfi was the rat's son. Yet the man who had brought Wolfi from Kiel and fended for him, building the tree house in the garden, lightly balancing the flute for him and laying his fingers along its body, did not appear to be the same man as had known these things. There seemed to Wolfi to have been two fathers; but only ever the one mother, the one Effi. She was indistinct, a snapshot in his mind, rather than a breathing woman. The photographer's hand had been unsteady. It had blurred her black-and-white image. Isolde was the colourful reality whose face now filled the horizon of his gaze and blocked out his childhood. *I say unto thee, every hair of thy head shall be numbered.*

My father disowned me.

Then we disown him. He drew her face to him again, stroking her lips and temples with his fingertips, breath soft in blessing. *We disown them.*

12

Lake Plön, 1958

Issie stood before the mirror, touching her lips, reliving that rush of novel intimacy, as boundaries went down. Weeping together. Wolfi's being unafraid to cry. Owen too had the gift of tears.

But Wolfi had said, *My father... your father.*

The throb of alarm at these words recurred now, a horror in her background, which somehow claimed kin, though she had never willed it, or cooperated with it in any way. Renate and she had crossed a continent, a sea, to confound it. Yet it always came in tow, like some sordid relative one yearns to ditch.

She turned from the mirror; remembered the rough softness of the contact on her lips, her body's ache of sweet disquiet. Breath on her cheek as they lay face to face, murmuring in German, in English, as though the languages had been discovered to be a seamless whole. Dialects of the one tongue. She had taken the lapels of his jacket between her fingers, rubbing the nap between her thumbs. Wolfi had kissed the palms and wrist, where blue veins fork beneath private skin.

Every hair of your head is numbered.

Faces so close. Eyes gazing into gazing eyes.

You could see every pore up so close. The small mole near her ear; Wolfi had kissed that. A blemish; she had always wished it away.

She had slid her hands beneath his jacket, into the layer of warmth between lining and shirt, reading the curves of shoulder blade and breast. A broken nail had snagged in a tiny tear of his jacket lining. She felt now the strange intimacy of that knowledge, of what, though ordinary, is never shown. Wolfi would not have much money; he tried to be modern without the means to do so. He had let her learn hidden things. She cradled the small messages she had gleaned. Though they had been fully clothed, there had been a nakedness.

At the same time, Issie was abashed at her own forwardness; a voice within her asked where did she think she was going? Wouldn't he think her fast? He'd throw her away when he'd used her: *Oh yes, my girl, and where will you be then?* But it wasn't her own voice. A thrilling ache went through her nerves, just on the right side of pain, at defying that voice.

Taking liberties, it accused, dull, platitudinous, like Swansea weekends when the rain fell steadily and Mrs Thomas over the road peered between net curtains with generalised disapproval. *Unfeminine behaviour*, the voice ticked her off, ending with the usual prophecy, *It will end in tears. Again.*

But Wolfi cancelled all that. Freedom and integrity could be one thing; they could. For Wolfi had said, *Anyone who would do that to you was not worth a hair of your head. Never cut it*, he urged. *Grow it all down your back. Promise.* Shame was a figment of other people's diseased imaginations. It was their own guilt and littleness they unloaded onto you. Wolfi and she would dive clear of all that, together.

The tap on the door broke up her reverie. 'Please, miss, Rachel Goldman's had an accident, miss.'

'Well, is it urgent? I'm not on duty, you know. Oh, all right, I'll come,' she grumbled, piqued that the petty troubles of kids should interfere with her self-absorption. 'Just hang on a minute while I get my keys.'

Pandemonium in the dormitory. A *Fräulein* shrieking. Girls' uproar.

'It's not my duty,' Issie asserted, before the matron had had time to open her mouth. 'Mrs B's on duty.'

Fräulein said in German: 'The little Jew has jumped off a wardrobe.'

Issie pushed past. Rachel was clenched in a ball at the top of her bed, dark hair in greasy waves all that could be seen of her head on the pillow. A child was leaping on a bed near the window, shouting some slogan about Singapore villages in an exultant blare that increased the vicious atmosphere of hysteria to near frenzy.

'Silence at once! You – get down from there. Now, who has done what to whom?'

The roaring girl seemed relieved to have her fit summarily aborted. She instantly became quiet and climbed down from her bed.

'Rachel, what is the matter?' Issie's testy voice, void of sympathy, bore the message *Why have you interrupted me with your unimportant plight?* as clearly as if she had spoken it aloud. Ashamed, she modulated her tone. 'Are you hurt? What happened? Can I see?'

The foetal child attempted to disappear into herself, skinny legs brought up as far as they would go, disclosing inches of thigh beneath the pleated grey skirt. Issie pulled down the skirt and saw the child's tremor of reaction.

She bent above the girl's head and stroked it. 'What is it, Rachel? Tell me what happened to you.'

'Miss, miss, she jumped off the wardrobe, miss.'

'I doubt it. Unless one of you dared her. Or pushed her.'

'We didn't so. We were messing about and she jumped. Ask her if you don't believe me.'

'Yes, well,' said Issie, her hand still on the silent child's head. 'If she did fall off the wardrobe, it was because you lot were doing your usual trick of going round the room without touching the floor.'

She caught the sly look that flickered from eye to eye.

'Matron, what happened?'

'The Jewish girl was trying to prove herself to the English by some stupid trick or other.'

'How dare you call her a Jewish girl? How dare you? And how dare you speak in German? This is an English school.' The *Fräulein* looked as perplexed as she was affronted.

'But she is a Jew,' she said in German.

'I shall report you,' said Issie in English. 'I shall report you for anti-Semitism. British people don't like it.'

'Oh please, no. I meant no harm. I like Jewish people,

Miss Dahl. I have no grudge against Jews, none in the world, they are a distinguished people, I don't envy their wealth, never have, ask anyone.'

'You disgust me,' said Issie in German.

The child swivelled round and said, thickly, through bruised lips, 'I fell off of the wardrobe.'

'She did, miss, she fell off,' Nadine said.

'Are you badly hurt? Show me.' The child showed a bruise on her knee. Issie fingered it softly, testing its tenderness, asking Rachel to bend her knee and instructing the matron to bring cold water to bathe it.

'Shall we send you to sick bay?' she asked the child. Probably it wasn't necessary; if people would go leaping around on furniture, they must expect knocks. But at least if she'd taken a tumble in some daft game, it showed she'd been joining in with the others. Perhaps she was on her way to acceptance. Perhaps the injury would act as a token of belonging. Rachel may even have dived off the wardrobe to achieve some such sign of comradeship. 'I don't think it should be necessary.'

A sour whiff came from the child. Didn't she ever wash herself?

And all the while, the memory of the momentous afternoon out there with Wolfi kept shining in, like sun through the weft of linen curtains, more urgently real than these petty calamities.

The child was nodding. She would like to go to sick bay.

'Well, I don't think it's essential. You can go tomorrow if the bruise hasn't gone down. Matron, give Rachel two aspirins and bathe the injury in cold water and witch hazel. Kindly: do it kindly,' she added harshly in German. She resolutely did not say 'please'. Her cold fury with the woman exceeded her sympathy for the child.

'I always do what is kind and right,' stated *Fräulein*, the epitome of injured rectitude. 'If the young *English* lady would cease to climb the furniture, she would not now be hurting,' she added, nodding at Rachel as she confided her subtle deduction.

'I didn't,' whispered Rachel.

'Are you saying you were pushed?'

'No.' Panic kindled the dark eyes raised to hers. The other girls' presence seemed to gather around them so that Issie heard their breathing. She felt their damage and how they were passing it on to the newcomer. She recognised, in the after-echo of the pleasure she had received this afternoon, how exquisite pain could also be. She should offer, from her own superfluity of joy, some fellowship to this child; yet she hungered to slip back to her room and recall the taste of Wolfi.

'Now, girls. Rachel is to rest on her bed and you are to be especially kind to her. Yes?'

'Yes Miss Dahl,' they droned.

'And, *Fräulein*, I think it would be nice if Rachel had a long soak in the bath. It will relax her.'

'It is not this group's bathing night,' came the objection.

'It is if I say it is, *Fräulein*.'

'But we are only allowed so much hot water and regulations state that each girl receives a full bath only once a week, and this, with a strip-wash every day, cleaning *under* the arms with a flannel, should be sufficient to keep each individual clean. Sadly young Rachel is shy to strip to the waist and hence misses her regular washes that are so essential to our hygiene and I have noticed too, if I may put this point to you now, Miss Dahl, that she does not take her clothes off to get into her weekly bath, with the result . . .'

'That's because you can't lock the doors, miss, and people look over the top of the wall and laugh at me . . .', the child blurted.

'We are not concerned with cleanliness,' Issie, red-faced and sickened, told the matron, 'but with kindness. *Fräulein*, I have asked that Rachel be given the opportunity of a hot soak. I don't see a problem about this.'

Matron drew herself up to her full height and raised her head. Issie saw where the cosmetic mask ended beneath her chin, exposing pouchy wrinkled skin.

'As you wish. Rachel Goldman, Miss Dahl wants that you take a bath to make you nice and clean.'

A mean titter passed round the girls: a collusion with

the Matron, in which they and she agreed to stigmatise the outsider as unclean.

'That is not what I said, Matron, and not what I meant. Rachel, I thought you might find a nice hot bath would make you feel better. Also a cup of tea, Matron, sweet, please, with two teaspoons of sugar. Don't let me hold you up in your duties.'

Issie stalked off, wishing she had never embarked on the subject of baths with that ghoul.

Had the woman never been de-Nazified? How did creatures like that get into the system? She knew there were decent matrons, for Miss Koch was a gentle young woman who mothered the boys and made their lives as homely as she could. Her youngsters loved her. And there were others. Should the rogue *Fräulein* be reported? Issie had heard Patterson declare that his *Fräuleins* were German ladies of the highest quality, whose price was far above rubies. She cast the matter aside in her mind, a bone already much gnawed which she would pick over again at her leisure.

But it appeared that *Fräulein* could not let the matter rest. She was trailing Issie down the corridor.

'Excuse me. I am not happy. Not at all. Nobody has ever questioned my work or my good feeling before, and humiliated me in front of the children. I must protest.'

'Yes?'

'Miss Dahl, I am shocked by your attitude.'

'That makes two of us. I'm shocked by yours.'

'You may not be aware that although the English insist on calling us Fräuliens, I am a widow. A war widow, Miss Dahl, as it happens. *Sudetendeutsch*. Driven out of home, estate, everything. I came here with only the clothes I stood up in. I have had to endure many hardships, in case you are interested, which I have done without complaint. I am a person alone. I have not been used to menial work such as this, but rather to have people serve me. But I do it to the best of my ability. Am I not entitled to respect? Young people are rash with their tongues and quick to judge. You constantly misunderstand my most simple words. Which surprises me, for I thought you were one of us.'

For some time afterwards Issie was visited by the memory of this phrase. What could the creature mean by it? How could they have anything in common? *Fräulein* had placed one ringed hand on her arm and gazed significantly into her eyes, shaking her head in disappointment. She reminded Issie for a moment of Renate, in gestures that obscurely cancelled one another out: a doctrinaire holding forth of nonsensical principles as mandatory. The bullying set of a tremulous jaw; the hard-as-nails softness of voice.

She shut her door on it all. Later there was a muffled stampede, catcalls. Some little tykes appeared to be riding others up and down the corridor, with leather case-straps for reins. Roy Rogers, Tonto and Silver. *Not my duty; let someone else subdue the Wild West.*

The view over the darkening lake failed to restore the stillness of that dreamy inwardness Wolfi had opened to her. He had been driven off by the prosaic furore of life that must be lived cheek by jowl with uncongenial neighbours. She lay down in bed and called Wolfi silently back.

***

Something from home at last. Heavy as a package, the letter was stowed in her patch pocket for later reading. All day it hid there, warm from her body. As she taught, ate, supervised the little ones' baths, her fingers stole in and played with it. Screeds of gossip probably – photos, or cuttings from the Western Mail. A P.S. from Owen. She watched the children with their post. How they'd thumb the envelopes open and go silent, breathing deeply as they read. Their letters assured them: *we are still here, still waiting for you, we have not ceased to exist.* Post was more important than tuck parcels, pale wafers which fed the soul.

She broke the seal. A livid scrawl dealt its sequence of shocks. She only skimmed the letter, then tried to stuff it back into the envelope, but it wouldn't go, wouldn't fit back in, so she thrust the wedge of papers under her pillow; rushed for the lake with bursting heart.

Oh my darling – You can have no idea how much I love you & have tried all our lives to spare you this knowledge. My eyes are streaming, I can hardly see to write so forgive the scrawl. You will judge me, no doubt of that – but please *meine Allerliebste* consider that you have had the good fortune to be brought up in a cosy Welsh world surrounded by aunties with their everlasting knitting, chapel and Welshcakes – a safe world where nothing ever happened to you much worse than a bumped knee – & you were never exposed to damaging influences. Please do not be too quick to judge anyone who has lived through terrible times of which you can never know, for one must have lived through them to understand. Put it to yourself: where sadness is normal, what ordinary person can see through it and stand against it? Ask yourself that question before you judge your mother. Are you so special? So intelligent? So incorruptible?

If not, spare me your blame.

If so, who made you this?

Issie stripped fast in the wooden shack and bundled her clothes on a shelf. Her body was a mass of shivers. It was really too late in the year for bathing. The water appeared gelid and pewter–grey, its surface puckered by rushes of wind. The door banged to and fro against the hut, as she ran down the sand to hesitate before the jetty that led to the pool. Why couldn't Owen have stopped Renate writing like that? Why did Tada have to be so milk-and-water meek? The pool was turbid, water slapping against the struts. She would not swim there but in the forbidden open water.

If I kept secrets from you, please Isolde try to believe it was for your own good. We started our lives anew once I'd got you out of Germany, and made it possible for you to grow up free of the horrible things I'd been through.

I am a stubborn woman & no doubt you get your temperament from me. I might have known you'd want to go poking round looking for your real father. As soon as I read the name Michael Quantz, I knew you'd started. God knows what lies that man has fed you. Your letter caused me such a sweat of nervous anguish I really thought I was having a heart attack. As a little girl, you had a frightful temper & tantrums round the clock. You used to pummel me: that was how your letter made me feel. I think it best I should explain things to you. So that you leave off your romantic hankerings after filthy people.

Issie was up to the knees when the ground shelved sharply: she went in up to the neck and gasping. But the cold would ease once her body became accustomed. She launched into the rhythm of a patient, disciplined breaststroke, making toward the gull island. There humans never went. Leaves eddied past her arms and mouth in patches of raw colour – yellow, ochre, scarlet – fleeing toward the shore.

So I must lay it all before you: or at least the bare facts, the skeleton. Firstly: I was not a mere nobody in Germany. I was a world-class swimmer who was only left out of the Olympic team for political reasons – but that came later. I make no bones & tell you, I was a fervent believer in the Fatherland. I was young, an idealist. We all were. Everyone saw, you had to be blind not to see, how much better off Germany was in every way. And the fun, excitement – marches, drums, flags, singing & torchlight, the feeling of being all in this new thing together, I was swept off my feet, it was quite unimaginably thrilling. A sporty young blonde like myself, from humble origins, who married the right person, could move in high glamorous circles.

What can I say? It was normal. I do not now like to see men in uniform, even the Sally Army gives me the creeps, or the Remembrance Day procession along the seafront. But the men in uniform were dashing. I did not like Jews. That was normal too. We took that in with our mothers' milk. I truly felt they would be happier in Madagascar where it was proposed to resettle them. But imagine my shock when my good friend Elisabeth was arrested. My friend – I can still see her face white and pinched – she was dragged away without slippers on her feet, all bare on the cold pavement, & we never saw her again. I didn't actually believe she was a Jew. Imagine your Jenny being taken away by Swansea Police, just for being English, that was the shock.

I protested. It has always been my way to speak my mind, you know that. You will believe that at least. I shouted my mouth off. I was a mere girl but I was a German girl with honour.

Into her rhythm now, Issie broke into a strenuous crawl. She powered into areas of deeper cold. When she paused to take breath, a sailing boat was gliding out from the far shore, its red sail a stiff triangle.

Oh my darling, this is all spilling out in the wrong order, it is my upset. Owen has just come in with a cup of tea and a shortbread biscuit & asked whether I really want to write all this to you?

I must. I should begin with your father. Paul Dahl was not all that bright 'up top' as Tada would say, but gorgeous, blond, vain as you like; a well-off schoolmaster's son – he was considered a prime catch. I was mad about him. Remember I was only 17 when I married, a child, & I have to admit I was pregnant with you. My husband rose rapidly in the Security Police, they all had blood on their hands & he got quite keen on the killing side of things. Took the racial theory of the time as gospel. When you were born, he was all over you. His golden girl, his angel, his blonde darling. Even though you were not a boy, which he was counting on. But you were not a blonde. Your hair as you became a toddler was almost black and I had to dye it. What is one to do? I take action. Namely, I bleach the child's hair, for its own good. You could not fault me there. But he spots the roots, you see, he spots the roots. You were his throwback, some Slav ancestor on the mother's side, but then he blames it on me! Me! My pedigree was pure back to 1711, so I must have been playing about, mustn't I? Can you imagine me throwing my eye at another man, no, of course not. Would I lower myself, would I stoop?

Our marriage was in trouble anyway, we women were just brood mares to them. I wanted some fun, & I had a great sporting gift which I wished to exercise for my country. Oh no, your father didn't like that one bit. Or that men fell for me (how could I help it? I ask you). There was, for instance, a sporting journalist from America, Fred Katcinski, such a hoot, a diversion from all our seriousness.

Your father got the idea that you were Fred's bastard, we quarrelled frightfully & made it up (at this time I remember the Quantz man who was thick with my husband, coming in, all very suave, helping to patch things up. I do beg you keep away from these people, they are not our sort. He had a dull little wife, I forget her name, & a child always grizzling. The husband was a terrible womaniser which Paul was not – he worshipped me.)

The red sail of the boat glided across Issie's eye and lost itself in one of the islands, to emerge, only to go into renewed hiding again. The sail's irregular rhythm mesmerised Isolde, as she breasted the sloshing waves.

I need hardly say you were not Fred's. He was a sweetie, & yes, he did once make a pass. He was tall & stooping, with a slouch & a shock of floppy hair. Giggled like a girl. Took me out on the razzle when Paul was away. What was I supposed to do? Sit indoors changing your nappies & cooking Wurst? We had Maria to do that. There was nothing in it, it was just fun. We were all mad about the American movies – Hollywood, Garbo, Chaplin – and the Amis gave us girls a thrill precisely because we lived such serious, idealistic lives.

Big mistake to tell Paul about the pass Fred made at me, it just slipped out. He went ranting up & down like an opera-star. Said, How shall I ever know Isolde's mine? The man's a Pole or a Rusky. I said, Don't be ridiculous, he's American. He said, They're all Yids & niggers & Slavs etc, etc. That was the level of his thinking. Now I'd got far more cosmopolitan since being in Munich, I could see farther than his nose even if he couldn't. At first I was defiant, then he began to strike & maltreat me, divorced & threatened to denounce me. I would have been put in 'protective custody', that was what they called it, so my pal Ingeborg helped us get out of Germany. I still dream of the official asking us for *Dokumente*.

You see now why I have kept all this from you, Isolde. My hand is shaking as I write. I was young & headstrong in those days, you remind me of myself.

Tiring, Issie began to flounder, churning a furrow through the water. She turned for home. Always she had been aware of Renate's power to protect her, swimming the Gower. Nobody else's mother had such strength. She had taken her on her back as a tiny child, Issie's thin arms lightly clasping her mother's neck, while bucking waters flashed past, like a dream.

I'm sorry you should have such a filthy father but you did & it can't be helped. When you were bad as a child I was disturbed because I feared to see him in you. I would correct & discipline you more than the Welsh children were corrected. Your cousins were brought up, according to my notion, in a sloppy way, whereas you were often smacked – you remember, no doubt – & no doubt you blame me for that too & think me a harsh unloving woman, which is why you adore Auntie Margiad & her eternal yakking, which drives me round the bend, though she means well. The Welsh are a sentimental lot.

You and I were never at home, we had to be each other's home. We were Category B 'Enemy Aliens' in the war. Interned on the Isle of Man. With one suitcase each, we were escorted to Cardiff under armed guard, with bayonets. Imagine that – a woman & a child of 7. What did they think we were going to do, you and I? Mine Cardiff Docks?

The crowd on Cardiff station pelted us with rubbish & called us foreign whores, you in your little green velvet coat, with your grave face saying 'Why are they shouting & throwing those nasties, Mama?' So much for good British justice, we might as well have been in Germany. I pointed this out to Dame Joanna Whatnot, camp commandant at Port St Mary, when she forbade us to wear trousers, can you believe it – wretched battle-axe. I & another Renate also imprisoned there said how can you do this to innocent refugees? Things did improve & I think they were sorry. The worst of it was, we were put in with Jews & no distinction made & although I was not offended by it, I think the Jewish family was. I told them about my protest over Elisabeth but something in my manner sickened them: it is still there & when I see you shrink from me in dislike or embarrassment, that is my cross.

As she turned on her back to get her breath, the welter chucked Issie from side to side, like trivial flotsam. Her limbs were leaden. She ploughed her way back towards the petty England of the school; the inexplicable Germany of her mother's fatherland; the blue-eyed viciousness of her father; and the two Quantzes.

Tada is quite well, he has come in again & said your Auntie Lennie is here. I do ask you darling to steer clear of the Quantz man & keep to your own kind. There must surely be some nice English company rather than these foreigners? They are foreigners now; we do not belong over there. Tada has been a rock to us, our life-line, a good man, who puts up with me because he loves me & loves you because you are his child.

It has all come tumbling out.

I sit back in the chair & look out through the window – the sea, the headland, white fluff of cloud – & I think to myself, 'I am not the woman I was.' It all seems crazy & unreal, a mad dance someone else got involved in – I am not that person any more. I could tear this up but I think the time has come & beg with tears your understanding & to go on loving me.

Issie's skin was scalding cold, covered in a dark flush like a rash. She dragged the weight of herself up the sand. Probably about to be sick.

Owen had used to stand at the edge of the sea with the blue bathing robe and a towel thick as a blanket, holding it out when she trotted from the surf, wrapping it round, saying, *Come on now, there's my beauty*. She scrubbed the towel to and fro over her back and flanks, teeth chattering. Owen not really Tada. Owen, just some friendly chap who happened to be around.

Enemy aliens. Amongst Jews on the Isle of Man. She had asked Renate *Are we Jews, Mummy?* on the Mumbles train, chuffing through Oystermouth from Black Pill: how the great beak snapped then, how the claws came out.

She wormed her way into her slacks, having to wriggle the chilled, not-quite-dry legs into them, legs like hams of pork, the wrong colour, as if they'd been skinned. Her cold fingers were puckered, clumsy. Sopping hair sluiced water down the neck of of her sweater.

Sins of fathers visited or not visited on sons? Pastor at chapel going on and on, hands waving so that you feared for the flowers perched either side of the communion table. Yes or no, visited on sons or not? On daughters?

One possible father, bloody and brutal. Black uniform, marching by torchlight, his seventeen-year-old bride baying with the mob. Another possible father a Polish American; a tall slick guy, giggling like a girl, lounging around on a barstool. And Tada, self-apologetic, with no claim at all, answering, *Well, there you are then!* indiscriminately to any question in lieu of *yes* or *no*.

And now she could remember spying on Owen and Renate in the gap between door and jamb, and hearing her mother saying, *Silver fox. I got it dirt cheap from Mrs Levi. She didn't need it where she was going. Oh God, oh God.*

And there sat Tada, masticating on nothing, swallowing draughts of his own saliva. He digested obscene absurdity into the stuff of his own normality. Was that capitulation or difficult mercy? Did he lie down as a human bridge between ethical worlds and offer his body for Renate Dahl to stagger belligerently across? Or just kowtow? Anything for the quiet life?

The spy had crept back upstairs and slid her hand between the coats in the wardrobe. The silver fox was cool, hanging among violet mothballs on strings. Pelts stitched together from long-shed lives. Renate didn't wear it nowadays.

Ostjuden, Renate had once said, shut up behind wire fences, sharing quarters. *East European Jews. Of course they can't help their parrot noses.*

Issie remembered looking for parrots.

A welling up of anguish now, as she bundled her clothes together. *Mutterseelenallein*. Even in her mother's keeping, she had been *mutterseelenallein*. The hungry wolf licks the whelp in its lair, as if to devour it.

She thought of the silver fox fur, still in the viscera of the wardrobe at home. *Where is the ash that once wore you?* Horror came to you clothed in the comfort of animal skins; and a mouth puckered in lipstick which stained your cheek red; but she herself was innocent of any such fur coat, and wore no cosmetic mask, and though the *Fräulein* was such a battleaxe, and the kids had to strip down in rows and crawl up and down the corridor, she and Wolfi had nothing to do with it.

Daylight was coming into question by the moment. The hut was a sour-smelling chamber of shadows. She opened the door, hoisting her shoulder bag, into a livid gloom: a storm on its way.

***

'I say,' said Lynne at table, 'you all right, Taf? You look quite green.'

'I went swimming. Got really cold.'

'Swimming in this weather. You must be off your rocker!'

Jugs of hot chocolate were placed on the table by the cooks, who executed small bows, with heel-clicking motions to Mr Patterson, who did not usually attend the tea-time free-for-all. The noise from the children was correspondingly muted.

'Shall I pour for you, *Herr Doktor* Headmaster?' asked the cook.

Patterson looked gratified at the honorary doctorate. 'No indeed, I'll do the honours,' he said democratically. Lifting the heavy jug, he vouchsafed the jest that he would 'play mother'. 'The swimming season is over, Miss Dahl. Pity really since you're so jolly keen, which is what we like to see. Pass this to Miss Dahl, would you, Miss Brierley? No, no, the pool is out of bounds. It will silt up and we will dredge it again next spring. Herr Poppendick locks up the huts and we can devote ourselves to our winter sporting pursuits – football, netball . . . '

Issie drank the hot sweetness, huddled in sweaters, her back against a radiator. The chill seemed to have lodged within, in marrow or liver, but as the chocolate slipped down, its hold loosened. Lassitude stole over her limbs and her mind lapsed into a conscious swoon in which the buffeting of the storm on the windows took precedence over the head's monologue.

'Well, Miss Dahl?'

'Oh, sorry, Mr Patterson, what was that?'

'I was enquiring as to whether you were fond of hockey. You've got the build for hockey.'

'Oh no.' She could not help staring as if he were mad.

'Netball then?'

'No – I don't much care for team sports.'

Not like team sports! Mr Patterson was aghast. How could this be? Nothing (Mr Norman would back him up) was more refreshing or character building than a good game of football or cricket and, for young ladies, netball, hockey or stoolball. John Norman nodded vigorously. Without cricket, Patterson wanted to know, eyebrows twitching with passion, how could we have had the supreme felicity of the Ashes? No cricket, no Commonwealth of Nations. Values of decency and fair play, valiant striving, good losers...

'How right you are, Mr Patterson,' purred Lynne. She adjusted the magenta scarf at her throat; admired her fingernails. Patterson also gazed at the painted nails, distaste spiced with fascination. These were hardly a sportswoman's hands.

'I hadn't realised you were so keen.'

'Well, only theoretically. It was never my – you know – thing,' she confided, with a smile of silken cynicism. 'I leave that to you big strong men. I don't try to compete.'

Patterson approved the sentiment. 'Even so,' he reflected, 'sportswomen can shine in their sphere. They don't have to compete with men. After all, you don't match a stallion against a... gazelle.'

'Quite,' agreed the gazelle. 'It might win. No, only joking.' She popped a piece of coffee cake into her mouth and winked at Issie. 'You don't usually honour us with your company at tea, Mr Patterson.'

'I thought I would, you know. Just to pass on some gen. Our marching orders are confirmed,' he told them. 'The school's to be handed back to the Germans in 1959. Well, we knew it was on the cards, didn't we? The Pioneer Batallion has taken over Dönitz's 'Trout' HQ over the way; soon our dear old Confessor's will be a school for German naval officers again. Jerry has proved he can be trusted. With our help. Sad for us. End of an era. Picturesque spot. I shall miss my cadets. And the end of conscription. Very bad step in my opinion: beginning of the rot. A taste of army discipline makes men of them. Still. We have done our duty – ambassadors in our modest way for democracy. Bit of a rum do for you, Miss Dahl – you've only just arrived and you're already told to up sticks.'

Susan rushed in with, 'But we've jobs promised us, haven't we?'

'Oh yes. But for me, it's carpet slippers, I fear. Old warhorse out to grass.'

'Oh, Mr Patterson,' crooned Lynne, 'you couldn't be called *old*.'

Issie watched the stegosaur leer. After years of annoying Patterson with her unsoldierly qualities, Lynne's mind was on her references.

'What will happen to all the helmets and swords – the Dönitz collection?' Issie asked. 'All the things you got out of the lake? I mean, whose are they really?'

'This is, er, moot,' said Patterson, reddening, and coughing into his hand. 'I have asserted a right to these objects but so, unfortunately, has the Ministry of Defence.'

Fools' gold, thought Issie. Of no more worth than the combings of a head, the nail clippings of dead men. How would poor old Patterson spend his retirement without his superior kit for toy soldiers? His sundering from these grave-goods brought her a fleeting spiteful pleasure. Her skull remembered its coronation with the iron helmet fetched from the lake.

'We shall see,' said Patterson philosophically. 'And by the way, I thought we ought to make this Christmas something truly festive. Since we are to go south and evacuate our northern so-to-speak stronghold, I think we might team up our English youngsters with the German children, carol concerts round the Christmas tree. There's an orphanage near here, charming children, well-behaved, you might have seen them out walking? All remarkably blond. Odd thing that. Anyone else noticed it?' Patterson looked round the table. 'No? Well, you take a close look next time. Hardly a dark child amongst them. Over Malente way they live. It would be a Christian thing to do, I think, to share the season with them. Show that all hard feelings are in the past. I have asked our good piano teacher, Mr Quantz, to devise a programme of carols.'

'*Non Angli sed Angeli*,' said the padre.

'I beg your...?'

'Pope Gregory when he saw the fair-haired English slaves,' repeated the padre beaming. 'Not Angles (the tribe) but Angels. Play upon Latin words, so dazzled was he by the beauty of these young exiles...'

Issie stared, with a sensation of unreality, as if she were not present at the table, an island in the commotion of grey-cardiganed children. The clatter of plates as they were passed along the rows, the wind's hand shaking the windows with a dull booming sound.

'I was always an angel at our nativity play at primary school. Never a shepherd.' Lynne preened herself.

'The reason there are so many blond kids around,' Issie burst out, 'is that the dark ones were culled – killed. It would have spoken better for the Pope's morals, surely, padre, if he could have taken to ugly, snotty, urchins and called them God's angels? The ones that are hard to love and easy to bully?'

Uneasy silence circled the table, as if they could not believe their ears. One of their number had compromised herself with an outrageous solecism. They were ashamed on her behalf and took the English way of covering up for her bad taste with politeness. Issie felt eyes making swift reappraisal of her own dark looks and marking her aberration as the sour grapes of a disaffected brunette.

Patterson hemmed. He rose, scraping his chair, shaking out the wings of his black gown sleeves and clasping his hands before him. The school followed him with a diminishing roar.

'For what we have received,' the padre intoned.

'May the Lord make us truly thankful,' the three

hundred and fifty lambs bleated.

'My dear Miss Dahl,' said Patterson, accompanying the black sheep out of the refectory. 'I do think we have to call the past the past and carry on into the future.'

'I don't suppose we have much option.'

'No one is more disgusted than myself at Nazzy atrocities. Believe me. But we've put the worst scoundrels away or hanged them.'

'Have we?'

'One or two may have got through the net,' he allowed. 'That may be. But no more than a handful. There will always be drawbacks to a non-totalitarian system of justice. On the whole we've purged the bad apples, set Jerry on his feet, and given him the means to start again. I personally,' he confided, bending to her ear, 'shall never particularly take to Jerry. But Jerry is our ally now. So I think it would be nice if you and Miss Williams would arrange matters between you at the orphanage. After all, you speak the lingo like a native. I do hope you are happy with us, Miss Dahl? That you feel at home in our little community?'

It rose in her mind to mention Rachel to him. She drew breath to say, *Yes, I've been made welcome enough but I'm worried about the bullying. There's one child in particular . . .*

She could and should have said it, and perhaps he would have heeded her fears, for he was by no means a bad man and believed in cricket.

13

Eutin and Lake Plön, 1958, 1945

'The admiral attacked his own beans, you know.'

Michael, scanning the newspaper in the bar, was arrested by the voice behind him. He had watched them arriving, the businessmen and bureaucrats, in coachloads or in limousines, overflowing from the accommodation at the *Blütehof* to pack out local lodging houses. Some had been billeted on local residents, who were recompensed with a largesse which raised spirits to an almost tangible degree. Michael experienced a complex sense of déjà vu, for persons he recognised with a spasm of recoil had transformed themselves, and been transformed, by age, good living and adaptation to prevailing codes of respectability. Their bearing and manner defied recognition; they had been abolished and reconstructed according to new dimensions. Many had tended to swell through years of good eating to a gravid corpulence, accreting layers of flesh which sank their old selves until just the eyes peeped out. They wore their acquired girth with geniality, whether august or modest, tendering it to public view, as if it were evidence of unimpeachable character. The group at the table behind him was unknown to Michael and Heini, who had paid little attention to its subdued chat until the matter of the admiral's beans had arisen.

'Yes, really. And Schirach hacked the heads off his prize blooms.'

'Why would he do that?'

'Apparently Funk was made to remove his sunflowers – they were interfering with the observation of the prisoners – so he beheaded them in protest. The chief decimated his beans in solidarity.'

'I hear the admiral was a great gardener in Spandau.'

'A genius. Brilliant with tomatoes: could grow forty or fifty on a plant – yes, really – and he tended them like children. You see, that is how it is with truly great men. Humiliate them, spit upon them, lock them up: the more they flourish. It was quite touching to hear about his tendance of that plot – how he loved planting lupin seeds, poked the holes with his finger, all planned out meticulously, and every day he would wait. And watch. In due time, the shoots would unfurl. Nature, you see, he said, was on his side. A very German thing, this. The British did not grasp it at all. And when he and Schirach sabotaged their own sunflowers and beans, the guards just gaped. The most precious things they had, they sacrificed. And started again.'

'A parable.'

The speaker, having paused to moisten his mouth with beer, joined in the general murmur of approval, saying, 'Absolutely. But of course they treated him barbarously. I said to Stricker, "This doesn't surprise me one bit." Stricker is a great apologist for the British. I said to him, "Did you know they had the admiral sweeping floors?" Naturally, this had not a jot of effect on the chief's morale. A naval officer is accustomed to spartan discipline.'

Heini stared straight ahead. He rolled his beer glass between his palms. Michael returned his newspaper to the table and fiddled among the wooden rods, selecting another. From the corner of his eye, he surveyed the group in the window seat. The monologist evidently counted for something in this group, for his know-all manner commanded deference. Something about him was queasily familiar. A well-built, tall type with pale, receding hair and no eyebrows to speak of, poor skin, well padded. As Michael returned to his seat, the man swivelled round, snared his eye in passing, signalled to the landlady with a raising of the eyebrow, and then fixed his gaze on Michael.

'Pardon me, but aren't we acqainted?'

'No, I don't think so.'

'Odd. Perhaps it will come back to me.'

Michael erected his paper as a wall between himself and the old comrades. Anyone examining that wall would have seen that it was quivering. An artery in his neck beat irregularly.

'... grow tomatoes myself, or rather my wife does. Got a fine crop the year before last ...' '

... grand old man ... never lost his dignity, never ...'

'... lives near Hamburg, convenient for Kiel and the U-boat reunions ... simple apartment, nothing ostentatious, but still one knows when one is in his presence, that one is in The Presence. That sort of thing has an intangible quality... deeply moving.'

'... Elected Successor ... laying on of hands, almost ...' A voice breathless with romantic reverence: a voice venerable itself, belonging to the elderly gent with a distinguished head of silver hair, who went on, shaking with emotion, '... our model of courage, loyalty and chivalry'. Faltering, the silver voice went silent. *Chivalry*, *Ritterlichkeit*, thought Michael. He had not heard the formulae for many years. Quaintness strove with a menace at once banal and operatic – a reanimated corpse raising its head from a Wagnerian lake, to the applause of businessmen.

'But of course,' went on the loudmouth who might have been (could it be?) Paul, grappling the conversation back into his own control. 'He quietly considers himself still to be the sole legitimate Head of State and I believe he would accept the position, were the Old Fox to pass away.'

'... love this place. The landscape. Brings back so much. You too? The lakes.'

'... good times ...'

'... nothing like them ...'

'... comradeship, possibly the only human bond that lasts for ever. Are you sure I don't know you?' asked Paul Dahl suddenly. 'I pride myself on seldom forgetting a face. The kind of mind you need in business. Your name is on the tip of my tongue. Help me out.'

'Neumann,' replied Michael.

'Uh *huh*. Right you are.' The Old Comrades were cautious and politic: ever vigilant to protect another's changed identity.

Michael examined the vacuum-cleaner magnate with a forensic stare. Heini half rose but Michael laid a hand on his coat cuff, quietly drawing him down. His own trembling had subsided. Like a spider whose reflex is to curl into a ball of vigilance, he became only an eye. Paul's skin that had been so fine and transparent was a rougher hide, stained with a rosy rash of what might be eczema. The fair hair had receded and dulled. Paul's piercingly blue eyes were magnified and blurred by horn-rimmed spectacles, so that his gaze seemed perpetually thrown forward. The effect was at once interrogative and vague. He looked more intelligent but less outstanding, a man capable of fading into any crowd. Nor was his bearing martial. Young Narcissus had adopted in middle age a prosaic gentility in a well-cut but well-worn suit; his 'Old Comrades' tie appeared a sentimental token worn by a civilian whose mind was on the legitimate pursuit of wealth.

'Are you here on holiday?' Michael asked Paul.

'Old sailors' reunion.'

'You say you were a *sailor*?' Michael choked.

'Indeed, yes. I was a humble junior officer stationed on Sylt when the end came. I have a feeling for the dear old peninsula.'

'Fortress Schleswig-Holstein,' Michael could not resist giving the crazed label the diehards had stuck on the area as the *Reich* perished. With the idea that it could somehow be broken off the mass of Germany and floated out into the Baltic and North Sea, with Denmark attached.

'Look, let me buy you a beer,' said Dahl. His wary smile broadened. 'Come and join us, Mr Neumann. No, do, I insist. My friends... Mr *Neumann*.'

Curiosity overcame Michael. He picked up his coffee, winked to the rigid Heini, and pulled up his chair to the table of old comrades. He was aware of his friend Joachim at the *Stammtisch* pondering the group with phlegmatic eyes. And not only Joachim: Michael's antennae were alert to the twitching of others in the room. Men with turned backs held listening postures, the whole room tuned to the murmurous group he was joining.

So that was where Paul had dived to, the navy, a safer refuge than the army for one who had so distinguished himself at Minsk.

'And how is life treating you?' Paul asked. One saw in the light from the window a landscape of pocking and scarring, tiny pits of shadow, like miniature craters.

'I teach piano.'

'Ah. My own calling is vacuum cleaners.'

'Indeed.' Michael sipped his cold coffee. He repressed a deep-rooted grin. 'That is where the future lies, I'm told.'

'Certainly. Find out what the housewife wants and give it to her. We accord a central role to the wishes of the consumer. And then to getting the message over to her that the thing she wants is available and just waiting for her to come along. The export market looks especially promising at the moment. You may be interested to know that our factory and offices are located in old naval warehouses in Kiel?' On he went. And on. Now he was describing with a zealot's conscientiousness the unique characteristics of some filter mechanism in one of their newest models. This, it seemed, was in itself a technological miracle, destined to make a contribution to the consolidation of Germany as a commercial world power. Evidently, Michael thought, glazed, his childhood friend had turned into a first-class bore.

Hadn't he always been a first-class bore? From passion about racial hygiene, how far was the step to devotion to dust sucking?

The silver-haired gentleman, while giving every sign of attention to Dahl's account of his new calling, signalled to the landlady for a beer for Michael, who shook his head.

'No, really.'

'Forgive me,' said Paul. 'I have not introduced my associates.' Names, naval affiliations (bogus or otherwise) and present professions were supplied. Here around the table at Eutin, above the blue-green lake, Michael felt enmeshed in a network of . . . why did the word come to him, rather than 'comrades', marriages? A web of intermarriage. They were corporately married, one to another, for life. But unlike the insecure bondings between man and wife, this grand male marriage consummated and bonded in blood could never be sundered. *True to the grave*, Paul Dahl had affirmed all those years ago here at Plön, in his drainpipe boots and the black glamour of his uniform, medal at his throat. Not so many years ago, come to that, Michael reckoned up: thirteen years, yet what an external alteration. And what similarity. He had sloughed his skin, as the times dictated. Behind Himmler's darling came into focus the altar boy with the white-gold hair. Isolde Dahl – was she really his child? Was that conceivable? He stared, trying to see Isolde in that face. He thought he did. But then again . . . A cold faintness came over Michael; he wiped the palms of his hands on his handkerchief.

'If I am right,' Paul was saying, 'you are one of us?' He waited for no answer but ploughed straight on. 'You may like to come along to the grand reunion. It should be a moving occasion. We are expecting notable guests. I think you would be interested, Mr Neumann. And we mourn, you know, our glorious naval dead. Now, if you will excuse us. This is not merely an occasion for old chums to get together but also an opportunity to do business. We have engagements to keep.'

Michael remained seated in precisely the same position when the group had departed, watched by every drinker out of the corner of his eye.

The door closed behind them. No one said a word, yet the air was alive with competing signals. Unnatural stillness and strain gave way to shufflings and coughs. Joachim yawned convulsively; held and kneaded his stubbly jaw, still yawning.

'*Scheiße*,' said a young farmer, and made a motion of spitting.

Eyes met eyes; glanced away.

'Pity about those beans,' murmured Michael to Heini.

Heini shook his head mournfully. 'Tragic,' he agreed and they drank to the slaughter of the admiral's beans.

'It was for you he suffered in Spandau,' a voice rebuked them, high and nasal, raw with righteous indignation. 'You Judases. Yes, that's right, go on, mock. Martyrs are mocked.'

'Where would martyrs be without mockers?' enquired Michael.

'What?'

'Never mind.'

'Karl Dönitz was a simple sailor,' said the older farmer. 'He did his duty.'

'*Scheiße*,' repeated the younger farmer, as if he acknowledged himself to be master of one single word, but in the application of that one word claimed infallibility. There was sudden, deafening uproar. Men were on their feet, bellowing.

'That old shit,' bawled Heini, 'him and his *Jagdkommandos*. Hanged my best mate from a tree. If you want to know about martyrs: Günther was a martyr.'

'And we know why! Damn deserter! And we know you too. Another coward. Pity they didn't string you up too, you filthy queer.'

Heini took a pensive mouthful of beer. It confirmed his reputation as a quietist committed to the turning of the other cheek. He looked down, swilling beer around his mouth, then spat straight into the red face of his accuser. A small, muscular figure in late middle age, the older man went for him. He took Heini by the lapels, rushed him against a wall, and smashed punches, right, left, into his nose. Heini's 'Oof' sounded oddly like a ball deflating. Then again: 'Oof.' He reeled sideways, blood streaming from his nose. The landlady shouted for her husband and let forth a torrent of *Plattdeutsch*. Joachim and the young farmer were on their feet. Michael lunged for Heini's assailant; and as he did so was punched in the kidneys from behind. Glasses smashed; a table was upended. Under Michael's stagger, the floor keeled like a deck.

As suddenly as it had begun, the mayhem ended. The farmer kicked at Heini, struggling up, and left.

Michael helped Heini to his feet. He looked dazed, fingered his nose.

'Christ, do you think it's broken?'

'Not if you can straighten it. Let's see,' said Joachim. He took Heini's nose between finger and thumb and clicked it straight. 'There you are. Be fine.'

Heini dabbed his split lip with the wet pad of a handkerchief.

'Sure, I deserted too,' said the young farmer. 'As soon as old Dönitz's tinny voice came over the radio, "the fight must go on," me and my pals were out the window of those barracks, you couldn't see us for dust, and then we laid low in fields for days. The farmers told us, "watch out for the naval police, lads, they're worse than the SS", and then one day a jeep stopped near us with four Englishmen and they were singing, wearing webbing belts. Singing! Webbing belts! We went crazy with joy. I'll never forget it. There among the dock leaves. "Webbing belts!" we yelled. "Webbing belts have conquered the leather belts!" Laughing, crying, rolling around in the dirt. We made it.'

'Except for Günther,' said Heini. 'So nearly made it, that was the ridiculous thing. Only just seventeen. Seventeen.'

'I can't be doing with this,' chivvied the landlady. 'Not on my premises.'

She bent grumbling with a dustpan and brush, to clear the shards of glass.

'If people want to talk politics, I wish they would do it somewhere else,' she complained. 'I don't hold with it here and neither does my husband. I've never taken sides.' She straightened up and addressed the drinkers. 'In all my life, never taken sides. I've seen them come and seen them go. We never have trouble here, it's peaceful and that's how we want it. I can't be doing with fighting and mess in my nice clean house.'

Who did she remind Michael of, as she went on grumbling, her tone of resignation contradicting her words? Effi, it was the self-styled apolitical Effi.

***

Framed in the open doorway, Isolde Dahl was sitting in the window seat, legs drawn up under a long, soft skirt of some russet material, sombre except where it caught the slanted light in auburn swathes. In that double frame, of the window within the door, Isolde seemed distanced like a woman made of paint, someone you could never reach through and touch. That very distance urged you to reach, impossibly, in. Wolfi was playing the cello. And she was listening.

Michael thought: *I saw your father today, miss.*

The thought weighted him with a burden of power over her. He had it in his grasp to crash a fist through the brittle, transparent walls of her fragile world and change it, and her, for ever.

Wolfi was playing an improvised version of the cello half of Brahms' Double Concerto. It was melancholy to hear it as a solo, lonely. The cello, bereft of dialogue, bore its mutilation as best it could; it cried out for a mate in a way Michael doubted the listening Isolde could comprehend.

Quantz kept watching. The Dahl girl's stillness was as complete as stillness could ever be. *We are made of motion*, he thought, *it never stops, even underground. Even in the grave motion never stops.* He saw Dahl, beautiful and thirty, coming toward him across the pit, striding in his boots, his finery bloodied. Smiling. Extending a hand in cordial irony as he marched on a shifting ground of Russian Jews, the dead and the dying. Ribs and fingers cracked and skulls tamped down under Dahl's heels.

Michael's insides shook, an influenza trembling that nauseated him so that he groped his way to a chair. His guts knotted. Speckles of Heini's nosebleed spotted his shirtsleeves and had dried on his wrist. He licked it off the skin and swallowed his friend's blood, his heart storming. The cello rose to its highest reaches, full and sensuous, for Brahms is testing its strength in the upper reaches here, and the instrument must soar in order to twin with the depths of the balancing violin; but the necessary violin was absent; the cellist out of his depth;

and the survivors said *Scheiße* in his mind's ear, but also *webbing belts*. Dahl still came walking forward over the crowding sea of shot bodies, smiling.

Bottomless bestiality. And now this renovated Dahl with the pudgy hand saying, *I thought you were one of us*. But the landlady said, *No politics here, please*. And the little Pole he nearly had that day by the lake saying, *Mister, I will forget anything what I am told to forget*. And Wolfi saying, *You knew, your generation knew it all and did nothing, you were in it up to your necks. You could have done something but you did nothing*. And Maria had offered the slender body which was her sole currency, in exchange for chocolate, and all he took was the cream of her tongue's lispings, and left her there to live or die.

All this while Isolde did not stir. Like a model for a portrait so real that it appears to breathe, the woman in the double frame had a quality of listening inwardness. Her attention was concentrated in her ears and eyes. She was Wolfi's. Wolfi was hers. Michael could hear his son repeat this over and over through his cello.

A pearl of light picked out Isolde's moist underlip, relaxedly open as she listened. He could see the slow, unconscious rhythm of her breasts rise and fall in the soft wool sweater. A tawny scarf was draped round her neck, silken and cool. Around the window the walls were packed with umber shadow but restless autumn boughs outside were fraught, beat about, a halo the colour of dried blood.

Her father's boot squelched through blood, slithered. He smiled a carrion smile.

Looking at Isolde's dreamy stillness failed to calm Michael. He stared through the doorway at a face nakedly open to view and yet illegible, to hunt down resemblances. Wolfi took after Effi, he read the resemblance daily, like a chastening haunting, a refusal on Effi's part to turn away mercifully into the past and leave him be. But was Isolde anything like her father? Or was Dahl not her father at all? Her striking colouring, dark curls and eyes, flushed cheeks, mocked the comparison. Still, there might be something. There might. At this angle, the wide oval of the face was narrowed, seemed longer, its expression of intensity pronounced. A dangerous girl. A girl who might have been called *konsequent*: no question but that, like her parents, once she limpeted on to an idea, she would act upon it, carry it through to the bitter end.

But whatever it was that she aroused in Wolfi also leapt in Michael. She came like a honeyed gift culled from the bitter past, seeming to ask for touch. The textures of her clothes repeated the plea, or invitation, of the contours that moulded them.

Wolfi fumbled a handful of notes; muttered, 'Blast it. I'm not actually much good on this thing.'

Isolde laughed. 'Go on,' she said. 'I wouldn't have noticed it was wrong if you hadn't told me.'

'You have a go.'

She swung down from the window seat. Wolfi came into view, and said, 'Part your legs then.'

Michael's face burned.

He could not stop himself watching, though it felt indecent. His son saying in that casual, tender way, *Part your legs then*. As if to make love to a wife after years of a good marriage, to whom you could say anything, in that tone, and be lovingly received. Which she did, accepting the cello gravely, carefully, taking the body of honey-gold wood, between spread legs, and the bow in her left hand. She leant the cello against her shoulder while she fingered the horsehair of the bow and glanced into Michael's son's eyes, saying, 'It feels so alive.'

Feels so alive, thought Michael. *The tail of a dead horse*. The room seemed full of the furniture of death, upholstered in hide and stuffed with down.

'Hold the bow like this... that's it... and just rest the cello in the other hand, we'll start with open strings. Now if you angle the bow, darling, and draw it across them... yes... that's lovely.'

Past Wolfi's kneeling figure, Michael could read her face's wonder. She played the open strings again. Wolfi reached over and created a vibrato for her. Her spread legs enclosed both cello and lover, seen from the perspective at which Michael viewed them, the soft stuff of the skirt fringing their one shape at either side.

'I love it, I totally love it. Will you really teach me?'

'Of course. You'll be better than me in no time at all, not that that's saying much.'

'So you think I'm a natural genius?'

'Definitely. And we'll have lots of child prodigies for our children.'

'Oh, I don't think so, Wolfi,' Michael heard Isolde say, with a clear rebuke. 'I'm not thinking of having children.'

Wolfi sat back on his heels. 'Well, not immediately, but . . . I thought all women wanted children?'

'I don't. That's not what I want. I want . . . to live my life. *My* life.'

She's trouble, thought Michael. *She'll walk all over him and he'll love it.*

'Okay,' said Wolfi, good-naturedly. 'In that case I don't want them either. Where do you want to live, Issie? Had you thought? Not here,' he went on, and a harsh, hoarse note crept into his voice. 'I can't stand it here. Anyway, it's shutting. We can make a clean break. Can't we?'

She handed back the cello, relinquishing it with evident reluctance. Michael turned away and slipped out of the door, to avoid overhearing any further disparagement from his son; laying the sins of the world at his father's door, the most convenient and least original place in the world to dump them.

Lake Eutin, wind whipped, was a bilious mass of peaks and crests. Michael walked out on to the jetty where he and Wolfi kept their boat. It slapped to and fro, slamming tight its twin lines, the bottom awash with bilge. It couldn't ever be the same between himself and Wolfi. But that was natural, he reminded himself, and high time Wolfi set up for himself. He played out that rope in his mind, slackening its tension.

Above Malente the old men were gathering. That they should still have power to create a rough house in their wake in a local hostelry caused Michael no surprise. Everything he had seen that morning had raised to the surface tensions which were not so much alive as undead. That was it, the undead. Dahl was one of the undead. That rough rind, the crude hide of an animal that survives by virtue of coarseness and cunning through any and every adversity. But what if Michael went to the authorities and told them all he had garnered over the years about the *Blütehof*, its personnel and purposes? Suppose he unburdened himself to someone, unloading secrets picked up over the years?

The water surged beneath the jetty, spewing itself on the sand, doubling over and sucking back.

He almost laughed aloud. The naivety of it. For what was secret about the *Blütehof*? There was no one to tell who didn't already know. Schleswig-Holstein was a nest of rats, many of whom wore their badges facing out. Who believed that the *Blütehof* was the innocent orphanage it claimed to be? Appeal beyond Schleswig-Holstein then? But they were all in it together, it was common knowledge. Chancellery, Foreign Office, Economics, Transport, mayors and judges, presidents and civil servants . . . arachnids presiding at the centre of a network of networks, angling a line here, a strand there. They watched with cynical amusement the desecration of Jewish graveyards; old comrades' gatherings that turned into rallies with mass-murderers parading in field grey, thousand upon thousand, with banners, bands, songs and swastikas.

He re-entered his house noisily, so as to make sure of being audible. The young couple was sitting in opposite easy chairs when he entered the living room. The room seemed to be charged with the aftermath of their tenderness. The lovers had obviously bolted for their seats as soon as they heard him enter. He watched Isolde's full skirts subside. The sensation of their blissful intimacy crawled on the surface of his body, and he felt as if they were surreptitiously winking at one another behind his back, though he knew they were not.

'May I offer you coffee, Miss Dahl?' Saying her name seemed a way of threatening her; offering a naked blade to the blind.

'No, really, thank you, I should be getting back. Wolfi is going to teach me the cello.'

'That's nice. I met an old acquaintance in the village. He invited me to the *Blütehof*,' he taunted her, perversely, since she was blind to the blade. 'It seems they are having a naval reunion. A big do.'

Wolfi yawned. He traditionally yawned at any mention of the Navy. U-boat anecdotes prostrated him. The destroyer *Dresden* brought on suicidal boredom. Nostalgia for the sea made him itch. It had always worked out very neatly until now: Wolfi never wanting to know what Michael had never wanted to tell.

***

An hour later Isolde was on the telephone, her low voice shaking.

'Mr Quantz, the little girl I was telling you about – that I was worried about – she's missing. Would you come over? They want everyone out searching. I feel so awful. I knew there was something badly wrong, I should have spoken. Rachel, we were talking about her, your pupil, Rachel Goldman?'

'Hang on there. I'll be right over.'

***

He heard the matron say, in a tranquil, comfortable tone, sewing hooks and eyes on to a child's frock, 'She was a very dirty little girl. I tried, believe me, I tried. To take her under my wing. To show her the uses of soap and flannel. No good at all.'

'No good,' echoed *Fräulein*'s colleague. 'Still, you tried.'

'Of course,' said *Fräulein*, 'it was hopeless from the start. *They* could tell, you see, the girls, from the outset. Tell the difference.'

'What difference was that, Mrs Meier?' asked Michael. Looking into the common room for Isolde, he had found only the matrons having a thick gossip in *Plattdeutsch*. They looked mildly shocked at this incursion into their female zone. He tickled the old trout on her underbelly. And indeed her mottled hands reminded him signally of that fish. 'I presume you mean that she is an unhealthy example of world Jewry?'

Beneath the mask of powder, a flush spread. She bent to her sewing, dabbing the needle through the cotton with a thimbled finger, while she negotiated the possibility of irony. Michael smiled at her quandary.

'Was she indeed, Mr Quantz? That I didn't know.'

'Come, come, Mrs Meier. We are not so naive.' He slid down his fingers again, steadily, into the soupy green of polluted water, reaching round for her belly. 'A Jew can always be smelt,' he whispered in *Plattdeutsch*. 'Or even a half-Jew. A quarter-Jew. The bad blood overcomes the good. Aren't I right?'

'Certainly, this girl gave off a bad smell,' she agreed, not quitting her cover. 'The English are less than particular about these things – either that, or they pretend for good manners' sake not to notice. A pity for all concerned.' She put down the frock on her lap, needle between thumb and forefinger. 'Cleanliness is everything, I think you will agree?'

She put this proposition to Michael with banal finality. Then stared, and they all stared, balefully, as if through a compound eye, hoping to drive him off. The moment was broken by the young matron from the boys' block, just entering, who said that it was dreadful for the little girl, she was sure she had been bullied, which was horrible, and nothing to do with Jews. All the new ones were bullied, stripped and doused in cold baths, dive-bombed in their sleep, their undergarments thrown out of the window and their tuck taken. Children could be so cruel and also sly, making it hard to intervene.

'She is no doubt hiding somewhere and will be found,' prophesied Mrs Meier. 'And a great fuss made of her. Quite rightly, Mr Quantz, for don't we read in the Bible of the prodigal son?'

'Pardon my obtuseness,' said Michael. 'But in what respect has this child been prodigal?'

'Well, obviously, in dirtiness. Pigsty behaviour. There you are, all ready for ironing.' She folded the pink-checked gingham dress with punctilious attention to alignment of sleeves and waistband, and laid it beside her, patting it, smiling lugubriously at Michael. 'I must now go and inspect the girls' beds and lockers, it is time, and I always do my duty to the best of my ability, on which Mr Patterson has been good enough to congratulate me, not that as a Christian one should boast. I merely mention it to reassure you, Mr Quantz, of my correctness in all things to do with my profession. In case you had any doubts, and I make no distinction between Protestant or Catholic, Gentile or Jew, or even, if there were any niggers here, niggers and white men, just to set your mind at rest. I am widowed and alone in the world. The Poles have my house and estates. The Russians have killed my husband and sons. But duty,' she asserted, standing tall on her high heels, 'duty is my all.'

It was an old stale tune. Its singsong came out from behind the stricken, stupid eyes like peepholes in her baggy face, with an odd edge, so that Michael seemed to see the child in the woman, learning by rote a rubric devised to serve in place of knowledge.

As he continued his search for Isolde, he saw the girls in their dormitories standing like soldiers by their beds. Hysteria was in the air. One roomful of girls was in full cry, chanting 'Kampong's gone! Gone Kampong!' It was a ritual slogan, dull and strained, which seemed to express not only cruelty but the sour taste of such cruelty.

'Cogs I have her cake at tea.'

'No, me. Me.'

'Me, I want it.'

'Don't be so mean,' a voice shrieked. 'You're disgusting, you. Rachel's lost, and you're after nicking her cake.'

There was a silence. Then, 'Of course she's not. She's just hiding. Kampong. Kampong.' But no one joined in and the chorus tailed off. A brawl broke out. Scuffles. A baying, which ended in a mass paroxysm of giggling while one girl cried. The children were silenced by braying orders. Inspection began.

'Anyhow, I'm having Kampong's cake, *so*!' came a final shrill.

'This is not,' said the duty-teacher, Miss Brierley, with a certain stately impotence, 'the behaviour of young ladies.'

The girls stood to attention beside their beds. Mrs Meier with Miss Brierley conducted inspection, collecting laundry and dealing out starched clean linen. Michael noted the military aspect of the scene. He might have been on board training again at Mürwik, the cadets having their kit inspected. Sonia with the frizzy hair and the spectacles who had the luxury of a corner bed gazed out of the window as the English teacher bossed the German matron, who hectored the English girls. He was struck by the expression on Sonia's intelligent face: not just absent-minded but absent. She had taken a leap beyond this exile. Like Rachel she was a promising musician, a sensitive only child and Quantz had seen her bullied too. But she had access to some other private dimension, proof against assault. Had taken shrewd leave, posting her soul way out of reach, beyond barracks and lake, like a letter on its way home; while somewhere out there the pariah Rachel was roaming lost.

14

Lake Plön, 1958, 1945

In waning light, Michael and Isolde combed the shore. Police and soldiers scoured the countryside, divers preparing to trawl the lake. The child's name was called and called until the air ached with 'Rachel'.

Isolde agonised to Michael. She knew she was to blame. She ought to have told Mr Patterson of the bullying and cruelty she was seeing; why in God's name hadn't she? They walked the shoreline in the direction of Malente. The lake beneath the darkening turquoise of the sky looked deadly cold. Michael didn't for a minute think Rachel would come to any harm, he told her. The child would show up in some hidey-hole, hungry and weepy, wondering at all the attention she had aroused. Or she would be picked up halfway home, having hitched a lift in a car headed south on the *Autobahn*, and would be quietly expelled from the school.

'She is a desperate child. I saw. I did nothing.'

'You can't blame yourself, Miss Dahl. You did everything you could. You alerted me. You stood up for her. Anyway, she's probably, as I said, halfway home by now, looking forward to a scolding and a fish and chip supper. Where is it her people are stationed? Hildesheim. Well, that's not so very far.'

'I hope so but I doubt it – she's such a hopeless little scrap, she can hardly keep her hair combed, let alone find her way south. It's a foreign country to her, Mr Quantz, isn't it? How could she find her way through a foreign country?'

It was strange to him how, when she'd appealed to him, turning to his age and experience for aid, the painful arousal had quietened. As they walked along side by side, she seemed more ordinary, naive and raw: almost, Michael thought, a banal young person. A nice, modern, rather uppity young person. With a gorgeous figure.

'You'd be surprised, Miss Dahl,' he said, 'how much initiative we can all call up in extremity. There are innumerable stories of children in the not so distant past who've found their way home across foreign countries, even across a continent. Rachel will have been far, far more terrified by her dear little friends here than by the open road. Truly. It's always our own people from whom we have most to fear.'

She darted him a funny, brooding stare. 'You think so?'

'Sure of it.' There had been the girl in the woods that time, looking for Poland. *Excuse me but how do I get to Poland, please?* As if blood and fire had shrunk continents. Just after he'd jettisoned all his medals in the lake, the little Polish girl had appeared out of the woods. How simple had been the sloughing of an old self. The medals went under, plop, plop, plop. So easy and so trite.

A back molar twinged and his stomach griped. He was tired after all the furore in the pub, fatigued and jaundiced. Michael underwent a customary dismay that at this moment and perhaps at every point in his life, his own minor pains should be more important than the major afflictions of others. But so it was. We jettisoned our medals. We turned our backs, looked to number one. And we learned to live with that, or rather, the carapace that hardened with years accommodated to it pragmatically, while on occasion the tender interior still started from such self-knowledge.

'Still, I should have told Mr Patterson,' Isolde was still going on relentlessly. It was like the skinny lads from the orphanage at Lübeck reciting the *Confiteor*, banging their chests like little drums with their right fists: *I have sinned, I have sinned*... a mindless rigmarole. 'I really should have told him. I was on the point of telling him and then for no reason – no reason I can really put my finger on,' she frowned, 'I... didn't. I let the opportunity slide.'

'Coincidence of timing,' Michael said. The canopy of trees above them darkened their walk to a green gloom. They were not really searching any more, just walking.

'My dad back home, Owen, used to say, *You can't take the world on your shoulder, girlie,*' Isolde said. 'I don't know how many times he said it.'

'And he was right. You can't. Common sense.' Michael thought, *I don't envy Wolfi this eternal chest banging*. It was beginning to get on his nerves.

'You think so?'

'Certainly.'

'Oh, so what are we supposed to do then, just lie down in rows and let the bastards steamroller us? You have to protest, Mr Quantz, don't you? Otherwise what is it all worth?'

'We may protest all we like, but who is listening?' *And my God*, Michael thought, *she is opinionated. How wearisome to come home to a female on her high horse in a continuous fuming state of mutiny.*

'We must have ideals. We must.'

'Oh, don't give me idealists. Idealists terrify me. Idealists are the worst of all.'

'I don't see that. That seems to me perverse, if you don't mind my saying so, Mr Quantz.'

She stumbled over a log lying in the way. It was growing dark and they were getting nowhere. He thought, *She has stopped thinking of Rachel. All she is concerned with is her own stupid virtue*. How arrogant these people of conscience were, boring the socks off you with their everlasting navel gazing and cant. And he thought, *The attraction and repulsion she exerts both come from my love for Paul. They don't apply to her at all.* He almost halted in his tracks at the recognition. His feeling for her was nothing but an anachronistic displacement. The tension in him slackened further like a boat's sails when the wind subsides. Odd; relieving, as if he'd been let off something.

'I don't mind your saying so, of course, but you have seen little of life as yet. Idealism is like milk, it doesn't keep. Believe me.'

He yawned. She tossed her head; positively flounced

along beside him. 'Should I believe you just because you're older than me, Mr Quantz? Did you believe everything your father told you?'

She and Effi would not have got on at all, he thought. Effi would have been horrified at this headlong straight talking. *Ill-bred*, Effi would have thought at this refusal of deference. *Too full of herself by half*. The two of them were walking so close, often brushing against one another, yet Michael felt the remoteness between their generations. He could never have suffered a woman with such a tongue. The recognition further released him from the eroticised image that had possessed him. He couldn't be bothered, hadn't the energy, he thought, to hurt her. And his love for Wolfi required that he stand back and hold his peace. Wolfi was the one human being to whom he had devoted himself. If he let go now, Wolfi would perhaps in course of time circle back. Perhaps.

'I think we should go back,' he said. 'She'll never have come this far.'

But, as he had intuited, Isolde was not thinking of Rachel. The mind begins at self, and it returns to self, he thought: the people it sees serve as mirrors along the way.

'Excuse me if I ask you something, Mr Quantz,' she said, 'since we're on our own.'

'Indeed.'

'Wolfi said,' and Michael heard her breath catch, 'Wolfi said, you knew my parents. Is that right?'

And she had put the sword back in his hand. She had bent her neck to the blade or offered to run upon it.

'Wolfi is remarkable for his facility in getting hold of the wrong end of the stick, absolutely remarkable, he should have a degree in it: I was merely hypothesising.'

There was a pause. He could hear the water slap and suck among the reeds, which rustled when the breeze gusted in a amongst them. The wild geese had all gone south. His stomach griped.

'Oh, so you don't, didn't, know my parents?'

'Hardly.'

Another pause. Not given herself to casuistry, Isolde was evidently finding it hard to deal with it in another.

But she stubbornly went on, 'So does that mean no?'

'You make take it as that. You must understand, with Wolfi – and Hansi, his good friend – they are reacting violently, and of course understandably, against the past; their world is full of real and imagined monsters and bugaboos.'

'So?'

'Just that. Wolfi took literally what was metaphorically intended.'

'So you're saying, Mr Quantz, that Wolfi is a fool?' she said quietly.

'Wolfi is no fool. But certain things are opaque to your generation. Shall we leave it at that, Miss Dahl?'

'Yes. Right. Only – my mother also mentioned a Quantz family. Actually.' Yet immediately she seemed to wish she had not mentioned her mother. She put her hand to her lips, as if to shush herself, to put away whatever admission had got out. She looked away; observed it was late, did he think they should call it a day? Then stood and listened. 'Whatever's that?'

'What?'

'Music. Sounds like a brass band. With full oompah.'

'It's their reunion up at the *Blütehof*, probably.'

'Let's just go and peek,' she said.

'Oh, I don't think so.' But she was bounding along the path and he followed. At the boundary of the *Blütehof* estate they paused. Brushing aside fronds of evergreen, Michael with a sudden stumbling shock found himself in the past. At intervals along the winding track to the *Blütehof* stood boys bearing flaming torches. Phalanxes of officers in *Wehrmacht* uniform, in naval full dress uniform, in air force blue, were moving between the larches, with swaying flags and standards, bright with medals, moving to drumbeat.

'Christ,' said Isolde.

Blond boys sang in piercing unison the 'Song of Youth':

Jugend ist Meer
Jugend ist Blut
Jugend ist Speer
Jugend ist Glut.

...Je heisser der Jugend
Stahlfeuerfluß
Desto härter formt sich
Der männliche Guß.

Hot youth tempering manly steel... the sick kitsch, with its call to eternal virility, fleetingly evoked in Michael a boyhood yearning to march free of the terrifying claims of tenderness.

'Hey,' Michael said to Isolde. 'No. Don't.'

For she was walking straight forwards, hands in pockets, without any attempt at stealth. Michael grasped her arm to restrain her. She wrenched it free.

'I'm going to see what this is.'

A band struck up, with a drum roll. Dogs barked, straining at the leash. She ran to the edge of the drive. Michael watched her go, with sinking heart: the skirts of her cream coat flapping as she ran, her hands still in her pockets, beret askew, as if in a casual hurry to catch a train. Michael had no option but to follow her. She was stationed beside one of the blond boys with a torch, speaking to him. The gangling lad, in leather shorts, with a scarf knotted round his neck, was visibly embarrassed by the interrogation but kept singing.

Karl Schmidt reached her before Michael.

'I do regret,' he was saying, 'this is a gentlemen only occasion. Old boys' reunion.'

'Really?' said Isolde, without budging.

'I hate to seem unchivalrous...'

'We're looking for a lost child.'

'I regret, I have seen no lost child.'

'What's going on up here?' Torchlight painted Isolde's face with flickering yellow. The last of the officers marched into the hall, their flags having been lowered and borne in before them.

'I *hate* to seem unchivalrous, but this really is an exclusive gathering. I shall have to invite you to leave.'

'What if I don't?'

'But I'm sure you will, my dear Miss Dahl.' Karl cupped her elbow in the palm of one hand, guiding her into the trees where Michael was standing. 'After all, you wouldn't want to spoil the occasion for a group of veterans, who rarely get the chance to meet. I mean, imagine you were at home and the... what shall we say... the veterans of the British Legion were having a get-together. Surely a young lady would not go thrusting herself in? Of course not. Now, Mr Quantz, do escort the young lady off the estate.'

'*British Legion?* You are kidding.'

Michael said, 'Come on, Miss Dahl, we've more important things to do than watch a pantomime.'

But Isolde took no notice. 'How do you propose to get rid of me, Mr Schmidt?'

Seeing her jutting chin, the trembling of her frame as she stood to her full height to confront Schmidt, Michael was visited by déjà vu: an athletic, belligerent woman standing up to her husband and being worsted.

'I will escort the young lady,' he intervened.

'I won't be escorted.'

And she sat plump down on the ground, folding her arms.

'Mr Quantz, we're expecting eminent visitors,' explained Schmidt swiftly, over her head, and looked at his watch, betraying embarrassment. 'They should be with us at any minute.' He spoke confidentially since Quantz, as a fellow male, however defective, must see things more rationally than a headstrong female.

'And another thing I want to know,' said Isolde, 'is why you only take blond children here? What is this, some kind of... stud farm, or what?'

She was winding herself up, Michael saw, into a distraught expression of hectic and inchoate pain. His heart suddenly went out to her in her turbulence. Out to the top of her beret set at a cocky angle, her cream coat, her arms defensively folded across her chest, the angry sulk on her mouth. It went out to the obstreperous child in her.

Karl Schmidt hunkered down, putting his face close up to Isolde's.

'The young lady's obsession with hair does not interest me. Just go,' he said quietly.

'Or?' She quailed.

'Or I will have you removed.'

'Oh, really?'

Michael thought, *But she's enjoying this, getting a kick out of it.* He marvelled at the adrenalin that overrode her rising panic. She went on, 'The British papers would be interested in all this crap you've got going on up here.'

'I wouldn't threaten if I were you.' Hauling her to her feet, Karl Schmidt snapped his fingers at a dark figure with an Alsatian dragging at a short leash. The animal's body surged forward, mouth spread. Then the handler set the dog loose and it bounded at her. Isolde yanked free. Crouching, she put out both hands; received the creature as it came snarling. Fondled its face authoritatively in both hands.

'Good boy, good boy then, have you come to see me?'

Bewildered under the vigour of her caresses, the dog slackened its jaws and allowed itself to be mastered. Panted as it burrowed the cold, wet ardour of its nose in her neck.

'Have you no respect for the dead?' Karl demanded of Isolde, with unfeigned indignation.

'For the *dead*? What do you mean, the dead?'

'It is for our drowned and murdered comrades that we meet. I am amazed that you should come barging in here, profaning a solemn gathering of men who have lost their friends.'

'Who are the dead?' asked Isolde, and her question eerily sang in Michael's mind, like wind in wires.

'They are all around us. The ancestors. They gave themselves for us. We see them again in the children.'

'What nationality are they then, the dead?'

She looked like a somnambulist, her eyes in the torchlight darkly inward. Michael heard once more the tuneless singing in the wires. Karl Schmidt stared, baffled. There was a purring of engines.

Michael said to him, 'I think your guests are arriving.'

In his quandary, Schmidt half turned, wavered, shrugged his shoulders and left them to it.

'Just let's go.' She was an impossible woman, Michael

thought, and marvelled. Once her jaw had set, the subtly intelligent heart was cancelled out. Down that road she would stampede, a one-woman herd, even if it led to a cliff edge. She stood beside him, looking pleased with herself for taming a security dog, while a man pure of scruple had hovered over her. But she knew nothing of his killings. Not knowing was the condition of her courage.

A fleet of limousines purred round the curving forecourt of gravel, drew up. Triangular flags flew from their bonnets. Out climbed the notables; a welcoming party swirled deferentially arond them. There was heel clicking, low-key hail fellowing. Michael recognised Globke, silky and urbane, dark-suited. Oberlaender. Admiral Dönitz in full dress uniform, his hat as large as his head, so that he seemed partitioned into black and white zones, was partly obscured by some fat fellow with a breastful of medals.

When shall we see one other again, comrades? The treble boys piped up the sea shanty like a choir of angels. Dönitz stepped out and looked cursorily round at the singing children, as they gave forth old men's songs, and nodded his pleasure.

Michael stood transfixed as the admiral appeared in the torchlight. The moment lengthened in his mind as it hooked onto memories bearing the same stamp. The thin lips, large ears. More gaunt than ever, with military bearing that no longer gave an impression of height, the admiral, phantasmal in the shifting light, wore a new look of frailty and the old look of anxious, frigid rectitude. The expression came free of the face in Michael's mind and lingered there like a life mask they had all worn. It had once done duty for a face, but was now daily shrinking, becoming wizened as a walnut.

When shall we see one another again, comrades? Globke and his officials stood aside for Dönitz. They gave place to the Berlin bunker's designated heir. Michael could scarcely believe his eyes. The Knight's Cross, with oakleaves and crossed swords, gleamed at the admiral's throat. Dönitz held back. For a moment there was an embarrassed pause in which no one knew what protocol required. The modest admiral would not go ahead. The deferential grandees of the Adenauer government refused precedence. They stood like puppets left to dangle by an absentee puppeteer. A dark figure who looked like Paul Dahl in naval costume hovered at the rim of the group, an unimportant extra, lord of the vacuum cleaners. Then all twitched into motion. Dönitz expressionlessly surrendered to pressure and moved forward, not as one who seeks pre-eminence but as a man who cannot allow himself to shirk the burden of inherited greatness.

From the innards of the building, men's voices were raised in a patriotic anthem. Lusty, self-pitying, archaic, the voices seemed to rise on some afflatus for ever in quest of a dying fall. A music of paranoia which required the existence of traitors for its justification, just as would-be martyrs need mockers.

The honourable company of butchers, thought Michael. *The fellowship of the spirit of Zyklon B.*

Isolde rose and accompanied him away from the house like a lamb. Michael thought: *She has seen her father now but she will never know it.* The certainty that he would never lift a finger to harm her brought a peace to his heart, a quality of balance that was sweet to know.

'Sorry about that,' she said. 'Sorry. It just came over me. Somehow I wasn't in the mood for all that out-of-date claptrap. Asses. Aren't they just pathetic?' The word had not struck Michael. It reduced these revived cadavers to a scale which removed them from the status of players on a world stage to ham actors in an out-of-date film. The girl's robust innocence reduced them, and Wolfi's bored scepticism for all things military and punitive reduced them, and the farmer who praised webbing belts reduced them. Perhaps, after all, that old nightmare would not come round again. Not, at least, in the original form.

They moved automatically toward the stone Madonna. A light had been rigged up beside her and shone obliquely on to the sterile monumentality of her face. She had been scrubbed clean of lichen and bird droppings and made presentable.

'That was him, wasn't it? Old Doughnut. Did you recognise him? I'm sure that was Dönitz.'

'Oh yes. That was him.'

'I was Dönitzed, you know. By Patterson. He made me put on an iron helmet. Dredged out of the lake. He does it to all of us. Fraternal rite of passage, even if you're a woman. Bet he didn't do it to Wolfi or you.'

'I've been Dönitzed already. In another life.'

'How do you mean?'

'I was on his staff, briefly.'

'Really? What was he like?'

'Rigid, limited, correct. Fine strategist and commander, old-style naval officer, anti-Semite, yes-man and, let's say, like many of us at that time, a bloody lousy judge of character. Crooked kind of uprightness.'

'That doesn't make sense,' said Isolde, smiling at the panache with which he brought off the colloquial English of 'bloody lousy'.

'No. That's right. It doesn't. We pass the baton to you. I hope,' he added gruffly, on a sudden impulse, 'I do hope it goes well for you and Wolfi. I really do. He deserves happiness. So much happiness.'

And the step back he took from their young lives was the renunciation of a claim. Valedictory, a blessing. He threw away a trove of hopes and expectations and felt the lighter for it.

***

Michael walked straight through a rainbow. Prismatic beads on a spider's web were strung between high ferns. As he passed through, the web lost all lustre and coherence; its tatters clung to his civilian jacket and he brushed them off. The architect must begin again, from scratch, inventing out of its own guts on a foundation of the fortuitous and the ephemeral.

He stood at the edge of the glassy lake, the medals and badges lying burnished on his palms. A delicate mist stood out in mid-water, into which the sun tipped light as the faintest of pale bronze sheens. A spring so calm and clement nobody could remember or had expected. It came from nowhere like irony or grace, in days when few spared time to meditate the difference.

Quantz hurled his Iron Cross in the air. It described a high arc and plopped into the water like a weighty stone. Then, bending his knees, Michael swung his arm to skim the badges like spinning pebbles, which bounced twice, three times and sank. The lake bottom, like a wishing well, was scattered with a maze of small change.

15

Lübeck, 1958

The hurt city glowed, its ancient red-brick churches the colour of chrysanthemums, comprehending a spectrum from ochre to russet. Across stepping stones of orange and tawny roofs, the eye skipped to the restored twin spires of the *Marienkirche*, green in the blue air. Magnificence was reborn; only vestigial scaffolding remained. Wounds which had seemed mortal were well-nigh closed, and only a knowing eye could tell which houses in the venerable terraces had been destroyed and which had endured. The holes were stopped, and the dwellings stood as if with their arms around one another, flanking their narrow medieval alleys. Isolde breathed sea salt on the air. Fishing trawlers with high masts and intricate ropes brooded upon underwater doubles in the canal. Colours lay like salve upon her eyes. She had never dreamed of such a city.

'My grandparents came from here,' said Wolfi. 'Now it's the doorway to the east. There's a bridge over there,' he gestured to some invisible point beyond the dream-like old town, 'the Wakenitz Bridge, it leads nowhere, it's just cut off on the eastern side. Do you hate the Russians, Issie?'

'I don't know any. I don't really ever hate people, except people who hate people. Wolfi, this is magical.'

It took forever for them to get to the *Marienkirche*, not only because of the press of people, meagre, ill-clad, striving along the narrow alleys, but because it seemed necessary to stop and kiss each other every few steps.

'Refugees,' said Wolfi, 'from the east.'

When you looked at architecture, your heart soared. When you looked at people, it sank. Isolde, running from Rachel, hunted by Rachel, gazed up at the sublime spires.

She dodged the proud old pauper sailor, with his beggar's tin, singing shanties to his accordion, a blanket covering his legs like an apron.

They were in the *Marienkirche*. Its Gothic height and beauty stunned her, the delicate flower painting across the ceiling, Christ Jesus hanging in harrowing pain. White-gold light that made gentle the splendour of altitude. But mostly the bells.

She had just lit a candle for Rachel. It burned coldly over there among other ephemeral flames. She had closed her eyes and tried to pray but no prayer came.

There was no prayer. Just the bells.

The remains of two great bells lay like buckled hearts where they had fallen when British planes had bombed the church that Palm Sunday, sixteen years ago. The ground beneath had crumpled. They would remain as a monument, with a cross of nails from Coventry. She stood holding the iron bars of the chapel with both hands, listening to the testament of the silenced bells. Tears stung her eyes.

A man in late middle age standing beside her said, as if in hectic riposte to some unanswerable accusation or reproof, 'Dresden.'

'Pardon me?'

'Dresden. Oh yes, the English have plenty to answer for.'

'We didn't want to fight,' she said in German.

'Who are "we"?'

Isolde did not answer.

'I presume you're not local. You would not believe,' he said with grumbling, defensive rancour, which was evidently habitual, 'what we Lübeckers went through. And afterwards, we had to suffer the disgusting ways of those beasts our good mayor calls "our unpleasant guests". Gangs of plundering, foul-mouthed, murdering Polacks. Ukrainians. Ruskies. They tore up our floors and burned them for firewood, they raped our women, my God, they had a field day.'

'Who are you talking about?' she asked, and the rigid material of his greatcoat seemed a horny carapace defending hidden innards of mush.

'The slave-workers,' said Wolfi in his hoarse, whispery voice. 'You old bastard, you mean the slaves, don't you?'

The man looked mortified. 'There were no slaves,' he muttered tonelessly. There was a scared, addled look in his eyes. Pulling his cap down over his brow, he strode rapidly away.

Wolfi suddenly found his voice and yelled after the retreating figure, and his yell rang round the transept, a litany of curses, a bellowing anthem like a roar of pain, whose words Isolde could not distinguish because of the echo.

16

Swansea, Christmas 1958

'So, Tada, what do you think of Wolfi?'

'A well-spoken young man, Issie. Yes, very well-spoken.' This from Owen counted as high praise. From the fountain of good English everything else flowed. Her stepfather's mother had forbidden the speaking of Welsh, the tongue of the underdog, in her house. But Owen praised Wolfi's English in the tone of a dirge, as if the excellence of a young man's vowels could not compensate for dearth of appropriate ancestry. 'You wash, I'll dry, is it?'

They were both wearing paper party hats from crackers, Owen's being a purple crown. His shoulders were draped with a festoon of tinsel but his look of vassalage belied his regalia. It had been a frosty meal, with much 'oohing' and 'aahing' over the tender meat that fell away from the chicken, the secret of which, Renate stated, was long slow cooking *upside down, the English way*. She had presided over the anatomisation and consumption of the bird as if commemorating its passing. Both Issie and Owen had been relieved to escape to the kitchen, away from the funereal Christmas tree strung with Woolworth's lights.

Issie swirled the hot water round with both hands. 'But?' she asked.

'Not for me to judge, see.'

She looked through the net curtain rather than directly at Owen. The backyard shelved steeply up to the flaking green gate; in the squally rain the rusty swinging seat heeled round, grating on its hinges. The swing belonged so deeply to her childhood – that and the giant pampas grass which plumed beside it – that she had only to see it to feel the years slide away. But this time it all oppressed her, together with the mingling of coal smoke and damp in the living room, and she longed to be anywhere else than in Mumbles washing up with the taciturn Owen on a dreary Christmas afternoon.

'We had a grand meal of plaice and chips at a new place they've opened up at Sketty. Did Mama tell you?' Owen tried to divert them from the festive gloom by recalling happier times.

'No.'

'Lovely, it was. With lemon quarters. You squeeze them on the fish.'

'Yes, I've had that.'

'You have?' He looked astonished at the thought of her having tasted such gastronomic novelty. 'Well.'

'It's quite common to have lemon with fish nowadays,' she said, blighting his conversational gambit. Typical of Tada to talk about anything but what mattered. In the past she had understood his difficulty in coming at things head-on, and made allowances for it. That was how he was: a mild soul who wanted everything to be nice.

Which was a lie. Everything wasn't nice. Her tongue had grown more bitter and caustic than she could well govern. Since they had found Rachel, she had scarcely slept a single night through, and found herself tired and irascible, out of temper with everyone but Wolfi, with whom she could give vent to bursts of weeping. She lay and soaked the shoulder of his shirt until she had emptied her conscience for the time being. And in the week of Rachel's death, Tada had written that five-line letter in the wake of Renate's revelations, about how she must always put her mother first, and how he was no letter writer but just to say: *Be kind to Mama, she's had a hell of a life. Just drop her a note to say you understand.*

Yes, and what if one did not understand?

Or, everything having clicked into place, understood all too well?

She was being asked to concur in Renate's account of how things stood, to forbear from interrogation, just accept that she was the child of depravity, bred of the coupling of wolves.

What should she think of herself now, with Rachel found face down in the lake, dragged out by fishermen, and all expressing shock at this awful accident? For a girl of such tender years could never have committed suicide. That was out of the question. And Patterson had given that speech to the school, enumerating Rachel's sterling qualities, omitting to mention that the dead child lauded in the chapel had been despised and neglected alive. There they had sat in the simple Lutheran chapel, built out of pale stone as a monumental arch in the heart of the woods, the first snows drifting past the porthole-shaped windows. A girl nobody had lifted a finger to comfort was committed to the care of the Almighty. Her parents (not Jews at all) had sat with dignity in the front row, looking old enough to be grandparents. And on the white driveway, beneath the white trees, they had sought out Issie to say that their daughter had told them in her letters that she was the kindest of the teachers. Tears had spurted from Issie's eyes. She had held out a mittened hand to the mother, who took it in her leather glove, their breaths mingling in the freezing air. Issie had felt that a partial absolution had been tendered by the only person qualified to offer it. But as she had turned away, and left the chapel steps, the absolution had dissolved away to nothing in her mouth, a wafer void of substance. How innocently barbed was the tribute: *kindest of the teachers*. As if one should congratulate the least venomous of snakes.

She had gone storming in to Patterson, now that it was too late, to have it out. She'd blurted it all, the bullying and the brutality, the way it was a system and not simply isolated instances of neglect.

The way he ought to be ashamed of this cult of Dönitz and his sailor boys. It was play-acting, sham, a farce. All those beastly relics, dredged up from the lake... while up there at the *Blütehof*... didn't he know?

Patterson, shrugging off the attack on his beastly relics as female vapours, had assured her he ran a well-ordered ship at Confessor's. Every care was taken for the welfare of his young charges. He'd urged Miss Dahl not to take things so much to heart, but to strive to see the larger view: which seemed to be the standpoint of an expatriate head, full of years if less full of honours than he might have wished, about to retire without a significant blot upon his name.

Not that there was any harm in soul-searching, he had felt. On the contrary. His gowned figure had leaned forward on his elbows, behind a glossily polished desk, to suggest a chat with the padre, as a means of setting Miss Dahl's mind at rest and enabling her to see this sad loss in a clearer light.

Then there had been the Christmas festivities to organise jointly with the *Blütehof* orphans. And Lynne sashaying round with Karl Schmidt showing off an elegant engagement ring. *Oh dear*, had been all Issie could say. *He won't be kind to you, Lynne*. She had tried to tell Lynne about the Dönitz night, the Lebensborn experiment; how men like that held women as chattels and breeding stock: some such phrase from Renate's letter had lodged in her mind. *He only wants you for your hair*, she had exploded, ludicrously, and the more she elaborated, the more fantastical it had seemed, even to herself. *You don't say, Taf*, Lynne had drawled, painting her nails, in the manner of the American films to which she was partial. *A bit far-fetched. But gentlemen do prefer blondes. Even out of a bottle. No offence to you, Issie, because you really are outstandingly good-looking, but it's a fact. All the film stars are blonde. Doris Day, Greta Garbo, Marilyn Monroe.*

Issie had shuddered to see Lynne tuck in under Karl's arm, snatch his riding whip and playfully swish it at the Alsatian. She had turned away with revulsion. Karl had made no allusion to what Issie had witnessed at the *Blütehof*. But something in his precise military bearing, his watchfulness, his way of looming over her on the few occasions they'd met had felt threatening. She had not been intimidated. Her mind had been obsessed by Rachel's death. The child seemed to shadow her, a long thin image attached by the heels which grew to an immense length in evening light.

The Christmas children had assembled adorably in the hall, in their foil wings, crowns of stars upon their heads. An overhead light had burnished them beneath the huge Christmas tree culled from the woods, which had wept the scent of resin through the hall. Picking out crosswise straps of silver over their chests, attaching the wings to their backs, it made of their white–gold hair something beyond the human. Amber foreheads, faces sweet as barley sugar, their voices rose as one, accompanied only by Wolfi's flute.

Es ist ein Ros' entsprungen
Aus einer Wurzel zart,
Und hat ein Blümlein bracht,
Wie uns die Alten sungen...

Issie had freely wept with the others, aching at the beauty of it.

***

'And for afters,' said Owen. 'Apple pie with custard. As much as you could eat. I had two helpings. Then coffee, and minty chocolate doodahs. It was as much as we could do to walk to the car. Maybe you and the boyfriend would like to go. We'll have to book, like, if you want to go, it's that popular.'

'Call him Wolfi, Tada. Not "The Boyfriend".' Owen had never learned more than the odd word of German in all these years with Renate. If English intimidated him, and made all writing a torment by its rich possibilities of misspelling, German was a minefield of gutturals and gnashings he scrupulously avoided.

'Isn't he your boyfriend then, Issie, if you don't mind my asking?'

'Well, yes, but . . . '

'Is it serious between you?' His eyes peeped piercingly between the wrinkles, from the habitually anxious face. He hoped, for Renate's sake, that Issie was going to say no.

'It's very serious. Wolfi's the best thing that's ever happened to me.'

'Well, there you are then.' He was drying knives and forks, lining them up according to Renate's laws in the correct compartments of the cutlery drawer.

'You don't sound very happy for me.'

'Of course I'm happy for you, girl,' Owen said lugubriously.

Issie laughed out loud. But inwardly she was dry of laughter. She recalled the single-ruled sheet of paper on which Owen had confided in his uneven hand his plea for a quiet life. For that was all it was. She looked over at his lean figure, in a rust-red cardigan of Renate's knitting, and reached into herself for the tenderness that usually came naturally enough but now eluded her. He had been her strength and stay. Still was (as he returned the dried 'best' plates to the dresser) the gentlest man she had ever known. But all she could think of was how he looked hand-knitted like a tea cosy in four-ply yarn. For he had asked her to believe that Renate's bombshell 'made no difference'. The prattle of a quisling. Issie had been urged to pen a nice note to her mother saying she 'understood', so that Renate could put her conscience away under its cold veneer, hidden in black velvet.

How long had it taken Owen to contrive that masterpiece? How many drafts, biting at the end of his biro, staring out of the window at the decaying garden seat and the potting shed, getting up to shovel a few coals from the scuttle on to the fire? How could he have allowed Renate to henpeck him into this state of spinelessness? He should have stood up to her long ago. So the Jenkins uncles and all but one of the *antis* firmly agreed: it was one of the family's few points of perfect concurrence. But that was not Owen's way. His persistent malleability was really, Issie felt, a mode of self-protection. Renate knew that. No doubt such knowledge made her rant and strut all the more. Who was the more impotent of the two when you came down to it? She had laid Renate's and Owen's letters aside, face down, like a brace of doubtful cards.

'But why do you not like Wolfi, Tada?' she persisted. Her voice was edgy, belligerent. It must have sounded to Owen like Renate's on a frosty morning.

'But I do.' He paused. She had washed down the draining board and now stripped off the obligatory rubber gloves. They came away like a pair of false and empty hands.

'But Mama doesn't?'

He coloured up. Played with the toggles of his cardigan, and that look came over his face that told her of the yearning to toddle off down Queen's Road for the snug of the Oystercatcher.

'Well, it's all the trouble in the past, see. She takes it personal that you would take up with . . . that family.'

Issie crossed the kitchen and took both her stepfather's hands in hers. The old tenderness seeped back in. She smiled and pulled the purple party hat down over his forehead, tightened the tinsel round his neck in a silver noose.

'Tada, what Wolfi's unpronounceable father did or didn't do is nothing to do with us, is it? We're a new generation. It's nothing to do with Wolfi or me in actual fact, is it? It's Mama's own bad conscience that's hurting her, and all the secrets she kept. That's what this is all about, isn't it?'

Suddenly Renate was in the doorway.

Owen faltered away from Issie, as if detected in some act of conspiracy. He folded the drying-up cloth impeccably in half and hung it from the oven door. This minor act of virtue was offered as a feeble sop to Renate's wrath. Issie felt herself blush fiercely, as though she too shared some guilt. But what guilt? The shame of truth. Breaking the taboo by bringing into the hard light of day facts that were scarifying. Renate refrained from interrogation of the whisperers behind her back. She shut the door behind her, cutting off Owen's retreat and ensuring that any words would not be audible to Wolfi.

Advancing over the kitchen, she swabbed down the draining board and wrung out the cloth, as a silent comment on her daughter's housewifery. She set the kettle on the gas and asserted that it was their duty to enjoy Christmas Day as far as possible, to show Isolde's friend how these things were done in England.

'Wales,' Issie corrected her.

'All I hope is that your aunts and cousins don't come round here tiddly and wanting to sing "Land of my Fathers" and "Rock of Ages" round the tree. Everything else I can bear,' said the martyr. 'But not that. Nasty nationalism and inbreedings I cannot stand.'

***

'Why don't we go down to the sea front? Have a wander?' Issie asked Wolfi, whose quiet and steadfast politeness had turned into stupefied silence under Renate's arctic freeze. He was seated askew in his chair, as if, in attempting to shrink his conspicuous tallness, he had got himself fixed at an ungainly angle.

'On Christmas *Day*?' asked Renate.

'Oh, I've always loved a walk after Christmas dinner,' said Issie. She persevered in keeping the tone light. 'Everything always used to seem so magical and mysterious.'

'In *this* weather?' Renate gestured balefully at the rainswept front window, buffeted by gusts from the sea.

'Oh, any weather.'

'Just to get out of the house,' stated her mother.

'Of course not.' Issie was beginning to run out of steam. Owen eyed the sitting-room door. Wolfi sidled his legs round in front of his chair, as if preparing to bolt, should the opportunity present itself. 'No. I just feel so fat.'

'Well, you are fat!' stated Renate, and the light of God appeared in her eye. 'You've always been heavily built, there's no help for it, Isolde, that's just how it is.'

'Charming,' said Issie. 'Thanks a million.' Suddenly she felt all blubber, beached like a whale in the easy chair. Yet at the same time, she thought: *Well, whatever, Wolfi loves me as I am.* She remembered in the quick of her the intimacy that was still so novel and young between them, and her body secretly glimmered with his touch. Deep touch, as they learned to know each other in a way the pastor had always strenuously admonished. She was spun on Wolfi's wheel like clay in the potter's hands; stroked with the fingers that guided the bow across the cello. She knew so much more about sensuality now. Flashed Wolfi a sudden radiant smile, which came and went on her lips as she remembered details of their loving.

Wolfi grinned back. Their eyes maintained a conspiratorial conversation across the lounge, while Owen remonstrated, hurt on Issie's behalf, 'Oh no, she's never fat, dear. Fair dos. She is beautifully made.'

'Yes,' said Wolfi in German. 'That's right. Your daughter is totally beautiful. In every sense of the word.'

Renate stared, flinching. Her heart hammered up into her throat. For this stranger to speak German at her hearth seemed not only a solecism but a wilful insult. If she could have spat out her native language she would have done so. And now this foreigner came and disputed rights and wrongs in her own home in that soiled tongue. She looked away from the three faces under the dingy festoons with which Owen had painstakingly decorated the sitting room, precisely as he did every year. They were ganging up against her. As always. Except that now there were three of them, three faces which corporately testified against her, including him of the winkle pickers, drainpipe trousers and quiff, no doubt even now the theme of every delighted tattler in Queen's Road. *Have you seen the boyo at Number 30? Give youself a laugh,* mun, *take a peep when they go past. Poor old stuck-up Rene, she'll be mort-y-fied.*

'Off you go then,' she said, evicting them, swiping off her yellow party crown, which she crumpled and threw on to the fire. 'Off you go into the rain, since you're so keen to get away. You too, Owen. Yes, go on,' she harried, making it seem as if she wanted him out from under her feet. And he sagged, and looked at her wearily, saying, no, he preferred to stay in here with her by the fire. Who wanted to go out in that lot? Nice and cosy here. He reached forward to jiggle the glowing coals with the poker, and poured on new ones from the scuttle.

The young ones were out of the door already. Renate shut her eyes as the door crashed shut, so as not to see them larking down the steep road past the window, with their arms round one another, Isolde's coat flapping open, her dark hair rushing upwards in the wind. Quantz must have told her all, every detail, distorted of course, and perhaps together they had gone to see Paul Dahl, whose face was forever young in her memory, with that arrogant male beauty and such a strange pearly quality to his skin, the blush that came and went, lashings of eau de cologne to cover his corruption. And to think that Isolde had visited this man of infamy, and perhaps been susceptible to his lies and slanders, was unbearable; it was death to think of; and she would rather be dead, thought Renate, than know that Isolde (who had been thoroughly insolent since her return, the German in tow) had made contact with that creature.

There was a genial knocking on the door. The chimes went; a thumb on the bell expressed determination to remain on the doorstep till the New Year if necessary.

She leapt to her feet.

'I can't see them, I'm not well, tell them I'm not well,' she said to Owen, striding past him and rushing up the stairs. 'Tell them to go away.'

Owen gave her time to hide and then slowly moved to answer the door, yawning theatrically as if just awakened from a nap.

But perhaps Dahl was dead, she thought. He had died in a Russian camp or in some witless last stand in the Austrian Alps; he had simply vanished off the face of the earth with all the other millions and there would not even be a grave, let there not be a grave, for Isolde to visit. And he was a stupid man, she thought, peering down from the bathroom window upon the heads of her merry in-laws; a crass, crude, stupid lump of manhood who had led her on. Without him she might have met a more decent and less tempting type, and come away intact, or as intact as anyone could be in that place and time. She plumped down on the pink frilled quilt in her daughter's bedroom, and listened to the to-do downstairs. The quilt needed dry-cleaning, which was yet another thing to see to.

All on your own, mun*? On Christmas Day?*

Oh no. Course not. Issie and the lad have just slipped out for a blow on the front. Renate's resting from all the excitement.

Has she got one of her headaches? That was Lennie, always solicitous, since she, as a North Walian and a head-turning beauty, was also considered a troubling outsider.

Aye, said Owen. *Not too bad but a lie down seemed the thing.*

I'll just tiptoe up and see if I can lay my cool palm on her brow.

And we've got all you presents, mun. Bring her down, Lennie, she's got to have her presents.

My God, thought Renate, this stifling captivity in a hen coop with clucking, cackling pullets and mangy cocks; their dopey, sly eyes; their small, inane pursuits. What had she done to deserve this? She heard Lennie bounce upstairs two at a time. And innumerable times it had come over her to unburden herself to Lennie (to whom she had refused to grant the silver fox), but every time she began she had feared the swift forfeit of a friendship that had never yet quite begun but was always arrested at the point of tacit confederacy. For if Lennie knew, if anybody knew, she would not be able to hold up her head.

***

The sea front was deserted; shops had their blinds down. Indoors, bloated families dozed in armchairs through the listless afternoon before cake came out, with reviving pots of tea and the Queen's Speech on the wireless. Issie and Wolfi sat in the empty bus shelter and kissed, while gulls hung static breasting the gale, and the stunted palm trees in the gardens bristled their spikes in roaring air. The masts of the sailing boats jingled like bells. Issie got up and spun round and round. She thanked the yelling heavens that they had escaped that horror of a Christmas. She grabbed Wolfi's hands and yanked him into the cold tide of sea wind.

'Come on, let's go down on the shore,' she said. Sure-footed she ran down the precipitous sea wall to the shingle, and he followed. The tide was far out, the broad crescent of mudflats a thick brown impasto. Past the mild stink of the overflow, she hopped from rock to rock, drinking in the smell of seaweed, gutted shells and live crabs in the pools.

'Lick your lips,' she ordered Wolfi. 'What do you taste?'

'You. I taste you.'

'And?'

'Salt. But mainly you.'

She broke away and scudded towards a sea which seemed to retreat at the same rate as she advanced upon it. Issie's cheeks burned with the thrill of the cold; she stopped to shed her shoes before she reached the flats, where the feet sank into the juicy richness of mud alive with lugworms and cockles. Looking back, she waved Wolfi on, watching him stoop to remove his shoes and roll up his trousers. The puckered mud stretched away from her, at once rank and pure, scattered with occasional gouts of tar cast ashore by the great ships.

But the child was dead.

She was dead for ever and could not reappear, though it felt impossible that the whole thing was not just a sham, a kids' game, and Rachel would reappear, elbows clenched in at her sides in that way she had, her pleated skirt somehow or other hitched up at one side and hanging all wrong, showing her petticoat, so that the children cried, 'Snowing! Snowing!' And how she could not take care of herself came over Issie in a bleak sweep of inner knowledge. If she, Issie, had spared time from her own so important life to take the child aside and sit down with her – she could so easily have invited her into her own room and offered her a cup of Ovaltine, and talked over the difficulties, trying to sort out a way of helping her cope. She could have told her how to become inconspicuous, the trick was to be inconspicuous so that they didn't keep picking on you. And after the child was dead, the Matron had presented Issie with a reliquary in the form of a drawerful of dirty green stockings, each bundled up as if trying to disappear into itself and smelling sour, which Rachel had been too shy to wash in front of the other girls.

'Frau Meier.' Issie's voice had shaken as she found herself taking the green, smelly hose in both hands and cramming the balls in her patch pockets as if to hide them from the cruelty of light, 'These relics should be on your conscience.' Tears of shame at the exposure of the child's sad secrets had sprung to her eyes as she had covered the stuffed pockets in the brightly chequered skirt with both hands. What did she harbour deep within her? What horror nested in herself, coded in her genes?

'I could not help it,' Frau Meier stated, but not on her high horse, merely as the chorus to some self-righteous chant which she had been taught to sing in childhood and now mumbled without conviction, 'This girl had not been taught hygienic habits, and it was too late.'

God tempers the wind to the shorn lamb. So the pastor had reassured them all, Sunday by Sunday, as the roast meat sizzled in the oven for lunch. It was not so. The father brought his cold metal tool from nape to crown and the child stood there in powerless bewilderment, to be shaven and thrown away. And the other child was dead. Children in their millions were dead.

And now it seemed that she was running away from land rather than towards the sea, the breath raw in her throat, mud sucking at her bare feet. Wolfi was catching up though, he was drawing level and close, and his mouth was drinking the salt from her cheeks.

***

Lennie crept in and sat beside Renate on the bed.

'Isn't it awful, Christmas?' She whispered this heresy.

'Frightful.'

'My two have been squabbling all morning over the train set. They were up at five and exhausted by six. The bird wouldn't cook, I got hot and bothered, Llew and I fell out and now we're here. You all right then? Is there anything I can do?'

'No, I don't think so,' said Renate, carefully circling her temples with her fingertips, as if consulting some inner list of possibilities. 'It's Isolde,' she said, 'and this young man. Not so young if you ask me, and a sight too old to be wearing these winkling pickers. They've gone off down to the front in the pouring rain, making such a noise as if they were drunk.'

'The winkling pickers should come in handy down there,' said Lennie.

Renate giggled. 'Honestly,' she said, 'you should see him, Lennie, such a freak. All he needs is a guitar to top him off. What will Mrs James say? It makes me come over all hot to think.'

'Oh, the young,' shrugged Lennie. 'Never mind, Rene, let them get on with it. Who cares?'

She took off her shoes and threw herself on the bed, arms crooked behind her head, her long, slender legs in the honey-pale nylons crossed at the ankles. Renate looked at the pretty curls all over Isolde's pillow and the couldn't-care-less grace of her sister-in-law and was suddenly bored by her own earnestness.

'We ought to go on a trip,' said Lennie. 'Without husbands. Just the two of us.'

Renate swivelled round, her face lighting up. 'Where though?'

'Oh God, I don't know. London?'

'I thought you were going to say Rhossili. Or at the most Ilfracombe.'

'Look here, Rene, we don't want to degenerate into puddings, do we, into *veg-ee-tubbles*?' She was parodying the laborious Jenkins lilt. 'We should have a bit of fun, see some musicals, why shouldn't we?'

'You know that old silver fox fur you wanted?'

'Yes.' Lennie's face stilled, the bubbles vanished. 'I understood about that, Rene.'

'It wasn't that I didn't want you to have it. You could have cut it down a treat and looked a million dollars in it. You could have been a model.'

Lennie sat up and took one of Renate's hands. It lay rigid in both her hands and she gently massaged the back between her thumbs. 'You don't have to go on. I could see it must have had a history for you. When I came to think of it afterwards, I could've bitten my tongue. Anyway it was too swanky for here.'

'It's still there,' said Renate. She was white to the gills.

'Where?'

'In there.' She gestured over to the great mahogany wardrobe which had belonged to Owen's childhood, and had once toppled on him, so he recalled, when the youngsters were playing mountaineering games. It was a wonder he hadn't been killed, but the bed caught the weight. And Mam was so cross he got no butter on his bread for a whole week. It was not possible to look at the dark brown beast of the wardrobe without thinking of the past through which it had travelled. And of its mothbally interior. It had a dull funerary massiveness, telling of the repetitiousness of what was, and is, and is to come. Of family.

Renate saw her own face in the long mirror Owen had affixed to its door. It wore a twisted look that she felt herself make in spasm, whenever a certain nerve was hit: a lipsticked mouth pursed up sideways in a face at war with itself. Around every corner lay ambush. The fur coat in that mausoleum asked Renate: *Where is the ash that once wore me?*

How could she have borne to coexist with it all this time? How? Knowing it was there, like a cadaver? That trophy she had snatched from the hands of Providence, whose gifts are not only never free, but rarely come cheap. How?

'What, Rene?'

'It's all mangy,' she croaked. 'Mangy and rotten.' She was unable to meet Lennie's eyes.

'Well, let's get rid of it, then, why don't we?' As Lennie bounded up from the bed, the springs twanged.

'Don't,' said Renate. Alarm went off in her chest and she shot off the bed.

'If it's all moth-eaten, let's bag it up and dump it, why not?' asked Lennie. Her forehead was rumpled, she looked older, betraying more awareness than Renate had guessed she possessed. How relieved she felt that she had not allowed her sister-in-law to burden herself with the rotten thing, cutting it down into a glamorous jacket, unconsciously fouling herself with Renate's carrion.

'I don't know... if I can,' she said uncertainly. How much could she confess without being cast off by the precious near-sister? Her timidity in the face of all Lennie knew and should not know made her voice small; yet at the same time something in her flashed, *If you'd been offered Mrs Levi's coat, ten to one you'd have taken it too*. But to Lennie no such offer could ever be made. And this unfair exemption from temptation brought a spurt of bile into Renate's throat, so that she was just about to say something haughty and chilling, when Lennie sailed out of the door, saying, 'Just a mo.'

Give us that bag, Iorwerth – that's right, the one with the presents in, just empty them out, I want the bag. That's right. No, she's just got one of her head pains. We're sorting out some junk.

Back in she came, threw open the wardrobe door and hauled out the weighty fur, which she began to stuff into the bag, without examining it, without mentioning that it was in perfectly good condition, that such a classy coat would last another century. Then she rushed the bag out, down the stairs and into the back of the Morris Minor. Renate watched her through the net curtain, slamming down the boot.

What you do-en, Mam?

Never you mind.

When you com-en for the cake?

In a bit.

She came back upstairs.

'You won't wear it, Lennie, will you?' asked Renate.

'Course not. I'll get rid of it, don't you fear. We've done what we can,' she told her sister-in-law, dusting her hands off on her skirt. 'Do you think I ought to have my hair tinted?'

Lennie turned her head from side to side in the mirror, and as she did so the curls forged there with chemicals and rollers, baked in the oven of the drier and teased into perfection by comb and brush, bounced gently and swung from side to side in the most natural way imaginable.

***

Between the pier's irregularly spaced wooden planks, the sea churned queasily, turning Issie's stomach over and over, as if the pier pitched on its moorings, and was not a sound construction. And this vertigo was all mixed up with a feeling of invigoration; it was familiar, and home, but she must dash for the wrought-iron railing for something to hold on to.

Wolfi said, 'This is fabulous. I wish we lived here, Issie. Do you think we might?'

'One day,' she said. 'That's where the lifeboat lives. And here at the end the fishermen come, and sit in their sou'westers.'

'It feels like being on a ship at sea,' said Wolfi. 'Marvellous.'

'I thought you didn't like boats.'

'I do when they're really a pier.'

They climbed down the metal steps beneath the pier, faces scalded red with wind. The rusted struts, encrusted with barnacles, were only reachable at low tide. They stood in one another's arms looking out to where the white pillar of the lighthouse stood homely and secure.

She was not the same Issie as had left Wales: where did it end, then, this process of metamorphosis that could hardly be called maturation? Did one just go on for ever, sloughing skins, struggling from egg to pupa to chrysalis, one coat after another?

No wonder, she thought, that Renate after so many years and such vicissitudes could not easily connect herself with the passionate member of the Band of German Maidens. Renate had not been making it up in that letter. Though recognisable, she was not the same. Yes, the thread was there that tied her back to her origins – the proud stance and thrusting gait, the high-handed behaviour, the possibility of racial remarks that made one's cheeks burn with shame that this cruel, stupid mouth should belong to one's mother, one's own mother (*What have I said? Why are you looking at me like that?*) Yet she was not the same.

And Wolfi had said, down there on the flats, that he wanted to marry her. She wanted Wolfi but did she want to marry? A dismal vision of arms in pink rubber gloves, plunged in sudsy water, had suggested itself to her. Peggings of white items on lines, where they would flap like flags of surrender. Mops. Brushes, sponges, the tackle of domestic life. Nose-against-pane like a trapped spaniel, awaiting the homecoming of a husband.

I don't want to get married, Wolfi.

Okay, he said equably. *We won't get married.*

It's very much overrated.

Probably.

So we'll just live instead, shall we?

And they might go and teach in a German school, they thought, hugging, huddling into one another as the water swept and sucked at the struts and the pier seemed to steady like some great liner berthed at a quay. And she imagined his fingers moving up, up the fine-skinned inside of her thigh, slowly, slowly, approaching the sweet, tingling place, feeling the juices, its give, fumbling his finger in the slick folds to find the place . . . yes. She would undress him cherishingly. The lamp would be on, she wanted to see. He was so beautiful, willowy and graceful. So intelligent in his sensuality. Her breath caught. And their fathers had seen men eviscerated, their guts flopping out, warm and bloodbathed. Men who saw and knew this undoing. But she and Wolfi had not seen, not done. She shut out Rachel, shut out Renate. She opened her coat to Wolfi and clasped it round his tender body.

The water was mounting as they stood engrossed, and surged up the top step, to glide across the platform as if putting out a hand, so that they had to retreat to the prow of the pier.